Cruel Havoc

Cruel Havoc

Montana Mayhem Book 4

Millie Copper

Written by Millie Copper

Edited by Ameryn Tucker

Proofread by MDC Proofreading and WMH Cheryl

Cover design by Dauntless Cover Design

Also by Millie Copper

Montana Mayhem Series

Unending Havoc: Montana Mayhem Book 1

Ruthless Havoc: Montana Mayhem Book 2

Merciless Havoc: Montana Mayhem Book 3

Havoc in Wyoming Series

Wyoming Refuge: A Havoc in Wyoming Prequel

Havoc in Wyoming: Part 1, Caldwell's Homestead

Havoc in Wyoming: Part 2, Katie's Journey

Havoc in Wyoming: Part 3, Mollie's Quest

Havoc Begins: A Havoc in Wyoming Story

Havoc in Wyoming: Part 4, Shields and Ramparts

Havoc in Wyoming: Part 5, Fowler's Snare

Havoc Rises: A Havoc in Wyoming Story

Havoc in Wyoming: Part 6, Pestilence in the Darkness

Christmas on the Mountain: A Havoc in Wyoming Novella

Havoc Peaks: A Havoc in Wyoming Story

Havoc in Wyoming: Part 7, My Refuge and Fortress

Nonfiction Books

Stretchy Beans: Nutritious, Economical Meals the Easy Way

Stock the Real Food Pantry: A Handbook for Making the Most of Your Pantry

Design a Dish: Save Your Food Dollars

Real Food Hits the Road: Budget Friendly Tips, Ideas, and Recipes for Enjoying Real Food Away from Home

Join My Reader's Club!

Receive a complimentary copy of *Wicked Havoc: A Montana Mayhem Prequel.* As part of my reader's club, you'll be the first to know about new releases and specials. I also share info on books I'm reading, preparedness tips, and more. Please sign up at:

MillieCopper.com/Wicked

Who's Who

The Dawson Family: After her husband's atrocious acts made her family outcasts, Victoria Dawson and her two sons, Brett and Jameson, need a fresh start. Through the kindness of Jennifer Dosen and her family, they have an opportunity for a new life. With only over a hundred miles left on their multi-month journey, tragedy strikes. Will Victoria's plans change?

The Dosen Family: Away from home when the attacks started, Jennifer and her sons, Atticus and Axel, are determined to return to their small ranch outside of Great Falls, Montana. Grieving the recent death of eighteen-year-old Asher, the Dosens are determined to reach home before winter.

The Hoffmann Family: Kimba and Rey Hoffmann, along with their three children—Nicole, Nate, and Naomi—fled Denver after the bridges exploded. They're invaluable members of the group and are committed to helping the other families in their quests.

The Monroe Family: Finally reaching the safety of Aunt Karla's lodge outside of Lewistown, Montana, Leanne and her two kids—sixteen-year-old Sadie and eight-year-old Sebastian—are ready to begin a new life. Donnie McCullough, a traveling companion of the Monroes, asked Leanne to marry him. She said yes! As they settle into their new community, taking on the daily tasks of gardening, tending livestock, and everything else needed in today's powerless world, their excitement is suddenly overshadowed by a new danger.

Rochelle Bennet, PJ Cameron, and Robyn Sorensen: When the traveling group reached Lockwood, Montana, Robyn Sorensen, who was injured after being underwater for too long after slipping into a cold creek, was handed over to the care of the military and her parents. Rochelle and PJ headed off on their own in search of Rochelle's son, who was away at summer camp when the attacks started.

Tamra: A twice-widowed mom of two daughters, thirteen-year-old Beth and seven-year-old Debbie. Her first marriage was built on love and trust—her second one, convenience and security needed at the end of the world. Turns out, what she thought was security was nothing more than a lie. After traveling for two weeks with Sadie and her group, they're safe in the small town she grew up in.

Chapter 1

Near Lewistown, Montana
Sunday, June 7, Early Morning

Victoria

His hand comes out of nowhere, landing solidly against my cheek. I don't even have time to cry out before he grabs me by the collar of my jacket and shakes me. I hurt—my face, my head, my arm. "Stop!" I cry. "Stop. I'm sorry. It won't happen again!"

"Mom? Mom, are you okay?"

"Mmm."

"I think she's coming around."

"Look at her arm. It must be broken."

Who's arm? I turn my head to look, then wince at the motion. "Ah!"

"Just hold still, Mom. We'll . . . we're going to figure out how to get you back to camp."

I lick my lips, feeling the grit of the dry earth. Opening an eye, a wave of nausea surges through me. My head hurts, my arm. My breath comes in short gasps. "What? What'd he do to me?"

"You fell and slid down the hill. Do you remember?"

My son's face is blurry, out of focus. "Brett?"

"Yeah, Mom. Atticus and Nate will stay with you. They'll keep you safe. You cut your head, but Atticus is stopping the bleeding. I'm going for help. We'll find a doctor. You'll be okay."

I look beyond my son, my eyes searching. "Where's your dad?"

"Mom?"

There's something in Brett's voice. Concern? Dismay? I take a breath and close my eyes. They pop open again. The sun is bright—too bright. I squeeze them shut.

There's a light touch on my shoulder. I lift my arm. Pain shoots through me. I let out a cry, then clamp my mouth shut, willing myself to ride out the wave of pain.

I test opening my eyes again, rolling my head to look at the source of my agony. My forearm looks peculiar. *Wrong.* The strange bend to it is obvious, even under the long sleeve of my ugly pale-blue shirt.

The hand of my uninjured arm goes to the fabric, lightly touching the cheap cotton. *I don't remember this shirt.* I glance at my pants. They're ridged, brown, and ugly. I can just see the tips of my shoes—*jogging* shoes. I don't jog.

My stomach heaves. I turn my head and vomit, choking on bile and spit.

Someone's holding my head, keeping my hair back. "You're okay, Victoria. We're going to take care of you."

<center>~~~~~</center>

Birds. Sunshine. I open my eyes. Blue eyes stare back at me, young and scared. "Brett will be back any time. My dad'll know what to do." His voice cracks as he talks.

My head is in his lap. Embarrassment covers me like a blanket. I attempt to roll on my side. Pain shoots from my head, my arm, and my back.

"Hold still," a different voice orders. "The bleeding stopped. We don't want it to start again."

I pant out a few shallow breaths. "Atticus?" I say his name but can't remember how I know him.

He furrows his brow and gives a slow nod.

"My arm . . . hurts."

"You broke it when you fell."

"When I fell . . . " I close my eyes. A wave of memories rush over me—walking day after day, these people I didn't know treating me like family . . . climbing a dusty hillside. I was following my oldest son, Brett, and his friend Atticus. Someone else too. Who was it?

The blue-eyed boy! Nate Hoffmann.

We were looking for deer. *Hunting deer.* We need the food.

We didn't see any, so we decided to see if the man—the one who held a gun to Atticus—was still in his house. They looked through their binoculars. Brett asked if I wanted to look. I took a step toward

2

him and then . . . then what? I close my eyes, trying to remember what happened next.

~~~~

"You're hurting her!"

"It can't be helped."

A shudder runs through me. There's a burst of bright light and an explosion of pain in my head . . . my arm, my back. I'm panting. Everything's gray, with little white lights. Fireflies. Thousands of them. Too bright. No, that's not right. There're no fireflies here. I left those behind when I moved from Tennessee.

"Victoria? We're going to move you. It's going to hurt."

"Mmm. I hurt."

"We're going to take care of you, get you back to camp and set your arm. Here, drink some of this."

Bitter liquid drips in my mouth. Booze. I spit it out. "I don't drink."

"It's the willow bark tincture, the one you helped make." The voice is calm, slightly accented. Familiar. What's his name?

"You have to drink it, Mom. It'll help with the pain." Jameson, my youngest son. His voice is too high. Stressed. *Scared.*

"I'm giving you more," the calm voice says. "Don't spit it out."

I crack open an eye. Jameson stares back. His face is pinched, his mouth tight.

"Hey." My voice comes out in a croak. I swallow. Dirt. Gravel.

"We're going to move you, Mom. Rey says it'll hurt. We'll carry you back. Brett's looking for a doctor for your arm."

"My arm . . . hurts."

"It's broken. It looks— "

"We're about ready, Victoria." The man with the calm voice smiles at me.

Rey. This is Rey Hoffmann. Atticus Dosen is next to him. No, not Atticus, a slightly younger version of him. I close my eyes and try to focus, try to remember. Asher, Atticus's twin. Not him. *He's dead.* The younger brother, he's still alive. A . . . he's an A Boy.

I let out a long breath, floating on a cloud. Everything goes gray.

"One. Two. Three."
~~~~

"Ah!" I cry out. White lights fill my vision. The fireflies are back, starry and bright. Impossibly bright. Then blackness. Faraway voices.

Let's move. Get her back to camp. Try not to rock her.

I'm no longer moving. There's a new man, wearing a cowboy hat.

Of course he is. We may not have fireflies in Wyoming, but we have cowboy hats.

No, that's not right.

I'm in Montana. I'm *moving* to Montana. Walking. Walking to start a new life.

"Her lip needs a stitch or two. The cheek also."

"What about her head?"

"She whacked it good. Seven, eight stitches probably. I'll set the arm first."

Set the arm? "No. No! I can't— "

"Shh. Shh. You'll be all right." Jennifer smiles at me. Jennifer Dosen. She's the A Boys' mom. She looks to the man in the cowboy hat and lowers her chin. "I'll help hold her."

"It's going to take more than just you. Someone hold her legs. I don't want her to buck." Cowboy Hat points at something. There's pressure on my legs, on my left arm . . . at my head. "Here we go."

I cry out. *Pain.* Intense, grating pain.

Chapter 2

Fergus Peak Lodge
Near Lewistown, Montana
Sunday, June 7, Early Morning

Sadie

"Sadie, you ready to go?" My mom steps into Aunt Karla's bedroom.

"We're just catching up," my great-aunt says. "It's been too long." She scooches up and elevates her head on the pillows. I reach my hand to help, but she shoos me away. "I'm fine. About had enough of this bed and the recliner. Lying around is for the birds."

Mom gives her an amused smile. "Just a few more days, then you'll be up and causing trouble like you're used to doing."

"Ha! I plan on causing trouble from here. Daniela seems to be getting a little too big for her britches while I've been down."

I hide the smile playing on my lips. Ms. Daniela Reynolds definitely wasn't happy about my mom, my brother, and me showing up here. And she was even less happy about Donnie McCullough.

After walking halfway across Montana to get here, we found Aunt Karla laid up with a severely sprained ankle and possible concussion. Sebastian, my younger brother, was particularly upset and insisted we shouldn't stay here. He thought we should, instead, convince Aunt Karla to leave with us. He said it'd be much better for us to keep walking with our friends until we reached their ranch on the other side of Great Falls.

I'm not sure why Sebastian thought the way he did. We hadn't even seen Aunt Karla yet; we were still outside the compound.

Yesterday, after passing through the barricade and walking the almost five miles to Aunt Karla's lodge nestled at the base of the mountains, he started to relax.

I understand.

As we rounded the corner and the lodge came into view, we saw lush gardens, children running and playing, horses, dogs, everything normal. *Happy.* Not like it's been for the last year.

Seeing my tiny aunt, looking frail and fragile in the oversized recliner, with her face cut and bruised, her ankle wrapped and elevated, but with the most brilliant smile imaginable, took every worry I had away.

Sebastian was already smitten by what he'd seen and only needed a few extra minutes to agree it was the right choice to stay at Fergus Peak Lodge.

We'll make a good life here, one that doesn't involve walking every day. We've walked so many miles; I don't even dare to think in exact numbers.

Too many.

We started in La Grande, Oregon, where we were stranded after a series of terrorist attacks—including an EMP—which changed everything. Then we took backroads to reach our home next door to my grandpa and grandma's—Aunt Karla's sister—north of Spokane, Washington.

When we found them dead, Ben Ferguson, the man we were traveling with, convinced us to go with him to Wyoming, where he hoped his wife and child were waiting at a friend's home.

My mom was such a wreck after what she'd been through. When she found her parents dead, she did little more than nod her agreement.

We walked from Eastern Washington to Wyoming in the dead of winter, barely surviving the multi-month trip. After finding Ben's family and friends, I thought we were done. We could finally rest and begin to heal, carve out a life in this new, powerless world.

Mom had other ideas.

She was miserable, completely unhappy about . . . well, everything. She didn't want to live at the ski lodge with Ben's friends. When she heard about a group leaving for Montana and planning to travel near Aunt Karla's lodge outside of Lewistown, Montana, Mom decided we were leaving. That was nearly three months ago.

Today, our journey is officially over.

We're going to our friends' camping spot to say our goodbyes, and to announce my mom will be marrying Donnie McCullough, a man we've been traveling with.

"Sadie?" The tone of my mom's voice suggests this isn't the first time she's said my name.

"Um, yeah?"

She narrows her eyes and gives a slight shake of her head. "I said, I need you to help me get Aunt Karla out of bed."

"Sure, let's do it."

Once Aunt Karla is up and steady, Mom asks me to make sure Sebastian's ready to leave.

"Where's Donnie?" I ask. "Have you seen him this morning?"

Mom's cheeks color slightly. "We went for a walk along the creek, saw the cabin Jack was talking about yesterday."

Jack Mosher, Mom's old friend from when she worked summers here at the lodge, is the leader of this community. "The cabin the mom and kid almost froze to death in last winter?"

Aunt Karla chuckles. "It wasn't that cold. But when they woke up one morning and their little dog's water had a film of ice in it, we decided to move them elsewhere."

"Do you need help dressing?" I motion to Aunt Karla, sitting on the edge of her bed in pajamas.

"We'll be fine, dear. You don't need to see my wrinkly, old body."

"You're not that old." My mom shakes her head.

"Maybe not before the lights went out. Then, sixty-three didn't seem old. But now, I feel like I've aged a lifetime in less than a year."

As Mom weakly attempts to argue with her, I step out into the main room. My little brother's lying all the way back in the recliner, staring at the ceiling.

"You ready to go, squirt?"

"I'm glad we're staying here. I don't know why I didn't want to before, but now that we're here—in this apartment—I like it."

"We're not going to live with Aunt Karla, in her apartment, you know. We'll probably only be here a few days while everything gets sorted out."

"And Mom and Donnie have their wedding. Then, I guess we'll all live together, right? We'll be a family. I've never . . . I don't remember having a dad. It'll be kind of weird."

I dip my chin in agreement. It *will* be weird. Our dad died when Sebastian was just a toddler and I was ten. He'd been sick a long time, but I didn't really know it. I didn't find out until he was so thin and feeble that he couldn't hide it. My Uncle Wes and Grandpa Martin were certainly father figures in our lives, especially for Sebastian.

"We'll get used to it. Besides, we've been around Donnie for months now. It's not like we don't know him."

"And how loud he snores."

I let out a laugh. "That's for sure. I'm sure he kept us safe by keeping all the wild animals away from camp. Mom wants to leave as soon as she's done helping Aunt Karla get dressed. You ready to go?"

"Yeah. Maybe we could take a couple horses?"

"I don't think so. We'll walk out and probably camp with everyone tonight, then bring all our stuff and Donnie's horse back tomorrow. Maybe he'll let you ride Gordie back."

"Who'll take care of Aunt Karla while we're gone?"

I lift a shoulder. "I guess Ms. Reynolds and Samantha. They've been taking care of her since she fell."

"Ms. Reynolds doesn't like us much."

I purse my lips, remembering the way she was yesterday, all bossy and demanding. She was totally upset when Mom said she and Donnie are getting married, especially since he'll live here at the lodge. Right now, it's women and children only—way back here away from the rest of the community, a half mile from the nearest house.

And they have a rule here about only trained people carrying guns. That's why the rest of our group is camping outside the compound. Mom's friend Jack Mosher said he was happy to lock everyone's firearms up, but they couldn't carry them inside the compound.

That was a solid no.

We've been attacked too many times to risk it. I was surprised when, the day before yesterday, my mom and Kimba Hoffmann made the first trip back to the lodge, both went in unarmed. At least officially. Kimba had a pistol tucked in a holster under her arm.

When the four of us—Mom, Sebastian, Donnie, and me—walked in yesterday, escorted by Mosher, I had my knife hanging off my hip, which wasn't a problem. It's just the guns.

I guess I can understand it, after seeing how Ms. Reynolds totally freaked out yesterday, not only with the idea of Donnie living at the lodge, but also being one of the community members approved to carry a gun. Seems she has a huge aversion to firearms, even saying we have a fetish with weapons and making a point of being disgusted by Mom letting me carry a giant knife on my hip.

A few weeks ago, Mom would've given the woman an earful, telling her what she could do with her opinion. But not now. Not since she's found Jesus.

The door to the bedroom opens with a squeak. "Sadie, can you give us a hand?"

"Really, Leanne," Aunt Karla chastises, "your help is enough."

My mom reluctantly agrees, but I still try and do my part. "Out of the chair, squirt." I motion for my brother to move.

He struggles to put the recliner upright, his tiny body not getting the momentum needed. I hold his hand while kicking down the footrest.

"Thanks. I forget how strong chairs can be."

"Yeah, I guess we don't really sit in them anymore. Just the ground for us."

Mom frets over Aunt Karla for a moment, getting her situated in the chair.

"Thank you, Leanne." My aunt turns to me. "Sadie, I forgot my bag in the bedroom. Will you be a dear and bring it to me?"

I find her messenger bag on the floor by her bed. When I hand it to her, she opens it and pulls out a compact and a tube of lipstick. I grin at her need to fix her makeup in the middle of the apocalypse, especially when she has a black eye and other bruises.

Mom lets out a long breath. "We should get going. We'll be back tomorrow. You'll be okay until then?"

Aunt Karla waves a hand. "I'm sure Daniela will be fretting over me as soon as she sees you leave. I'll have a talk with her. She'll be less . . . *prickly* when you return. She means well, just forgets the world doesn't revolve around her. I think, once you get to know her, it'll be fine. You'll probably even be friends."

Mom smiles. "It's easy to see she cares deeply about you."

"She does. And she's a real asset here, a master herbalist and wild forager. She's been keeping us healthy and has planted a lot of medicinals in the garden—things she brought from her home after . . . " Aunt Karla clears her throat. "After she realized it's safer here. She's even transplanted wild things so we can cultivate them. We've all learned so much from her." She purses her lips and furrows her brow.

"What is it?" Mom asks.

"Oh, I was just thinking of Patti Hyde."

My back stiffens. A few days ago, a man named Ledger Hyde held Atticus Dosen and me at gunpoint. "Is she— "

"She's Ledger's wife."

Mom opens her mouth.

Aunt Karla lifts a hand. "I know your experience with Ledger was bad. He's had a hard time, went over the edge maybe. But his wife and babies, Ledger too, we love them all. He was a huge asset when things went bad and was Jack's right-hand man."

"Really?" I gasp. "I thought Jack hated him."

Aunt Karla lifts a shoulder. "They had a falling out."

"Because?" Mom asks.

"Who knows. I've heard Jack's version and heard Patti's version. But I didn't talk to Ledger about it, so I don't know what he thinks. Loomer says something entirely different."

"Loomer?"

Aunt Karla rolls her eyes. "Randy Loomer. He's the reason—never mind. This is a long, drawn-out story, and you all need to get going. Or, as I suggested earlier, Sebastian and Sadie can stay here if you'd like."

I'll admit, I did want to stay when she first mentioned it. But I want to say my goodbyes. We've all become very close while traveling together over these last several months.

Nicole Hoffmann, who at seventeen is just a year older than me, has become a good friend. Same with her little brother, Nate, and the Dosen brothers. My breath catches as I think of Asher Dosen. He was the best. Asher was killed a couple weeks ago in an explosion. It still hurts to think about him.

After telling Aunt Karla goodbye and meeting up with Donnie, who spent last night in one of the outbuildings, we begin the walk back to our camping spot. We're about halfway, having just turned from the road the lodge is on to the road Jack Mosher lives on and where our friends are camped, when an ATV comes roaring toward us.

"Someone's in a hurry," Donnie grumbles.

Mom squints in the morning sun. "Jack, I think."

Donnie grunts. "Figures."

The quad slows as it nears us. Jack Mosher lets off the engine, still shouting to be heard. "One of your friends is hurt, fell down a hill and broke her arm. Who knows what else? She's knocked out."

Mom lets out a gasp. "Who?"

Jack scrunches his mouth. "Um . . . the one with the stringy, gray hair?"

"Victoria?"

"Maybe. She carries an ax on each hip?"

"That's her." Donnie nods.

"One of our people, Chuck Rice, will set the arm. Thought I'd get Daniela too. She'll know how to help."

Mom bites on her lip, fighting tears. Victoria hasn't been the nicest person in our group. Far from it. Since Mom's conversion to Christianity, she's taken to praying for Victoria and especially her son Jameson. Believe me, they need all the prayers they can get. Both are less than kind. Even so, any injury is terrible. In today's world, a broken arm could mean permanent disability.

It could even be a death sentence.

Chapter 3

Near Lewistown, Montana
Sunday, June 7

Sadie

We're nearing the compound barricade when Donnie points to the ditch. "Dead rabbit."

Mom shakes her head. "Aunt Karla and I were talking about that this morning, about the rabbit disease. Someone in the community was raising meat rabbits before everything fell apart. Later, they trapped wild ones, trying to domesticate them for food. Do you think this— " She lifts a hand. "What'd they call it?"

"Some sort of hemorrhagic disease. Highly contagious. If you're wondering if it could spread to the caged rabbits, I think so. It's not new, been around awhile. We just didn't hear much about it unless we had a reason to, I suspect."

"What kind of reason?" Sebastian asks.

Donnie lifts a shoulder. "Maybe if you had a pet rabbit? You might be worried it could spread to them."

"Now it's not just about pets," Mom says. "How many people do you think are, or *were*, relying on rabbits as their main source of food? Now they're dropping dead. People will— "

"Living only on rabbit is hard too," Donnie says.

Mom waves her hand and lets out a sigh. "I know. Rabbit starvation. But it can be combated by eating the organs to add some fat and finding a carbohydrate source."

I give a slight shake of my head. I know about hunger. Going for days without food or having only a few morsels at a time is miserable. A plague that affects rabbits could mean death for many people. Is it selfish for me to feel happy we're here, at Aunt Karla's, and safe from starving to death?

"Rabbits dropping dead, deer and elk getting the wasting disease . . ." Donnie shakes his head. "It's not enough other men are trying to kill us, now our food sources are dwindling away. It'll be a miracle if our species survives."

Mom rolls her eyes. "Really, Donnie?"

"Well, you know. I'm just saying . . . never mind."

The men at the barricade wave us through. Nate Hoffmann is the first person we see as we approach camp. He's standing well away from the tents, looking drawn and pale. Is he also injured? Sick? Seeing us, he drops his head.

"Hey, Nate," Donnie says. "Mosher said Victoria's hurt."

Nate doesn't look up. "She fell."

Mom steps next to Nate. "Jack said she broke her arm?"

His head bobs slightly. "It's bad, I think. She hit her head too. Lots of blood, and it knocked her out."

"What hill?" Donnie looks around the flat land. There's a slight incline down to a creek, but other than that, the nearest hills are farther away.

"She went hunting with us."

"She did? That's not like her."

Nate scrunches his shoulders. "We talked her into it, thought she might like to do something different than just sit around camp. No deer, but we could see the cabin—you know, the one that Hyde guy lives in? We thought it looked empty, so we were trying to get a better look. That's when . . . " He shakes his head.

"What're you doing over here all by yourself?" Mom's voice is kind.

"It's— " Nate shakes his head. "The hillside wasn't very stable. I started to slip. She grabbed for me, then . . . she just disappeared. This is the second time she's saved me." A tear travels down his cheek.

"The second time?" Sebastian repeats. "Oh! You mean at the creek when she kept you from falling in?"

Nate gives a weary nod. Several months ago, Mom and most of the others from our group were gathering water along a frozen creekbank. The ice gave way, landing pretty much everyone but Victoria in the icy water. She grabbed Nate, who was dangling off the edge, and pulled him to safety. My mom ended up with pneumonia from being in the water. Another woman, Robyn, practically drowned.

I didn't realize until now, but after that day, Nate's been particularly kind to Victoria, offering to help her put up her tent and other things. I guess he felt he had a debt to repay to her. And now, if he thinks she's injured because of helping him . . . poor kid.

At almost fourteen, Nate's only two years younger than me. But until a few days ago, everyone thought he was the elder. At my mom's insistence, I'd been lying about my age. Because of my small stature, I've easily been passing myself off as a twelve-year-old. It was Mom's idea, a way to keep me safe. It wasn't until my mom asked God for forgiveness of her sins that the truth came out about my actual age.

She said she couldn't lie anymore.

I thought then, and still think, pretending I was young was smart. The more people looked at me as a child, the less was expected of me. In today's world, sixteen is pretty much considered an adult. I guess I don't mind in most ways, but in some . . . it's good to just be a kid.

Nate doesn't really act like a kid. Sure, he'll tease his sisters sometimes, especially Naomi, who's Sebastian's age, but he's usually pretty intense. He's taken on a role of provider in our group, using his slingshot to take down almost as much game as those with guns. Grouse, chukar, partridge, even a turkey. And he sets snares for small game. He can use the rifles and handguns, too, but the slingshot is where he shines.

"Ah, Nate." My mom offers him a slight smile. "It wasn't your fault Victoria fell. Things . . . " She shakes her head. "Things just happen, that's all."

"I guess."

"Mosher said someone's here to set her arm?" Donnie asks.

"Yeah, and he stitched up her head. Said someone else is coming, too, someone who knows about medicine."

"That woman with a stick up her— "

Mom clears her throat and gives Donnie a warning look.

"Sorry," he mutters. "Guess God still has a heap of work to do on me."

I resist the urge to roll my eyes. Just like my mom, Donnie recently chose to follow Christ. Sebastian has long believed God is with us, being almost annoyingly devout, even suggesting God tells him things—*talks* to him.

I'm the one in our family who isn't sure, the one with more questions than answers. In our traveling group, I've been subjected to daily Bible readings and continual prayers. Jennifer Dosen is the worst, always coming up with some sort of scripture and saying, "Praise Jesus," and other stuff.

As we near the man in a worn cowboy hat working on Victoria, Mom motions Sebastian and I to keep back. Even from here, it's easy to see what a terrible mess she's in. Blood covers her face and dots her shirt.

The man leans back on his heels. "Guess that's about all that can be done. Stitched up the cut on her head and set the arm. Someone should clean her up a bit." He lifts his head slightly and looks toward the barricade. "Pretty sure I hear the quad. Jack'll have *Mizz Reynolds* with him. Yeehaw."

I cock my head to one side, listening. It takes a couple seconds before I hear the faint sound of a motor. That guy has some good ears.

A few minutes later, Mosher and Ms. Reynolds—she made it very clear yesterday we are not to call her Daniela—putter into our camp.

"You already set the arm?" she asks the man in the cowboy hat.

"Yup. Broke both bones. Figured there was no sense in waiting."

"Compound?"

"Nope. Thank God."

Ms. Reynolds purses her lips. "You should've waited. We could've put some knitbone—*comfrey*—on it."

"Give it a couple days. We'll want to rewrap it once the swelling goes down a bit anyway. Then you can start your voodoo on it."

She lifts her chin at him then makes a noise of disgust. "Wrapping the arm in comfrey leaves twice a day will give her the best healing. It might even save the use of her arm. You should've waited for me." She looks around our group. Her eyes quickly dismiss my mom before resting on Kimba. "Will you be caring for her?"

"We all will be," Jennifer answers.

"Well, I don't want to have to explain this to everyone. You." She points to Kimba. "Come over here and listen in with— " She juts her chin in Jennifer's direction.

"I'm Jennifer. She's Kimba."

"Fine. Fine." Ms. Reynolds turns to the man with the cowboy hat. "Mr. Rice, would you be so kind as to give me a description of her injuries?"

The man's mustache twitches slightly. "Broken arm. Stitched up the back of her head. You can see the mess on her face."

Ms. Reynolds gives the man an impatient look. "Is that all?"

"Far as I know. She's not talking to tell us where it hurts. Did a quick check of her legs. They seem okay. She could have some internal injuries. Didn't see any bruising, but it's still early."

The woman lets out a disgusted sigh. "You two can help me give her a proper exam. The rest of you, we'll need some privacy."

I glance at Jameson and Brett, Victoria's sons. Jameson's red-rimmed eyes go wide. He looks like he's ready to argue.

Sixteen-year-old Brett places a hand on his younger brother's arm. "She's right. Mom wouldn't want us gawking."

"Isn't there a doctor?" Jameson asks. "A real one somewhere?"

The man in the cowboy hat grunts. "Had some good ones. And a right fine hospital, too, before all this happened. The hospital's trying to function, but we're short on docs."

"Why's that?" Kimba asks.

"Some left. Some died. Some were killed."

"But there must be someone." Jameson's voice raises in pitch.

"You're better off with Daniela here. She knows how to make medicine out of weeds and eye of newt— "

Ms. Reynolds crosses her arms and shoots him an evil look.

"Or some such thing." He gives her a wink. "Trust me on this. The doctors we have left, they don't know—well, never mind."

Jameson shakes his head. "You'll tell us when we can be with our mom?"

"We'll let you know." Jennifer gives him a kind smile. "We'll make sure we have her all taken care of."

My mom ushers us away. "Let's talk with Rey and see which of our supplies they want to keep. Everything's a little ratty, but maybe there will be things they can use. Then we'll have lunch."

Her voice drops to a whisper, and she motions us to step closer. "I didn't say anything before, but Aunt Karla gave us some stew to share with everyone and greens from the garden and things Daniela foraged. Even olive oil to drizzle over it."

My jaw drops and my mouth begins to water. Lettuce? We've been pulling weeds and eating them along the way, pretending it's salad and hoping none of them made us sick. We really have little idea what is edible in the wild and what isn't. Could this be real lettuce?

"Where is it?" Sebastian asks.

"In our packs, mine and Donnie's. I thought it'd be a nice surprise for everyone. But this . . . " Her smile quickly fades. "We'll still enjoy it, I'm sure."

While Mom talks to Rey, I empty out my large backpack. I want to sort through it for stuff I'm definitely keeping. A second pair of pants and a shirt, a tank top, undergarments, night clothes, and socks are all staying with me, as well as a few toiletry items I've collected along the way.

I spend several seconds running my finger over the smooth wood of the plaque the Dosen family gave me for my birthday, handcrafted by Asher.

Aunt Karla said they'd do some rearranging to find us a place of our own. Maybe it'll be one of the third-floor rooms with a loft, where we slept when I was younger. The loft room was like a tree house, with big windows looking out over the forest. Once we're settled, I'll find a spot to hang the plaque.

I pull out a small photo of my dad. Last fall, after finding my grandma and grandpa dead and their house ransacked, we went to our home next door. It was also a mess, and everything useful was taken. The framed picture of my dad and mom on their wedding day, a picture of my dad in his uniform, and one of him holding me when I was a baby were all on the floor, the frames busted.

I took the photos and put them in an electric bill envelope. *An electric bill.* No one pays bills now. Not power bills, garbage bills, not even mortgages. Of course, there are no grocery stores or anything to buy stuff from either. Money isn't even our currency. Instead, we trade for the things we need. Or steal them from empty houses.

Maybe now things will start to feel somewhat normal again.

And safe.

I wrinkle my nose. I guess nowhere is truly safe. Look at the mess Victoria's in.

"Sadie?" Mom steps around the tent, causing me to jump. "Sorry. They'd like to keep our tent, the sleeping bags you and Sebastian have, and the plastic tarps. I'm also giving them my backpack since it has the gun sling on it. Nate's going to use it to carry the .22."

"What about your guns? Donnie's guns?"

"I'm keeping my rifle and pistol, though they'll be locked in Jack's safe. Donnie will have his guns. Jack's going to put him through a quick training course this afternoon to make sure he's safe with them."

I shake my head. "That seems silly."

"It's their way. And we'll respect it. You heard how nervous guns make Ms. Reynolds." There's a twinkle in her eye as she exaggerates the *Ms.*

The quad roars to life.

"Are they finished with Victoria already?"

"They are. She was even starting to stir. Sounds like Daniela left quite the treasure trove of medicine for her."

"No other injuries?"

"Doesn't seem so. We'll have some lunch and spend the night here. They're going to stay a week or so until Victoria can travel. I thought we'd come back and tell them goodbye before they leave."

Chapter 4

*Near Lewistown, Montana
Sunday, June 7, Late Morning*

Victoria

"I made some tea, Victoria. Want to sit up?" Jennifer's voice is cheery. Too cheery. She helps me get upright and puts an insulated mug to my mouth. It's not hot, barely even warm. Some dripples down my chin. She dutifully wipes it.

The sleeve of my ugly blue shirt is gone, and my arm's in a pink-toned sling. Underneath, thin pieces of wood are wrapped with strips of flowery yellow cloth. My arm aches, throbs. "Who did this?" I blink, waiting for Jennifer to answer.

"A doctor. Well, something like that anyway. Brett was going to go into town, but people from Mosher's compound took care of you."

"Where's Brett? Jameson?" I lift my left hand—the unbroken one—to the back of my head, gingerly touching the long, puckered line. When I pull my fingers back, there's a spot of blood.

"Here. Let me get that." Jennifer dips a cloth in a small bowl of water before carefully wiping at the wound.

"Was it seven or eight?"

"Pardon?" She wrinkles her brow.

"The doctor said my head needed seven or eight stitches."

"It was eleven. Your boys are both on projects. Jameson is with Donnie, watering the horse at the creek. Brett's on patrol with Kimba."

I close my eyes. "The horse?"

"Donnie's— "

"Oh!" I blurt out, as memories rush over me. Donnie McCullough's horse. He's the only one of us not on foot. And he'll likely be staying here or heading back to Bakerville.

He only came along to make sure Leanne Monroe and her two children arrived at her aunt's house safely. They went to visit the aunt within the compound. The rest of us are camped on the outskirts because of their rules against firearms within the community.

"Are you having trouble with your memory?" Jennifer's concern is evident on her face.

I shake my head, instantly regretting the motion. "I'm just a little . . . confused. Everything was a blur, but it's starting to make more sense." When Leanne returns to our camp, she'll tell us more about her aunt and what the community—or cult, according to those in the nearby town of Lewistown, Montana—is like.

Cult. Such an interesting word.

For Leanne's sake, I certainly hope it's a word just being thrown around because of lack of knowledge. The rest of us are supposed to move on, keep going until we reach Jennifer's ranch outside of Great Falls.

But if Kimba and Rey aren't convinced Leanne will be safe here, they may . . . what will they do? Stay and make sure all is well? I guess we'll be staying anyway. I don't know how I'll be able to travel, walking many miles each day, with the way I'm feeling right now.

"Leanne's still at her aunt's?"

"They're back. They even brought us lunch. Wait until you see it!"

My stomach gives a weird grumble, more sickness than hunger. "What time is it?"

Jennifer looks to the sky. "Eleven, maybe."

I touch my face. "My glasses?"

"Sorry, hon. Broken. We can't fix them."

My lips become a hard line. My vision is terrible without them. I knew I should've had the stupid laser surgery years ago, then I'd be able to see in the distance. That's all those were good for anyway. They were a backup pair. I'd started wearing progressive lenses a few months before the attacks. Thankfully, I still have an old pair.

I close my eyes. I'll worry about being able to see later. What a mess this is. Brett, Atticus, Nate, and I left the camp just as the sky was beginning to lighten. They wanted to be in place early, while the deer were grazing for breakfast.

The plan was to check the meadow and then try a few other possible spots before returning to camp in time for lunch. I guess I messed that up.

"Want a snack before lunch? I made bone broth."

My stomach churns at the thought. "Not now. I think— " My eyes drift closed.

~~~~~

The laughter is light and airy. *Happy.* I slowly open one eye, but the brightness of the day encourages me to keep it closed. I focus on the sounds. A party.

"Hey, Mom? Are you awake?"

"What's going on?" My voice is harsh, gravelly. "Water?"

Jameson holds the insulated mug to my mouth. The cool water coats my throat and drops in my stomach. I pull my head back.

"Was that enough?" he asks.

"For now." My voice doesn't sound much better.

"We're getting ready for lunch. Everyone wanted to wait for you. You won't believe what they brought."

"They sound . . . happy."

"Yeah, I guess they are. Leanne's aunt's place sounds nice. Even Sebastian wants to stay. You're not going to believe this, but Leanne and Donnie are getting married."

"Humph. I believe it. Those two— " I move wrong, sending a shock of pain from the tips of my fingers up my arm and into my shoulder, then my head. I let out a moan.

"What's wrong?" Jameson's voice is panicked.

"Hurts. My arm."

"I'll get Jennifer. She has stuff for you."

A few minutes later, Jennifer gives me a squirt of the bitter liquid Rey forced down me earlier and then some tea.

"You ready for some food?" she asks.

"A little. Maybe."

"We set up a second seating area, but we thought we'd move over here and eat together . . . if you're up to it?"

"Okay, yeah, sure." I stumble over my words. "Just let me close my eyes for a minute."
~~~~~

Chapter 5

Near Lewistown, Montana
Sunday, June 7, Evening

Victoria

It's nearly dark when I wake again, the campfire putting off a soothing glow. As always, Jennifer's by my side. She's humming as she sews.

I clear my throat.

She looks up from her work with a smile. "Good morning again, Victoria. Or I should say, good evening. I was just thinking about waking you to ask if you wanted to move to the tent." She swats at something on her arm.

"What're you working on?"

"Your pants. You got a hole in them. It may not look great, but they'll work."

I squint my eyes. The brown corduroy sports a line of red. Our small sewing kit contains few thread options. Even so, red wouldn't have been my first choice.

"Your shirt has one sleeve now. I can't sew it back on. Guess it doesn't matter since you'll be in the sling for a while. It'll be easy to get over the cast."

I swallow the lump in my throat. At one time, I had a 5,200-square-foot house full of beautiful clothing, feminine shoes, furniture, dishes, and other treasures.

Now everything I own is in a backpack. The ugly pants are one of only two pairs, plus a pair of yoga pants for sleeping. The light long-sleeved shirt, which is necessary to keep my arms from burning, usually goes over a tank top.

I look at the clothes I'm wearing. Someone helped me into the yoga pants and one of my tanks. I wonder when that happened? Who did it?

"Mom? You're awake?" Fourteen-year-old Jameson's voice floats on the air.

I turn my head slowly, carefully. He and most of the group, other than Jennifer and me, are sitting around a second campfire.

"Hey, why are you over there?"

Both he and Brett scramble to their feet.

"Remember?" Jennifer asks. "We set up a second seating area to give you a little peace and quiet."

"Mmm. I missed lunch?"

She smiles. "And supper. We saved you some soup and a little salad."

Brett, now kneeling at my side, reaches for my hand. "You look better, more alert."

"Does your lip hurt?" Jameson asks, taking a knee next to his brother.

My tongue moves to the spot just above my lip. It's crusted over and rough. "I must look a sight."

"You look good." Brett squeezes my hand.

"He cut your hair so he could stitch up your head," Jameson says. "But he left it long on top. Kimba says no one will even notice."

A small laugh escapes me. "Really?"

Jameson lifts a shoulder in response. "We'll probably stay here a week or so, give you time to feel better before we start traveling."

"A week?" I'm torn between telling him that's not nearly long enough and saying I'll only need a few days. "Will my arm heal properly?"

The boys share a look.

"Uh, well, we don't— " Brett stutters out a response.

Jennifer jumps in. "It'll take some time, and you'll need to be very careful not to move it at all, but you should be able to use it."

"Use it?" I furrow my brow.

"It was worse than when Dad broke his arm." Jameson shakes his head.

"Worse?"

"You broke both bones, the ulna and the radius. Before the collapse, you would've needed surgery to repair it. Plates and screws added, all that good stuff." Jennifer gives me a half smile. "But now, well, it's not an option."

"Of course not," I say, remembering Jon's surgery. It was supposed to be day surgery, but he had a reaction to the anesthesia and stayed overnight. He was in a cast for three months and didn't even go into the office for five weeks. Five long weeks. Miserable weeks. "But will it heal correctly? I know that— "

"We don't know, Mom." Brett's voice is soft. "There's no way to be certain. Chuck Rice, the man who set your arm, said you could possibly have it repaired once things get back to normal. And he also thinks Great Falls may have surgeons. Maybe the Air Force— "

"Humph," Jameson scoffs. "You heard Donnie. The Air Force may be taking care of things from a military police standpoint, but any resources they have will be kept for themselves. Including their doctors."

Jennifer puts out a hand. "This is a worry for another day. We'll pray your mom's arm heals as it should."

"Just like you prayed we'd all reach your house safely?" The brutal words, and even harsher tone, blurt out of me.

Jennifer pales. Her eyes fill with tears as she shakes her head. "I know it's hard to understand. With this injury, with Asher's death, it may be easy to think God isn't with us, that our prayers are useless."

"But if God's so powerful . . . " I shake my head, wincing at the motion.

"I know. It seems He could've stopped it—*should* have stopped it. I don't know why Asher was taken from us. I don't blame God, though. Asher's death was the result of what a man did."

"Well, you're a better woman than I am, because I definitely blame Him—for Asher dying and for . . . for this whole mess we're in." I refrain from pointing to my broken arm as further proof of God's negligence.

Brett gives my hand a slight squeeze. "Asher wasn't afraid to die. If anything, he was afraid his life didn't glorify God. It did. He used to say he was going to use the gifts God gave him to bring praise to Jesus. He did that. Everyday."

Jennifer blinks several times. When she speaks, her voice is husky. "Thank you, Brett. Your saying so fills my heart with happiness."

I glance to Jameson. His chin is on his chest, his eyes closed. He lets out a loud sigh. "I miss Asher. He was . . . he was always kind to me, even when I didn't deserve it. I don't know much about God, about Jesus."

The way my son looks at me squeezes my heart. I want to argue and remind him how we took him to church almost every Sunday. The preacher told him about God. But the truth is, whatever he may have heard on Sunday was left in the building.

Jameson's eyes fill with tears. "Brett's right. Asher made no secret about who he was and how much he believed—*trusted*—in God. I heard him say once that his dad was walking on streets paved with gold, worshipping with Jesus. He missed his dad, but he was still happy for him. And he said he was looking forward to that himself someday." Jameson wipes his eyes.

Jennifer rests a hand on his arm. "He loved you, both you and Brett. When we— " She clears her throat. "It was Asher who first suggested we ask the three of you to come to the ranch with us." Jennifer's eyes meet mine, her lashes starred with tears, glittering in the firelight. "I wasn't sure. It hadn't been long since my sister died."

I lift my chin slightly. Her sister was killed at the hands of my husband. While he may not have pulled the trigger, his actions resulted in her death and the death of several others in our tiny community.

"I was still hurting. Angry. When Nina died, I was devastated. Losing my husband, while being stranded so far from home, was almost too much. While I tried to rejoice in—as Jameson said—him worshipping with Jesus, the loss was still hard. My sister helped me through it. She wasn't . . . "

Jennifer bites her lip. "She wasn't a Christian. Not then. And to my knowledge, not on the day she died either. Her death, in many ways, was harder than losing Archer, my husband. I don't have the assurance I'll see her again. Oh, I hope in those final minutes, as she laid on the floor gasping for breath, she reached out to God and accepted Jesus as her Lord and Savior."

She lifts a shoulder. "But I don't know. I wasn't with her. I was serving the food, excited about the wedding celebration and talking with someone in line before the shooting started. She died without me by her side."

"And you blamed me." My voice is quiet.

"No, Victoria. Not you. Not exactly. But it was still hard to . . . to . . . Asher was insistent. He knew my anger wasn't doing me any good. He reminded me of my emphasis on treating others the way I wished to be treated. He reminded me I was treating you poorly, blaming you for something of which you were innocent."

"I wouldn't say completely innocent," Brett blurts out.

My eyes go wide as they shoot to my oldest son. "Why do you say that?"

He gives my hand a squeeze. "We all knew Dad was losing it. You, me, and Jameson— " he looks at his little brother, who's no longer relaxed but is now giving Brett a hard stare " —we knew he was completely . . . "

"Nuts?" Jameson offers.

Brett lifts a shoulder before turning slightly toward Jennifer. "He'd been progressively getting worse. We should've known he was up to something. The way he'd disappear . . . Mom thought— "

I take in a loud breath. "Brett, please. You don't need to air all our dirty laundry."

"Mom thought he had a girlfriend," Jameson says. "Wouldn't be the first one."

I close my eyes. The pounding in my head is increasing. I was foolish to think my children didn't know.

"I'm so sorry for the difficulties you've had." Jennifer's voice is kind. "And I hope you—all of you—will forgive me if my actions added to those difficulties."

"You're giving us a fresh start. We needed that. Right, Mom?" Brett squeezes my hand again.

I blink a few times, clearing the moisture from my eyes. "We do. Very much so, Jennifer. Staying in Bakerville, knowing my husband was the cause of so much heartache, would've been very difficult. Running away may seem, um, cowardly." I meet her eyes with an embarrassed smile. "But it's truly what we need, what my boys need."

"I could've stayed." Jameson crosses his arms, a hard look taking over his face. "I would've shown them— "

"Shown them what?" Brett asks. "That we're just like him? Cruel and unyielding? Murderers?"

"I'm not a murderer!" Jameson's voice booms, causing those at the other fire to look over at us.

"Shh," I admonish. "That's not what your brother said." The pain in my head ratchets up several notches, along with the ache in my arm.

Jennifer must register my discomfort. "Want a pain pill?"

I furrow my brow. "Pain pill?"

"Mosher gave us a couple, remember? To get you through the first few days. We're combining them with the willow bark tea and tincture, along with some other things Daniela Reynolds left. She's even growing turmeric to use for long-term pain management, just like we did in the ski lodge greenhouse."

Again, my tongue finds the stitch above my lip. "Does that stuff really work?"

"Does the willow bark?"

"Well, it helps. Maybe. But turmeric . . . I don't know."

"We'll see. She said you can't use it right now, to wait until you aren't taking the pain pills since the turmeric can lessen their effectiveness. She's sending a rhizome with us to plant once we reach the ranch. I sure wish I knew more about herbs and natural remedies."

"Maybe there'll be someone who knows those things," Brett suggests. "You know, a neighbor."

"Maybe in Simms." Jennifer nods. "But not my nearest neighbor. They're . . . anyway, we'll ask around. I may have books in my mother-in-law's things. Many of her things were just boxed up and put in the attic above the garage. It'll be a true treasure hunt to see what of hers may be useful." Jennifer hoists herself off the ground. "I'll be right back with water and a pill."

After she leaves, Brett asks, "Can I get you anything else?"

"Will you find my extra glasses? They're in a hard case in one of my backpack pockets."

"The taped-together pair?" Jameson narrows his eyes.

I tilt my head to the side. "Jennifer said mine broke and can't be fixed."

"She's right." Brett nods.

"I'll look for them." Jameson lets out a noisy breath. "Too bad Dad— " He shakes his head.

I close my eyes. Yes, too bad Jon got so mad at me he smacked me and sent my glasses flying across the room, snapping off the bow. I put them in a drawer, choosing to wear the backup pair. It wasn't the first time Jon was physically violent with me, but it was the last. The next day was the day he died.

When we were packing to leave on this trip, Jameson found the glasses and used a roll of electrical tape to put them back together, saying I may need them. I open my eyes to meet those of my young son. "Thank you. I'm grateful you repaired them for me."

He gives me a tight smile before bouncing up.

"Need anything else?" Brett asks.

"No. I think I just need a little time to heal. I'll have one of the women help me to the bathroom and then get something to eat before going to my tent. I'm ready to call it a night."

"You'll probably feel a lot better tomorrow." Brett gives me a sweet little-boy smile.

I want to agree with him, but I suspect I'll feel a lot worse tomorrow. Even as I sit here, I feel new aches and pains. No, tomorrow probably won't be good at all.

Chapter 6

Near Lewistown, Montana
Monday, June 8, Midmorning

Sadie

On our way back to the lodge, Mom leaves her pistol and rifle with the men manning the roadblock, but Donnie's allowed to bring his in. He's now an official member of the protection squad. Even after taking Mom's guns, they make a point of telling her she isn't allowed to use any weapons within the borders of the community.

She smiles sweetly. "I understand."

Mom doesn't mention the gift Kimba gave her before we left camp: a tank top with an underarm holster and a pistol. She's wearing it now, just like Kimba did a few days ago when she and my mom first visited Aunt Karla. Mom tried to refuse the gift, saying Kimba might need it, but our friend insisted.

"Do you guys know anything about Ledger Hyde's place being deserted?" Donnie asks.

The two men look at each other, then one starts muttering all kinds of things about Hyde being a loser.

The younger man clears his throat. "Hey, Loomer, there's kids here."

"Whatever," the muttering one says as he spits on the ground.

The younger one, or as I've come to think of as *the nice one*, shakes his head and tells us he didn't know about it until they started their shift and were told to keep an eye out for Hyde in case he tries something funny.

We're a dozen feet from the checkpoint when I ask, "Where do you think they went?"

Donnie shakes his head. "Sounds like Hyde finally realized he wasn't welcome here."

"I'm not so sure," Mom says. "Yesterday, before we left, Aunt Karla was talking about Hyde and his wife. She said they were a respected part of the community. The man worked side-by-side with Jack, setting things up so they could all survive. She sounded sad about the whole thing."

It's hard for me to imagine the man who held me at gunpoint—in such a careless way that I could get the drop on him and send his weapon flying from his hands—could be someone to be counted on. I mean, *look at me*. I'm not even five feet tall and only ninety pounds.

Whatever Aunt Karla thinks of Ledger Hyde, I think he's probably lost a marble or two since she's been around him. I guess that's understandable. Being driven from your home and forced to live in a shack with your babies and young wife would be hard on anyone. Aunt Karla whispered to Mom about the large age gap between the two, but they never let it bother them. Especially if it's true he was previously a leader in the community.

"Well, whatever's going on now, it's probably best Hyde isn't here. Too much animosity, if the guy at the barricade is any indication of how people feel about him."

"The other man seemed nice," Sebastian says. "But the one who was mad . . . is he the same guy who was at camp the other night?"

Of course! I thought he looked familiar. The loud one, Loomer, was one of the men Jack Mosher had take Hyde back to his home the night Atticus and I were held at gunpoint.

I glance to the house on the right side of the road—Mosher's place. The large, single-story home sits back from the road. What was probably once a beautiful green lawn is now overgrown with horses in it. Gordie, Donnie's horse, sees the equines and lets out a soft whinny.

"Is he happy to be going to Aunt Karla's?" Sebastian asks from Gordie's back. "He'll have other horse friends again."

With one hand on the horse's lead rope, Donnie lifts the other to Gordie's soft brown neck. "Whatta ya think, old friend? You ready to be around some of your own kind again?"

"Maybe he'll make a baby horse?" Sebastian's voice is hopeful.

Gordie and Donnie snicker at the same time.

Mom smiles up at Sebastian. "Gordie's a gelding, honey. He can't make babies."

Sebastian furrows his brow. "Like when Uncle Wes's dog Lucy Lou had that surgery?"

I squeeze my eyes tight and let out a silent breath. Uncle Wes was with us when the attacks started and the EMP hit. At the time, we didn't really know what was happening. Warnings had gone off, telling us of a missile strike. We hid in a church basement for many days, thinking we were being bombed. After it was determined the imminent danger had passed, we started planning how to get home.

Some of the church people found bikes for Mom and Wes with a bike trailer for Sebastian and me to ride in. It was Uncle Wes who suggested we take roads less traveled. That choice ended up costing him his life. We did finally make it home, to find Grandma and Grandpa dead, and Lucy Lou along with Grandpa's dog, Rover, missing. I hate to think about what might have happened to the dogs.

There's a quiver in Mom's voice when she answers. "Yes, very similar."

"So, no baby horses? Um, what's a baby horse called? A pony?"

"A foal, colt if it's a male," Donnie answers. "A pony is a breed of horse smaller than a full-sized horse like old Gordie here. Your aunt has a couple of ponies in her string."

"String?"

"Her stable."

Sebastian shakes his head.

"He means in her herd," Mom says. "There are a lot of names for a group of horses. Remember the horse last night that you said was just your size? She's a pony."

"She seemed nice."

Donnie snorts. "Ain't no such thing as a *nice* mare. 'Specially a pony."

With Sebastian riding Gordie, we walk the five miles without stopping to rest. While we were traveling, we limited our walking to ten miles a day so Sebastian and Naomi Hoffmann didn't get too tired. We'd go a couple of miles, stop and rest for half an hour or an hour, and keep it up until we made our daily quota.

After Mom got sick, she rode Gordie. When she started feeling better, Sebastian and Naomi took turns. I've ridden him before, too, when we first started walking and I was still weak from our winter travels, just like my mom and brother.

Now I'm feeling good. Strong. Mom is too. And five miles is nothing.

As we begin the final bend in the road before the lodge comes into view, Donnie points to the trees. "I think I'll talk to Mosher about how we can fortify this area."

"Like with a roadblock?" Mom asks.

"Don't think so. Maybe an early warning system of some sort, figure out a way to let us know if someone's approaching."

"You really think it's necessary? They have the barricade back at the intersection." Mom motions behind us.

We've only seen two of the roadblocks the community set up. One by where we were camping, and a second where we turned from the road where Mosher's house is and onto the dead-end road leading to Aunt Karla's lodge. We were told there's another barricade toward the state highway. There's also an old fire cabin on the mountain top used as a lookout.

"We're sitting ducks back here all alone. I don't know what they were thinking, putting the women and children here, isolated, without even a means to protect themselves."

"Oh, I wouldn't say completely without." Mom winks at Donnie.

He answers with a shake of his head.

As the lodge comes into view, I can't help but smile. *We're here.* We'll be making our home with Aunt Karla, settling in to one place. No more walking for miles and miles each day.

Kimba promised she'd send word via Mosher when Victoria's well enough to travel. We'll return to camp to say our goodbyes, and that'll be it. No more traveling and daily walking.

Daniela Reynolds is working in one of the flower gardens. She quickly sets her tools aside and rushes toward us. "How's your friend this morning?"

"More lucid." Mom gives the woman a light smile.

"Her pain level?"

"Okay. Mosher left a couple of pills, and Jennifer's using the teas and tinctures just like you said, plus the salve you left for the cut on her face and the back of her head."

"Looking at her arm, I suspect four or five days and it'll need to be rewrapped."

"They're going to send word when Victoria feels ready to leave."

"I can't imagine that'll be any time soon. Too bad your friends are so stubborn. The woman needs a bed, not sleeping on the hard ground."

I glance to Donnie just in time to see his eyes narrow and his mouth open.

Mom puts a hand on his arm. "I'm sure they're making her comfortable."

Ms. Reynolds darts her eyes to Donnie's hip. She lets out a growl. "How dare you. How dare you come here, wearing that . . . that thing. I've told you this is a place of peace and rest. Jack is going to hear about this. You're defying our mandates!"

"Who do you think told the guards to let me in with it?" Donnie's tone is even, controlled. "I'm an official member of The Little Dogies Protection Squad." He gives a slight bow.

The woman spits out several choice words before turning on her heel and flouncing off.

"That went well," Donnie mutters.

"She certainly has a bee in her bonnet about firearms. Good thing she doesn't know about Aunt Karla's stash."

Donnie lets out a laugh.

I tilt my head toward my mom. "Meaning?"

"Meaning, your aunt doesn't share the same hatred for firearms as Ms. Reynolds. She doesn't flaunt what she has but can protect herself if necessary."

"The problem is, one frail old woman isn't going to do a hill of beans against an actual attack," Donnie says. "Every single one of these women, the children too, need to know how to defend themselves. Look at Sadie and Sebastian. They fought their way out of their kidnapping. You think those little girls could do the same?" Donnie motions to a couple of children around my brother's age who are working alongside a woman in the vegetable garden.

"Or those kids?" He points to a boy and girl chasing each other in a game of tag. One of the women hollers for them to wrap it up and get back to work.

I chew the nail of my thumb, thinking about the nutty man who took Sebastian and me hostage in Roundup. He kept talking about taking sister wives and having a bunch of children. He'd met another man who was doing the same thing, taking several wives so he could help rebuild the country, creating the large family he always wanted.

My crazy captor thought it sounded like a good idea. And the way he talked, he wanted me to be one of the wives. *Gross.*

I look at the children. "Maybe they could. We don't know if they have training. What about before?"

"True. But I think you know that, unless you keep up on it and practice moves over and over, you aren't going to summon your inner Bruce Lee."

"Who's Bruce Lee?" Sebastian asks.

"He was a martial arts expert," Mom says. "He was in a lot of movies. It's a good point, Donnie. Too many people think it's like TV and everything will go just right. It doesn't. And it's over in seconds."

"Maybe we could teach them the things we've learned?" my brother offers.

"I think that's a fine idea." Donnie nods. "Ms. Snooty Pants might not believe in self-defense, but I have a hunch there're plenty here who'd be happy to learn how to defend themselves."

"You're going to teach them how to use the guns?" I ask.

He lifts a shoulder. "Not sure that'd go over too good. But the other stuff, the escapes, kicks, blocks, maybe even the knife defenses . . . I can't imagine that'd be a problem."

I lift my eyebrows. I think he may be wrong, considering the way Ms. Reynolds reacted yesterday to me carrying a knife on my hip. Of course, learning how to defend against a knife attack, and understanding you'll be cut during that defense, is different than having a knife strictly as a tool. Everyone in our group, even Sebastian and Naomi, carried a knife . . . or two.

I wish Kimba could do a class for everyone. She's a master with blades and is the best teacher. Maybe we should go back to camp and convince her it's a good idea, have her do a couple of good self-defense classes to get everyone started. I turn to ask Mom what she thinks when a scream breaks the quiet of the lodge.

Donnie's hand goes to his sidearm. Mom reaches for hers, too, seeming to forget she's not wearing one on her hip.

"What is it?" Sebastian torques his body in the saddle, trying to find the source of the noise.

The woman in the vegetable garden with the children lifts her hand. "We're fine. It's just a garden snake."

One of the little girls is laughing while the other is shaking her head and moving backward.

Mom lets out a loud breath. "I completely forgot I don't have a gun on my hip. And I didn't even think about . . . " She raises her eyebrows before lightly touching her armpit.

"See?" Donnie crosses his arms. "This whole thing of keeping the women unarmed just makes you a victim. And *you* are no victim."

"Let's not be so dramatic. I'm going to talk with Aunt Karla and see what we can do."

Chapter 7

Fergus Peak Lodge
Near Lewistown, Montana
Sunday, June 14, After Breakfast

Sadie

"All right, Li'l Partner. Show me what to do with these."

I roll my eyes at the fake accent and annoying manner of Cassie, one of Aunt Karla's wranglers.

Sebastian gives her a shy, adoring look before taking the reins in his hand.

"Yup, that's it. Don't pull too tight. Old Rosie doesn't think much of having her mouth yanked on. Now what if you want her to turn?"

"Which way?"

"Left."

Sebastian gives a nod. "I look to the left, then shift my weight a little so more is on my left side. Now move my leg into her and lift up the left side of my rein."

"Well, fine then. Let's see you do it."

Sebastian flawlessly moves Old Rosie to face the left.

"G'job, Sebby. You're a natural horseman."

Sebastian's cheeks color from the praise.

I shake my head at the fake gushing. It seems Cassie doesn't realize she no longer works for tips. She's always overly dramatic, especially with *Sebby.* Why she even started calling him that, I'll never know.

Mom planned to teach us to ride, and has spent some time with us, but Aunt Karla said Cassie's the best, especially with the children. She and Brooke, another wrangler, were both working here with three others when everything happened.

The other three, all from homes in the Midwest, left together after the bridges exploded. Aunt Karla was in contact with them for several days and knows they ended up on foot because of the fuel issues. When the cyberattack happened, she didn't hear from them again. She hopes they each got where they were going but has no way of knowing.

Cassie and Brooke, one from Southern Oregon and the other from Northern California, decided to wait it out—mainly because they were able to reach their parents, who told them to stay put.

Cassie puts Sebastian through several drills before she has me do all the things she just had him do.

"You two are turning into right fine horsemen. Here come your folks. I'll tell them you're ready to go."

Mom gives us a wave as she walks toward the stables. "Looking good."

"They're doing fine, Ms. Monroe. Just fine." Cassie beams. She's so saccharine sweet. It's annoying, but at the same time I swell with pride. Sebastian, too, sits a little taller.

Mom and Donnie get their horses ready. While Donnie is, of course, on Gordie, Mom's on a black gelding named Legend. I'm riding a buckskin gelding called Boot. Sebastian is on a pony named Old Rosie.

Donnie said he thought riding a pony mare was a mistake. Cassie, Brooke, and Aunt Karla all say she's as gentle as a kitten and completely mild mannered. "We'll see about that," Donnie muttered.

Taking the horses and leaving just a little over an hour after sunup will put us back here tonight. Our friends would welcome us to stay, but Mom and Donnie figure they've already made use of the bedding and goods we left for them.

"Why upset the apple cart?" Donnie asked. "No reason we can't make this a day trip."

Like last time, we're taking fresh greens and several jars of soup. Aunt Karla is even sending a smoked elk roast with us as a gift for helping us get here.

She wanted to ride out and meet our friends but decided she's still too unsteady to be on a horse. Donnie offered to ride double to help keep her on, but after a stern look from Daniela Reynolds, Aunt Karla waved a hand and said, "I'd best not."

Since our friends leave tomorrow, Ms. Reynolds will have Jack Mosher take her out on the quad again to check on Victoria and how she's healing. Even though the woman is still uptight most of the time, especially when she's in Donnie's presence, I can see a kindness about her.

And she's definitely smart about medicine and foraging for food. She calls herself a wildcrafter, which is pretty much what we did while traveling, trying to find plants for food and medicine. But we didn't know anything compared to what she knows. My guess is our diet would've been a lot more varied if someone like Daniela Reynolds had been with us.

I got a good laugh the other day when I was on garden duty with her and she pulled a knife out of her pocket to cut a stem. The way she reacted to me wearing a knife on my hip, I was sure she had an aversion to them just like she does to guns. She saw me staring and lifted a shoulder before going back to her project.

In addition to Daniela, Samantha, Cassie, and Brooke, there are dozens of other women and children living at the lodge. I think I've met everyone, but it's hard to keep them all straight.

Mom and I have been added to work crews. Sebastian too, though he has two hours of school each day. We work not only in the gardens, but also in the kitchen, at the laundry, or taking care of the livestock. I'm surprised by how many different animals they're raising. Many, like rabbits, are wild ones they captured.

As the only adult male living at the lodge, Donnie's now staying in an unfinished cabin up the creek a bit—the same one the family was in last year when their dog's water dish froze. He's fixing the place up, getting it ready for all of us to live in after the wedding. He isn't on any of the official work crews but helps wherever he's needed.

A light breeze caresses my face as my horse, Boot, plods along. The lodge stable only has trail horses, and they're trained to follow each other. Donnie's horse, Gordie, wants nothing of that and is happy walking alongside Mom's. Sebastian's pony follows Mom's gelding, keeping right on his tail. Boot is last in line, never falling more than a few feet behind the pony.

We're talking and laughing, having such a great time you'd think it was just a casual stroll on a normal Sunday.

As we come within view of the first roadblock, Mom asks, "Should we stop?"

"No need," Donnie says. "It's just for those coming from the north. Outsiders."

"Outsiders?" Mom's eyebrows go up. "You're beginning to sound like Jack."

"Yeah, I guess."

"Do you know the men at the roadblock?"

Donnie squints. "Yup."

After the brief training he had with Jack, Donnie was assigned to monitor the barricade a couple of times. He's even being added to the rotation at the old fire watch cabin. He'll go up for a week when his turn comes.

Mom and he will probably be married by then. He said he's going to sneak her in his duffle bag and take her along, give her a honeymoon of sorts. Mom laughed like a schoolgirl when he told her that. It's good to see her like this. She was so miserable for so long. I love that she's happy.

"Why are there three men?" Sebastian points to the barricade. "Isn't there only two on duty at a time?"

"Hmm. Good point. Looks like one is Randy Loomer. He was on with me yesterday. Man's full of himself, probably just there to make sure the other two know he's all that."

I chuff out a laugh at Donnie's choice of words. Mom's laugh is merrier and lighter, the laugh of someone in love.

Once we're close enough, it's obvious Loomer isn't there just to show how important he is. He and another guy are standing toe to toe. The third man is making weak motions with his hands but staying well back.

"What's going on?" Mom whispers.

"Nothing good," Donnie says.

We're close enough now for me to recognize the second man. He was one of the two who showed up at our camp to take Ledger Hyde back to his home. Randy Loomer was the other one.

"Hang back," Donnie says with a nod.

"Sadie, Sebastian, stop your horses." Mom gently pulls back on her reins. "Whoa, Legend."

I do the same with Boot, while Sebastian stops Old Rosie.

Donnie moves Gordie forward at a slow, deliberate speed. "Hey, there," he says as he gets closer.

Even from this distance, I can see the shorter of the two guys narrow his eyes. "Whatta ya want, McCullough?"

"Nothing at all. Just heading out to see our people."

The taller guy lets his shoulders drop slightly. He gives Donnie a nod and a grimace, which may be an attempt at a smile.

"We're not done." The shorter one thumps the taller guy in the chest.

Tall Guy immediately straightens. "We're done, Randy. Completely done. Get out of my face."

Short guy, Randy Loomer, lets off a string of words that cause my eyes to bug out. I glance to Sebastian, whose eyes are not only protruding but also his mouth is in an *O*.

Donnie looks back at my mom.

She gives a slight shake of her head. "Let's go." Her voice is low, directed at my brother and me. "We don't need to be here for this."

Donnie turns Gordie in our direction. My eyes are still on the two arguing men. Tall Guy lifts his hands and takes a step away from Randy Loomer.

With a growl, Loomer launches himself and hits Tall Guy in the gut with a shoulder as his arms wrap around him. They hit the ground hard, both throwing punches.

"Hey!" the third guy yells.

"Go." Donnie motions toward Mom. "Cut across the corner."

Mom moves her horse, making a clicking noise with her mouth to get him going. Old Rosie is happy to fall in behind. I'm still watching the fight as Boot takes his place in line without any urging from me.

The third guy yells again for them to stop, which causes Old Rosie to falter in her steps.

"You're okay, old girl." Sebastian's voice is wobbly, unsure.

Mom turns in her saddle as she coaxes her horse to a stop. "Nudge her and come beside me. I'm taking your lead rope."

Just as my brother gives his pony a slight kick, the third man yells again. I glance over at him in time to see him raise his pistol, the barrel pointed to the sky. The percussion of the discharge shatters the morning.

Old Rosie takes off like a shot. Boot lifts his legs, jumps in the air, and follows after Rosie.

"Whoa! Whoa!" I cry, yanking on the reins. Boot pays no mind, trying to keep close to Rosie, who's running straight for a fence.

Sebastian is pulling back on her, yelling for her to stop. Just before hitting the fence, Old Rosie zigs, heading for the road.

My horse does something like a dance step, unsure if he's supposed to follow the pony. I tighten my legs and hold on to him, somehow bringing him to a stop. He shakes his head and makes several noises.

Donnie's instantly by my side. "Whoa, horse. Whoa." He grabs my lead rope.

Mom's almost to Sebastian. Old Rosie's slowing, a sheen of sweat covering her coat.

"You're a good boy," I croon. I hear the quiver in my voice. With my heart racing and my hands shaking, I try again. "That's it, Boot. We'll just wait until they get Old Rosie calmed down. That mean man shooting his gun has her all riled up. She'll be fine."

The words are no sooner out of my mouth when Rosie seems to give a shiver and come to a full stop, flinging Sebastian forward. Somehow, he manages to stay on, leaning just slightly off his saddle.

Seconds later, Mom's by his side and reaching for the lead rope. They're too far away for me to hear the conversation, but from the way Sebastian is moving, it's obvious he wants off the horse. While she doesn't let him off, Mom does dismount from Legend and checks to make sure Old Rosie's saddle is still secure.

A couple minutes of conversation follow before Mom gets back on her horse and leads Old Rosie and Sebastian toward me. My brother's shoulders are shaking, his face stained with tears.

"You got your horse?" Donnie asks me.

I give a hesitant nod.

"Yes or no, Sadie? Can you control this horse?"

"Yes. I've got him."

His eyes meet mine before he gives a nod and hands me back the lead rope. "Put it back like it was."

I close my eyes, trying to remember how the rope was secured.

"Wrap it around your saddle horn. Tuck the end so it isn't hanging loose," Donnie instructs.

I give a nod and do what he says.

Donnie steers Gordie toward the three men. The one who fired the gun looks embarrassed, his gun once again in its holster. Tall Guy is standing several feet away from the other two, his nose bloody. Randy Loomer glares at him, then shifts his angry gaze toward Donnie.

"What were you thinking?" Donnie calls out. "The kids could've been killed."

"I . . . I'm sorry." The man who shot the gun lifts his hands, palms facing the sky. "I didn't— " He shakes his head.

As I get a good look at the man who shot, I realize he's not much older than me. His beard is scraggly and uneven.

Using a string of profanities, Randy Loomer makes it clear the shooter is a fool. He finishes his tirade with, "Going to find himself in the hoosegow if he's not careful."

"Sadie." My mom motions to me as she reaches the road to the camp. "Let's go. Donnie will be right behind us."

With my heart pounding, I give a nod and a slight kick to my horse. He's more than happy to join the others. I let out a noisy breath, happy the horses are cooperating. As we move, I keep my eyes on Donnie and the men.

"What's this all about?" Donnie asks.

"None of your business," Loomer says. "You're new here, and some things don't concern you. Nelson and I just don't quite see eye to eye on things, that's all."

There's a roar of a motor in the distance, and Mom orders me to move quicker. As soon as I'm near them, she says, "Scoot up here. I'm holding your horse too."

Mom's already secured Old Rosie's lead rope to her own saddle horn. When I'm at her side, she reaches out to grab on to mine. We wait, holding the horses still until Mosher's quad comes into view.

"You okay?" Mosher asks after letting off the idle.

"You need to talk to your man," Mom bristles.

"On my way to do that. I heard the shot and called for a report. The numbskull told me about his foolish action." Mosher shakes his head. "Are your children okay? They didn't get bucked off, did they?"

Mom shoots us a smile. "They stayed on like champs."

Sebastian's shoulders shudder as he takes in a ragged breath. "I don't want to do that again. Mom said I have to keep riding, that I can't let her beat me."

"Your mom's right."

Donnie rides up behind us as Jack lifts a hand in farewell. There was some serious animosity—or maybe competition—between Donnie and Jack the first few days we were here. But now that Mom's made it clear she loves Donnie and is marrying him, the two have a truce.

"What was that about," Mom asks Donnie. She hands me back my rope, which I wrap and secure.

Donnie gives an exaggerated shrug. "Who knows? Couldn't get a straight answer out of Loomer. And Nelson wasn't talking either. The boy, don't know his name, was starting to talk until Loomer pointed at him and told him to zip it."

Having experienced Loomer's fondness for colorful words, I imagine there were several descriptive actions added to the instruction.

"We're done here?" Mom asks.

"Completely. Let Mosher take care of them."

Chapter 8

Near Lewistown, Montana
Sunday, June 14

Sadie

Visiting with our traveling companions—*our friends*—for what will likely be the last time we'll ever see them, is bittersweet. While we were all strangers when we left the ski lodge three months ago, it's no longer like that. Even Jameson, who has been nothing short of a brat for most of this trip, seems less annoying.

Is it because I know I don't have to spend any more time with him? Or is he softening, something like my mom did?

When we first arrived at the camp, Sebastian relayed the story of the fight, gunshot, and our horses taking off. He went into very vivid detail about how frightened he was. With wide eyes, Naomi told him how glad she was he didn't get hurt. Donnie made a less than kind remark about mare ponies and glue factories.

Kimba asked more about the fight and what it was all about. When Donnie told her who was involved, a long conversation about the missing Ledger Hyde and his family ensued.

The day after we last saw our friends, Atticus and Axel went to check out the house Hyde was living in, confirming what was suspected from the top of the hillside before Victoria and Nate lost their footing—the house is indeed empty.

"I asked Jack Mosher about it when he and the herb lady were here a couple of days ago," Atticus says. "Mosher said he didn't know they left until we mentioned it to Chuck Rice when he was working on Victoria, said he figured Ledger just decided to give it up. His wife has family in Western Montana, so they probably set out for there."

"You look like you're feeling better," Mom says to Victoria. "Are Daniela's herbs helping with the pain?"

"I'm much better than I was, that's for sure. Ready to walk again."

"You're even wearing your ax." Mom motions to Victoria's left hip, the side without the broken arm.

"Just the one." She nods. "Nate's going to take care of the other one for me."

Color rises to Nate's cheeks. "I asked Jameson and Brett first. They said they had their pistols, so . . . " The boy lifts his hands.

"Yeah." Jameson nods. "It's fine."

"We still practice together." Nate's words come out in a rush. "Victoria, Jameson, and me."

I furrow my brow. Nate isn't usually so nervous with words. I wonder if he still feels guilty about Victoria's tumble and is blaming himself for her injuries. I also wonder if Jameson might've said something to make Nate feel even more guilty.

Mom turns back to Victoria. "You can throw left-handed?"

Victoria lifts a shoulder. "Somewhat. It's not as easy as right-handed since that's my dominant hand. I used to throw two-handed when I first started out. And then I switched to just one. I've practiced with my left before, so . . . "

"She's still good," Jameson says, "hits the target like a pro, even with her left."

She gives a half smile. "A few weeks, and I'll be good as new. But I couldn't do this alone."

"We help her with the sharpening, either Nate or me. Mom can't do that very well with one hand."

"Everyone has been great about . . . well, everything. Jennifer makes sure I take my medicine. The boys are all great about helping me with things. Kimba, Rey—just everyone."

Victoria's smile and praise are genuine. There's something more, a different demeanor about her than she usually has. Less conceited maybe?

I've always felt like she thought she was better than the rest of us. I'm not really surprised. As the wife of a successful attorney, she had a pretty posh life, always the best of everything. But as we've gotten to know her, it seems it may not have been a very happy life.

Right now, sitting at this camp with a busted-up arm, she looks more relaxed and content than I ever remember.

~~~~
~~~~

It's midafternoon. After we linger over the lunch, eating and laughing, Mom and Donnie start making suggestions about it being time to leave.

Jameson quietly asks if he can talk to me for a minute.

I lift a hand, indicating he should go ahead.

"Privately?" He looks at his toes.

I cock my head to the side. "Want to walk?"

When we're out of hearing range of the others, he clears his throat. "I, uh, I wanted to say . . . to tell you . . . I'm just . . . I'm a jerk. I shouldn't . . . I don't know why I'm like this."

I want to laugh at his stammering. But he's so sincere with his words, his tone, he seems completely genuine.

While I'm sorting out what to say, he blurts out, "I shouldn't have been so mean, shouldn't have laughed at you or teased you. I hope . . . maybe you can forgive me?"

I lift my hands. "Sure."

He glances at me, and a slow smile creeps on to his face. "Yeah?"

"Yeah."

"Thanks, Sadie. Maybe we'll, um, we'll see each other again. Pretty soon, travel will be easier, right? And with the highway between Great Falls and Lewistown, maybe they'll even run buses or, I don't know, stagecoaches."

I let out a laugh. "Maybe so."

"You think you'll like it here? Living with your aunt?"

I chew on my lip as I consider my answer. "I like my aunt. And I'll like not walking every day. But there's lots of work to do."

"Ha. That's everywhere now, I think. We've been talking about all the things we'll need to do once we reach the Dosen ranch. Mom's worried it'll be too much for Jennifer. She hopes her arm's better so we can get everything done before winter. Hopefully, we can get to the ranch quickly so we have time. I guess the winters are as bad around here as they were at home in Bakerville. Cold, snow, wind. Guess I'll be learning to ride a horse too. That's how they take care of the cattle, you know."

I don't say anything about my concern they may not have any cattle once they get to the ranch. They left their home almost a year ago, leaving their hired man to take care of everything. Is he still there? Did marauders discover him? What will they find when they reach the ranch?

"So that's, uh, that's it. I just wanted to ask if you'd accept my apology."

After long, drawn-out goodbyes with everyone, we finally mount up and start for the lodge in the late afternoon. Mom holds her head high as she rides, but I still catch the back of her hand occasionally going to her eyes.

When we reach the second barricade, where the trouble was earlier, two different guards give us lazy waves.

"I wonder what Mosher did with the troublemakers?" Donnie asks in a low voice.

Once we're well passed the checkpoint, Mom asks, "Do they have a jail set up? The guy who started the fight—is his name Randy?"

"Randy was one of them. I'm not entirely sure who started the argument, but Randy surely knocked Nelson to the ground. Surprised me some. Nelson's built like a brick wall."

Mom gives a slight nod. "Randy said the guy who fired the shot was going to end up in jail. Is there a jail here?"

Donnie lifts a shoulder. "Not that anyone told me about."

"Didn't you get a tour of the whole place?" Sebastian asks, his pony on the tail of Mom's horse.

Old Rosie has certainly been on her best behavior since running off earlier. Maybe she heard Donnie's pointed remarks about finding a glue factory? Boot doesn't seem to have a care in the world and plods along sedately behind the other two.

"Got the nickel tour, yep. Probably just the stuff they thought I needed to know about as part of their protection team. I guess, if there is a jail, they didn't figure I needed to know about it."

"What do they do with bad guys?"

Mom and Donnie exchange a look before Mom turns in her saddle to meet Sebastian's eyes. "They haven't had much trouble here, sweetie. Maybe it isn't something they've considered."

He wrinkles his forehead. "They had a jail at the ski lodge. It was put in *before* they had any trouble, so it'd be there if they needed it."

"You going to help brush your pony when we get back?" Donnie asks, changing the subject. "A good buckaroo always cares for his horse."

"Am I a buckaroo?"

Donnie lets out a laugh. "The way you hung on to Old Rosie, you're a broncobuster."

Sebastian smiles at Donnie, then turns his head slightly and creases his forehead. He lifts his chin, using it as a pointer. "What kind of bush is that?"

Donnie looks over his shoulder. "Which one?"

This time, Sebastian risks removing a hand from his reins to point. "The red one."

I follow his finger, looking out over the landscape to the edge of a tree-lined creek as it meanders from the forest. There's a dot of bright red on the landscape.

"Huh," Donnie mutters. "Hold up a minute. I'll get the binoculars out."

"Is it Indian paintbrush?" Mom asks.

"I don't know what it is." Donnie shakes his head as he digs into his saddlebag for the binos. "Indian paintbrush is the Wyoming state flower, but it doesn't look like that. That looks more like— " He shakes his head.

"Blood?" Sebastian's voice is a whisper.

"Let's not get ahead of ourselves."

Donnie spends several minutes with the binoculars to his eyes. He scans not only the area where the blood-red bush is, but also to the left and right. Finally, he turns to Mom.

"What do you think?" Mom asks.

"Can't be sure. These binoculars aren't the best, especially at this distance."

"Should we get closer?" Sebastian asks.

"Wait here. I'll ride over and get a closer look."

Mom looks in all directions, scanning like Donnie did when he had the binoculars up. "Is it safe?"

"There don't seem to be any threats around. I could just ride back to the barricade and ask one of them to check it out. But if it's nothing . . . " He lifts a hand. "Guess I'd feel kind of stupid."

"We'll wait here," Mom says.

"You want the rifle?" Donnie motions to the scabbard on the offside of his horse.

Mom glances at Sebastian. "I don't think I'd be able to use it, not with as jumpy as the pony is."

Donnie's face registers his agreement before he again mutters something about glue.

"That doesn't help anything," Mom scolds. "Sebastian, come on up here. Let me have your lead rope again."

Donnie touches the tip of his cowboy hat. "Be right back."

Sebastian starts asking Mom questions as Donnie rides off. *What do you think it is?* She doesn't know. *Have you ever seen such a red bush before?* She has, but not in Central Montana.

Mom patiently answers his questions until she finally says, "Donnie's almost there. We'll know soon enough."

When Donnie reaches the bush, he doesn't get off the horse. Instead, he takes a wide berth around it. Gordie doesn't seem happy about the way he's being moved, and his nose keeps going in the air.

I look to Mom, who's chewing on her lip.

Donnie walked Gordie out to the bush, but he trots him back.

Mom doesn't wait until he reaches us. When she deems him close enough, she calls, "What is it?"

He waits a few seconds, getting closer before answering, "The bush is covered in blood."

"Blood?"

"Yup. And there's a body."

"A . . . a cow?"

"A man."

Chapter 9

Fergus Peak Lodge
Sunday, June 14, Late Afternoon

Sadie

"Do you know who it is?" Mom asks.

Donnie shakes his head. "He was face down. I didn't get off Gordie to make sure. I'll wait and see if Mosher needs my help. Maybe . . ." Donnie scratches his chin. "How about we keep this quiet until Mosher checks things out?"

"Won't it get out once it goes over the radio?"

"I'll try and make it vague, get him here without saying exactly why."

"You want us to wait here?"

"No need. Head on home. I'll see you later."

Mom takes us back to the lodge, while Donnie rides to the barricade so the men can call Jack Mosher on the walkie-talkie.

As soon as we reach the stables, Brooke, the second wrangler, gives us a cheery wave.

"Remember," Mom cautions, "we're waiting for Donnie before we say anything. Sebastian, are you okay?"

"I . . . I guess. It's just weird to think about a dead body. How much blood— "

"I know, honey. At least he can have a proper burial."

"Who do you think it is?"

"Donnie will tell us all he knows when he gets home."

After taking care of the horses, Mom tells Sebastian he should play on the lawn with the other children. He gives her a weak smile before joining in the pre-supper fun.

"This lawn is so inviting," Mom says, slipping off her boots. "Join me?"

I take off my shoes and socks and walk on the lush green grass, letting the blades run between my toes. It's been such a wet spring, the yard's green without any extra water.

"Glad to see you enjoying the grass," Ms. Reynolds says with a rare smile on her face. "You should walk barefoot daily. Try it in the morning. It's very good for you, boosts immunity and helps improve eyesight. I think we need to get your aunt out here tomorrow. It's time she got up and around." She gives us a final nod before walking off.

"Huh," Mom says. "First time for everything I guess."

"You mean first time she's been pleasant?"

"Exactly."

I can't help but laugh at the face Mom makes. I'll never be able to replicate it, but it's hilarious.

Then she ruins it by saying, "I need to remember to be kind, to pray for Ms. Reynolds. She's obviously hurting."

Can't she go more than five minutes without bringing God into everything?

Putting our shoes back on, we join Cassie and Brooke on the main patio. Back when the lodge had paying guests, this space used to function as an outdoor stage and bar. Now it's a working and cooking station. We sit at one of the tables and help clean the saddles and other tack.

"I just don't know what to say about Old Rosie," Cassie says, shaking her head. "I had no idea she was gun shy. She's always been so gentle."

"There's no way you would know," Mom says. "Trail horses aren't usually exposed to gunfire, not like a horse a hunter would use."

Brooke looks up from her work. "My dad hunts with horses. Not at home, but up in the backcountry."

"There's your man." Cassie points toward Donnie, riding in on Gordie. The rev of a motor sounds in the distance. "And it doesn't sound like he's alone."

Mom sets aside the leather rein she's working on. "I'll be right back."

"May I come?" I ask.

She shakes her head but then seems to rethink her response. "Sure, come on."

Donnie stops at the hitching post near the corrals. We speed walk to reach him and get there about the same time he dismounts and lands on the ground.

"Hey." He opens his arms. Mom doesn't hesitate before stepping into his embrace.

After a moment, which I spend looking at my toes, she asks, "Did you know him?"

"Gray Nelson."

"Nelson? The one fighting earlier?"

"Yup."

"Well, that's . . . interesting."

"Isn't it? Mosher seemed to think so too. He and Randy Loomer are right behind me."

"They're here." I motion to the quad as it rounds the final bend before the lodge. "Do you think he killed him?"

"He says he didn't and has an alibi. That's why they're here."

"What kind of alibi?" Mom asks.

"Samantha."

"Samantha? The one who helps care for Aunt Karla?"

"No way," I say under my breath.

"That's what I thought too." Donnie makes a face. "Seems she could do some better."

Mom gives him a look. "People can't help who they love."

"And I'm glad for that. Seems you could do some better too." He drops a kiss on her nose. "Lots better, in fact."

While Donnie isn't exactly handsome, he's not ugly either. Just kind of average looking. Mom once said he looks a little like the star of *Dances with Wolves.* Maybe . . . from later in the movie when he'd been living in the wild and not grooming. Not when he's a well-dressed officer in the beginning.

"They're here to ask Samantha?" I ask. "To confirm they were together?"

"That's the plan."

Jack stops the quad near the hitching post.

When both men are on the ground, Randy says, "Can we get this over with? It's been a long day, and I need to take care of my friend."

I shoot my mom a questioning look; she answers with a slight shrug.

"Your friend, huh?" Jack says. "Didn't seem like Gray was a friend when you knocked him to the ground earlier."

"I told ya, we just had a disagreement, that's all. Not something to knife him over. Besides— " Randy points his finger to Jack's chest. "He rode off with you, remember?"

Jack narrows his eyes. "I took him home so he could clean up. After *you* clobbered him."

"So you say."

"And you say you were with Samantha. Let's ask her."

Jack turns slightly to look at my mom. "You know where she is?"

Mom shakes her head.

"Um, I might." My voice is small—too small. I clear my throat. "I saw her heading up to her room earlier."

"Saw her earlier, huh?" Jack darts his eyes to Randy. "What time was that?"

"After we got back, maybe an hour or so ago. Before we started working on the saddles and stuff."

"Run and see if she's in her room, Sadie," Mom says.

"Don't tell her what this is about," Jack instructs as I step away.

I lift a hand in acknowledgment. Like I'd say anything. But if it's true . . . *ick*. She's not much older than me, only eighteen or nineteen, I think. And Randy, he's much older and is losing his hair! And there's something about him. He's just . . . ick.

I'm breathing hard by the time I reach the third floor of the lodge. All the rooms have private, outdoor access, and both flights are long and steep. Samantha's room, which she shares with another girl around her age, is at the front.

I have a vague memory of seeing this room when we visited years ago, when my dad was still alive and my mom was helping with the housekeeping. I think this room shares a bathroom with a room on the back of the building. If it's the one I'm thinking of, it was used for families, giving them a two-room suite. It's a nice space.

I tap on the door. It's too soft. Straightening my shoulders, I try again.

There's a scuffing sound from the other side before it opens slightly. "Oh, hey." Samantha's brown eyes are friendly. "I forget your name."

"Sadie." I step away from the door, motioning toward the quad with my arm. "Jack Mosher is here. He wants to talk to you."

"Jack? He wants to talk to me?" Her hands go to her smooth, black hair as she runs her fingers through it. "Um, he asked for me?"

I lift a shoulder.

"Sure. Okay. Tell him . . . tell him I'll be right out."

The door closes with a soft click of the lock. I shake my head. I guess she's not totally head over heels for Randy, not with the way she's fawning over Jack.

I'm almost to the others when I glance back and see her on the top step. When she answered the door, she was wearing sweats. Now she's in cut-off jean shorts, her long tan legs glistening, and has a huge smile on her face.

When I reach Mom and the others, I look at Samantha again. The smile's gone. Her pace slows.

"Samantha," Jack calls out to her. "Thanks for coming down.

"Um, yeah, sure. What's this . . . what'd you need?" She looks from Jack to Randy.

"Hey, babe. Will you tell him I was— "

"Randy," Jack growls.

"What?" Randy feigns innocence. "I was just— "

"I know what you were *just*." Jack turns back to Samantha. "I was wondering what your afternoon included."

"What my afternoon included?" She furrows her brow.

"He doesn't believe me when I tell him we were together." Randy blurts out, earning him a hard look from Jack.

"Oh . . . ." Samantha's cheeks color. "We, uh . . . " She looks at the ground.

"You were with Randy?" Jack's voice is soft, understanding.

Samantha lifts a shoulder.

Randy steps toward her. "C'mon, babe, don't be like that." He puts a hand on her bicep, rubbing up and down.

She stiffens before lifting her eyes and giving a very slight nod. "We were together."

"See?" Randy turns to Jack. "From about noon until, I don't know, four o'clock? Does that sound right, babe?"

A confused look crosses her face. "Four? I don't— "

"Definitely four." Randy nods.

"Okay, I guess. Maybe."

Randy pops a kiss on her cheek, then she steps away from him.

"Thanks, Samantha," Jack says. "I appreciate your help."

She looks at him with doe eyes. "Any time, Mr. Mosher."

He waves a hand. "Jack."

She giggles. "Okay, Jack."

Randy crosses his arms. "Run along now, babe. I'll see you in a few days."

Samantha looks at Jack, who gives a slight nod. "Thanks again for your help."

So weird. I'm not a detective or anything, but that didn't seem quite right.

"Let's go, Mosher," Randy says.

"Something isn't making sense to me," Jack says in an even tone. "Samantha didn't seem so sure about the time you were together. And four hours? Didn't you have obligations today?"

"Got 'em done early." He shoves his hands into his pockets. "Listen, I've already told you, Gray Nelson was my friend."

"Then what were you fighting about?" Mom asks.

Randy's eyes dart to her. "What concern is it of yours?"

"It's a good question," Donnie says. "I asked you earlier what the problem was. You hemmed and hawed instead of answering."

"That's because I don't answer to you."

"You do answer to me," Jack says.

Randy moves his tongue, pushing out the side of his cheek. Then he steps closer to Jack. "Do I, Mosher? Do I really?"

They stare each other down until, finally, Randy steps back. "You know who probably did this? Ledger Hyde. Probably getting revenge for kicking them out."

"Kicking them out?" Jack furrows his brow. "You forced them to leave? We had an agreement, Loomer. They were banished from our community, for now, but could live nearby. You kicked them out of that place? I thought you said they left on their own?"

"Um, yeah." Randy gives a vigorous bob of his head. "They did. He said he wanted to go, had enough and figured his wife's family would take them in. We just . . . Gray and I, we helped them pack, made sure he and his woman made it into town. We were just— "

"Just what?" Jack steps into Randy's space.

"Being neighborly. With you and him being friends, it was the least we could do. Help them. On account of your friendship."

Jack lets out a long, slow breath. "So help me, if you did anything even close to resembling kicking them out, I'll . . . " Jack turns and walks to the quad. He doesn't wait for Randy to get on before firing it up.

"Hey! Whadda ya doing?" Randy yells as Jack revs the engine and turns the machine around.

"You can walk."

With that, the quad takes off at full speed.

Randy's choice of words is equal to what we heard earlier today. Finally, he motions to Gordie. "How about giving me a ride?"

Donnie crosses his arms. "You heard him. You can walk."

"C'mon, man. I need to get back and help get my friend ready for burial."

"You really think Ledger Hyde killed him?" my mom asks.

"Makes sense." Randy nods. "The man's done lost his marbles. Hyde used to be a good guy, until he started thinking everyone was out to get him and his woman. Why, he even accused me of making googly eyes at her. Not that she isn't a fine-looking lady, but there's enough single women here to keep me busy." He gives Mom a leering look. "Know what I mean?"

Donnie steps closer to Mom. "You might not have heard, but we're getting married as soon as her aunt is up and around."

With a sneer, Randy says, "That right? Then I guess I've got some time to change her mind."

The next thing I know, Donnie's fist connects with Randy's nose.

As Randy's head bounces back, his hands go to his face. He quickly regains his composure and drops his shoulder, intending to ram Donnie—the same thing he did to Gray Nelson earlier today.

Donnie steps to the side, tripping Randy as he goes by. With Randy sprawled on the ground, Donnie says, "Stay away from us. Pick your sorry self up and get out of here."

Randy rolls to his bottom. "You can't tell me what to do."

"I can, Randy Loomer." Aunt Karla is standing at the edge of the lawn, balancing on a pair of crutches with Daniela Reynolds by her side. "Scoot on out of here."

"Now, Karla . . . " Randy lifts his hands.

"Go on now."

"This is . . . this is an overreaction on his part." He points at Donnie. "He misunderstood— "

"You heard what Karla said." Ms. Reynolds puts a hand on her hip.

"Well, ain't you tough, Mizz High and Mighty?"

"Enough, Randy." Aunt Karla takes a wobbly step forward. "I heard and saw enough to know exactly what happened here."

Randy picks himself up, muttering the entire time. He wipes his bloody nose with the back of his hand. "Be seeing you, sport." He motions his finger toward Donnie.

We're quiet as he walks away, waiting until he rounds the bend and is out of sight before talking.

Mom turns on Donnie. "Why'd you do that?"

His eyes go wide. "Uh . . . "

"I don't need you fighting my battles. I wanted to tell him what I thought of his . . . his proposition."

Donnie's face drops. "I don't know. He just . . . the way he was, so smug and arrogant, I didn't think. Sorry, Leanne."

Mom's face immediately softens. "Well, don't think you need to fight my battles for me. And punching him! That wasn't necessary."

"You're right. I overreacted. I told you earlier, God still has a lot of work to do with me."

My eyes go to the grass where Sebastian was playing. He, along with the other children, are all staring in this direction. Donnie also sees the kids and several adults gawking.

He lets out a sigh. "Guess I really made a mess of things."

"Well, no use worrying about it now," Aunt Karla says. "Give him some time to cool off, then you can apologize. Now tell me what is going on. Daniela said someone died?"

Chapter 10

Near Lewistown, Montana
Monday, June 15, Daylight

Victoria

"You're sure you're up to it, Mom?" Brett scrunches his mouth, biting the inside of his cheek. "We could wait a few more days."

"It's been a week already. And we don't plan on going far. I can handle it." I adjust the ax hanging from my left side. The last few days, I've been practicing getting to the ax with this stupid sling on my arm. It's awkward but doable. Nate Hoffmann, who's often by my side, was a great help retrieving my ax from the throwing block as I practiced.

"Let me go through your pack again and see what we can do to lighten your load."

"It's nearly bare. Just my survival items are left, things that'll keep me alive for a few days if I'm separated from the rest of you."

He lifts a shoulder. "I'll look anyway. It's good Nate's carrying the second ax. I think— " Brett glances toward Nate. "I think he feels responsible for your fall."

I let out a sigh. "I've told him it wasn't his fault."

"Yeah, well . . . " He lifts a shoulder. "At least we don't have to put the ax in a bag. That thing's heavy."

"True." I give a small smile. "He's getting pretty good at throwing, too, almost as good as you and Jameson."

"Not as good as you." My son gives me a wink. "Even with a broken arm, you're lethal."

"Go on now, Brett. Let's finish getting ready. I know everyone's excited to get going again. This unexpected delay is taking a toll on people's nerves."

His face lights up. "We got a deer out of it."

Brett and Atticus continued to hunt each day, coming back empty handed until a couple days ago. The buck isn't overly large, but we're all grateful for the additional dried meat. Brett feels especially accomplished since his shot took the young deer down.

He had never hunted before we started on this journey to Montana. Although he wanted to be on the mountain hunting crew, and be one of the apprentice butchers, his dad quickly squashed those dreams, forbidding both Brett and Jameson from participating in the community apprentice programs.

Jon insisted the boys spend their spare time reading his law books and other scholarly tomes in preparation for college. He was confident this was just a blip on the screen and things would be back to normal before they reached adulthood. College was the plan.

Both Jon and I were grateful for our educations. Jon, as a lawyer, more so than me. We met in college, and both of us planned to continue on to law school. We married and Jon went on while I got a job. The plan was he'd finish school and then, once he had a job, I'd go.

I didn't. Instead, as soon as he graduated and was working, I became a stay-at-home wife at his insistence. I went along with it, agreeing that if we were going to have a family, I'd want to be a full-time mom. Funny enough, each of his side women were all professionals he met at conferences and other meetings across the country—around the world even.

I hold my hand out to my son. "You did great, Brett. The extra meat should get us to the ranch."

He gives my hand a squeeze. "To our new home."

"Yes," I agree with a hesitant nod. *Our new home.*

~~~~

Day one of walking with a broken arm is a near disaster. I guess a week of rest wasn't enough. I'd been preparing myself, or so I thought, by walking around camp. Being on the road is not the same. The continual motion sends shockwaves through my body, jolting my arm. To help keep it from sliding out of place while the bones mend, Daniela Reynolds suggested taping my arm to my body. It helps, but just barely.

We make it the mile back to Lewistown by taking the highway, which is also the main street through town. The town has a flea market type thing set up on the street by the Fergus County Courthouse.
~~~~

While the others attempt some trades, I rest. When they return, it must be obvious I'm wiped out.

"There's a camp set up on the edge of town, about two miles from here," Rey says. "We'll take it slow and stay at the campground tonight."

"I can keep going." My voice is weak, unconvincing.

"We'll see."

Once we reach the tidy, little campground set up and maintained by the townsfolk, I'm sweating and shaky—to the point I'm not even thinking clearly. At this pace, it'll take us a month to travel the 140 miles to the ranch.

"Why don't you sit here?" Jennifer motions to a bench. "We can wait while Rey sorts everything out."

I answer with a weary nod.

Once we're seated, Jennifer lets out an exaggerated sigh. "I'm tired too. Not walking for several days has me out of shape. Isn't this place adorable? The little camp trailer looks like it was plopped in the middle of an English garden." She motions to the fenced-in yard. "I swear, I can even smell the roses from here."

"I don't think it's roses you're smelling. Didn't you see the outhouse?"

She lets out a hearty laugh. "Well, maybe. But even those are cute with the moon on the one marked *Hers* and a star on *His*. This place doesn't feel like the apocalypse."

I lift a shoulder, instantly wishing I wouldn't have. My head's pounding, and everything hurts.

As Rey and Kimba make their way to the gate of the yard, a young woman in her early twenties with two children—one at her side and the other on her hip—steps out and stops next to the *Camp Host* sign. "I'm telling you, he wouldn't leave us. Not like this. He wouldn't."

"I'm sure you're right," the voice of an older woman that's out of my view answers. "Maybe he's just delayed. I'm sure he'll be back."

"He would've already been here if he could. He always keeps his word." The young woman takes another step forward, allowing a silver-haired woman to come into view.

"Ah, my dear." The woman opens her arms. They spend several seconds like this, as the older woman makes soothing sounds. "Let's get you back to your place. LJ, do you want to walk with me?" She holds out her hand to the toddler.

The older lady has a bit of a start when she sees Rey and Kimba. "Oh! So sorry, I didn't . . . my husband can help you." She gives them a smile.

The younger woman keeps her eyes on the ground.

"Great. Drama," Jennifer whispers.

I dart my eyes to Jennifer. Such an odd thing for her to say. I open my mouth to ask what she means when an older man loudly declares, "Sorry 'bout that. You folks need a place to stay?"

A few minutes later, after being assigned two side-by-side campsites and given a list of handwritten rules, we make our way to our spot.

"Let's get you resting," Jennifer says, then she helps me remove my backpack. Within a matter of minutes, my mattress pad and bedding are set up by the cold fire ring. The rest of the group puts the tents up. I lean back and close my eyes.

I feel lazy. Worthless. This past week, I've been taken back to the days of my marriage with Jon. Not the early days when things were great between us, when we worked as a team. Oh, there was no doubt who the team leader was, but it was still fine.

After Jon finished law school, we moved to St. Louis where he worked as a public defender. He was passionate about the law, idealistic even about proper representation. Jon thought he'd find the perfect case, the one to catapult his career and get him noticed by some big firm.

His desire to relocate to Wyoming came as a shock. He'd met another attorney at a convention, a guy whose practice centered around oil. I didn't know what it was about the man or the work, but Jon decided it'd be better.

Looking back, I can see now how it made sense. Being a public defender wasn't easy. There wasn't much money in it, and most of his clients were found guilty—because they truly *were* guilty. Getting that one big case that would make headlines and change his career was unlikely. Working with contracts was much easier, more reliable. And the man was willing to train Jon.

We were happy in Prospect, Wyoming. At least at first. We were in Prospect about a year when I got pregnant. We'd been trying for a baby for several years and very much wanted a child. With month after month of disappointment, I was beginning to think there was something wrong. Our oldest son, Michael, was born at twenty-three weeks gestation. I didn't even realize I was in labor until he was coming out. I called 911, but he died in my arms before the ambulance arrived.

Michael's death was a turning point in our marriage. Looking back, I know it was never a truly healthy relationship. But it went noticeably bad after losing our baby. I still stuck it out, believing things would improve if I could just be a better wife. If I could just give Jon the baby he so desperately wanted.

Brett was born five years later, healthy and perfect, with Jameson following a couple years after. I was almost thirty-nine when Jameson was born—much too old to have a newborn, and definitely too old to try for a third. Unfortunately, having children didn't help our marriage.

We were still living in Prospect, with Jon owning the law firm he'd trained at so many years before after the previous owner died of a heart attack. Prospect suited me. It was a decent-sized town, at least by Wyoming standards, and had pretty much everything we needed. I'd made several good friends. We had a nice home, and the children were doing well in school.

Then Jon decided he wanted to build our dream home in the enclave of Bakerville about thirty miles north of Prospect—in a small, isolated community where I had no friends.

It wasn't terrible for the boys; they were able to catch the school bus on the highway and attend classes with their friends in Prospect. But for me, it was an adjustment made more difficult by my husband.

Prospect wasn't huge by any standards, only around ten thousand people, but I had my friends. *My tribe.* We'd get together once or twice a week for lunch or do other fun things, including quarterly girls' trips. Most of the trips were local, within driving distance. But a few times, we went away for long weekends and flew someplace fun.

At first, I kept that up and drove the half hour from Bakerville to Prospect. But then Jon started to complain about it, saying I was putting unnecessary wear and tear on the car, plus he didn't like me away from home for so long. It didn't matter he was working in Prospect and driving in almost every day.

The original plan was he'd only go into the Prospect office once or twice a week, scheduling all his appointments on the same days. That lasted less than a month before he started going in three, then four days, and eventually five or more. The home office, built to his elaborate specifications with all sorts of technology, wasn't good enough.

My guess is he was bored. Being isolated out in the middle of nowhere, on the edge of the national forest, wasn't what he'd thought it'd be.

Not only did the weekly lunches stop, but so did the girls' trips. After we moved, I only went on one trip before Jon came up with an excuse for me to miss the next one. Then, the girls and I started planning another trip and he threw an outright fit. Told me I was unfit as a wife and mother with all the gallivanting I did.

That argument came only a day after he returned from a business conference in Costa Rica. In the months leading up to the attacks on our country, living with Jon was hard. His temper was volatile. And while he never hit me during that time, I expected it. He came close on numerous occasions. One time, he shoved me up against the wall, with his hand around my neck. I thought he was going to . . .

I shake my head to stop the memories.

This injury's really messing with my brain. It has me almost living in the past, to the point I'm half wondering if Jon will suddenly appear. I let out a shaky breath. No, that won't happen. Jon is dead.

A hand lands on my shoulder.

I let out a yelp and jump, again jolting my arm.

"Oh, mercy," Jennifer says. "I'm so sorry I scared you. Are you all right?"

Tears of pain flood my eyes. "Y-yes. I just . . . um . . . it hurts."

"I was just going to tell you it's time for meds."

"Which one?"

"I'll make you a rosemary tea. And since you're having pain, let's get some willow bark for you to chew. It's been long enough since you had it last."

"Thanks, Jennifer. I . . . you've been very kind to me."

She smiles and lifts a shoulder. "With all we've been through, sometimes I feel we're more like sisters than friends."

My heart fills. *Sisters.* When we left the ski lodge, we were barely friends. In the three months since, things have certainly changed.

"Hello?" a timid voice calls out. It's the young woman from earlier, the one with the missing husband. This time, she's without the children as she ambles toward us.

Jennifer lifts her hand in a *stop* motion. "Something we can do for you?" Her voice has an uncommon edge to it. Usually, she's welcoming and inviting.

The woman must hear it too. With a wobbly smile, she says, "Lauren, the camp host, she says you came through town?"

"That's right." Jennifer crosses her arms.

The woman nods. "Okay. I just thought I'd ask to make sure. My husband— "

"We heard."

The young woman taps a finger to her chin. "Maybe you've seen him? Can I show you his picture?" She digs in her back pocket and then steps toward us.

Jennifer releases a noisy sigh.

I tilt my head in her direction before turning back to the woman. "We can take a look."

"I'm sure we haven't seen him," Jennifer mutters. "But if you insist."

"Thank you." She takes several steps forward, then leans toward me instead of Jennifer. "Oh, I didn't notice your arm. That looks . . . painful."

"It is."

"You're traveling on foot?"

I take the photo from her. "Mm-hmm."

"This is older, from when LJ was born. He's, uh, he'll be three in a few months."

It's a professional photo. She's in a flowing, dark blue dress with pink and white flowers. Her black hair is combed smooth and shiny, her brown eyes gleaming. She's holding a baby wrapped in a blue blanket with a blue hat covering his tiny head.

The man, wearing a button-up blue shirt, is slender and not much taller than her. His ice-blue eyes are bright, kind looking. As I gaze into them, he seems vaguely familiar.

"He has a beard now, of course," the woman says. "His hair's a little thinner. He's thinner."

Jennifer moves her head closer, finally interested in the photo. I'll have to ask her what her indifference to this woman is about. Usually, someone like her, someone obviously hurting, would receive all sorts of kindness from Jennifer.

Jennifer lets out a gasp. "Atticus! Rey! You'd better come here."

Those around the other camp lift their heads. "Mom? Are you okay?" Brett calls out.

"She's fine." Jennifer lifts a hand. "But you all need to see what this . . . this girl has here. The photo."

Chapter 11

Lewistown, Montana
Monday, June 15, Midafternoon

Victoria

Rey makes it to our firepit first. He gives the young woman a nod. "I'm Rey Hoffmann." His voice is calm and without his usual light British accent. While we've been traveling, he's slipped in and out of the accent like a winter coat, saving the Queen's English for when we're in private and sounding like a typical American whenever strangers are around. In some ways, he reminds me of myself.

After marrying Jon, he insisted I learn proper pronunciations and rid myself of my hillbilly accent. Growing up, I never even realized I had an accent. I talked just like everyone else around me.

It wasn't until I went away to college that I realized just how different my Mountain Speak sounded. I was truly surprised how cruel students, and even professors, could be about how I spoke.

We weren't even dating yet, were just friends, when Jon suggested I take classes to learn how to rid myself of my home talk. As a wedding gift, he bought me a package with a voice coach.

Rey's young daughter, Naomi, once said her dad fakes his American accent so people won't worry that he isn't one of them. It makes sense, especially with the way things are now, with not only our country a mess but, according to rumors we've heard, the entire world is at war.

Being in Montana, it'd probably be smart to go back to my forced-midwestern accent too. I just don't have the energy or desire to continue to fake it. Not having to pretend I'm someone I'm not has been freeing. Besides, even if I have reverted back to Mountain Speak, I don't hear it when I talk, so what does it matter? To me, I sound just like everyone else.

"I'm Patti." The young woman gives a small wave. "I think maybe she knows my husband." Patti points at Jennifer.

"Look." Jennifer thrusts the photo in Rey's direction.

"Whatcha got?" Atticus asks, appearing by Rey's side. Brett and Jameson are next to him, with the rest of our group only steps away.

Rey holds the picture so Atticus can see it.

His face registers surprise and then a flash of anger. He narrows his eyes. "This is your husband?"

"Yes, have you seen him? His name is— "

"Ledger Hyde," Atticus spits out.

Patti's eyes go wide. "Uh, yes. You know Ledger?"

"Humph," Atticus scoffs. "You could say that. He held a gun on me."

The young woman closes her eyes and breathes out a loud sigh. "You must be the people traveling through who camped by the Little Dogie Ranch."

"He told you?" Rey asks.

"Not Ledger. Randy Loomer did when he brought my husband home and told us to pack up and get out."

"What?" Atticus pales. "They forced you to move?"

Patti tilts her head. "We were talking about it anyway. Things were too hard there after we had to leave our home in the compound. We just couldn't make it on our own. We're heading to my family. We should've left as soon as the snow cleared, but— " Her voice catches. "Ledger thought we could make amends and Jack would let us back in."

"Jack Mosher said he kicked your husband out for stealing," Jameson says.

She vigorously shakes her head. "That's not what happened. Look, I'm sorry about what Ledger did, what he put you through." Her eyes meet Atticus's. "Have you seen Ledger since, uh, since then?"

There's a chorus of noes and head shakes.

"How long has he been missing?" Atticus asks.

"About a week."

"From here?"

"Yes. Randy Loomer and Gray Nelson made us pack up right after . . . after they brought Ledger home. Gray oversaw our packing, helped a little even. Randy, well, he's a bit of a bully. Anyway, they walked with us to the edge of town. Randy made all kinds of threats about seeing Ledger again and what he'd do. We planned to leave for St. Ignatius the next day."

"I knew it," Jennifer mutters.

Patti gives her a strange look.

Atticus rests a hand on his mom's shoulder. "You're from the Flathead Nation?"

"I'm Kootenai. My parents and sister are still there . . . or they were when I last spoke to them before the phones stopped working."

"Traveling to find loved ones is a risk."

She bobs her head. "So, Ledger went to see about a few supplies. He left here as the sky was starting to lighten. Said he'd be back before midmorning, then we'd go. But . . . he didn't come back."

"And no one's seen him? Have you gone into town?" Rey asks.

"No one has any information. He said he was going to the Court House. They have a swap meet set up."

Rey gives her a slight smile. "We did some trading on the way through."

"Lauren—she's the camp host here, along with her husband, Charlie—she watched the kids for me so I could look for Ledger. No one admits to seeing him. There're several people we knew. Friends."

"Do you think they were lying?" Atticus asks.

"Oh, no. It's just odd."

"Where else would he have gone?" Rey asks.

"Nowhere. That's the thing. We were finally getting out of here. By force, of course, but I think he'd accepted it and knew it was the right choice."

Atticus scratches his chin. "St. Ignatius is, what, three hundred miles away? How'd you expect to make it before winter? With the children?"

"We've heard there're people traveling for trade, hauling goods back and forth. We thought we could catch some rides. And the military, maybe ride with them?"

"We haven't seen any military up here," Rey says. "They're by Billings, working on securing Interstate 90. That'll probably change soon, and they'll be more spread out."

"That's what we're hoping. We heard about the interstates and thought maybe, once we reached I-15, they'd be there. But until I find Ledger, we're stuck here."

I drop my gaze, not wanting my eyes to tell the poor girl what I think. *What I believe.* If he's been gone a week, he isn't coming back. He either left of his own free will, looking for greener pastures without a wife and two young children, or he's dead.

Rey hands the photo back to her. "We'll be leaving in the morning. If we see him along the way, we'll let him know you're still here."

One corner of her mouth lifts slightly. "I appreciate that. Safe travels to you." She lifts a hand in farewell before returning to her camp.

Rey motions for everyone to sit around the firepit. In a low voice, he asks, "What do you all make of that?"

"He skipped out on her," Atticus answers immediately. "The scoundrel left his family."

"Maybe so," Rey agrees.

"Wouldn't surprise me one bit." Jennifer stares at Patti's camp. "Probably got tired of worrying about being killed in his sleep."

My mouth gapes open as my head swivels to look at Jennifer.

"Mom," Atticus says under his breath as his neck becomes crimson.

Jennifer rolls her eyes. She gives her head a slight shake as she puts her hand to her mouth. "I don't . . . I shouldn't have said that."

Rey gives Jennifer a long look. "Well, it does seem Ledger is gone. I hope she comes to realize that soon and comes up with a plan."

"Mosher made it sound like she was welcome in his community, that her husband is the issue, right?" I ask.

"That's the way I took it."

"She should go back. We should encourage her to go back. She and her children could live at the lodge with Leanne." My head bobs as I talk, sending a wave of pain through my entire body as I finish my sentence. *That was dumb.*

Jennifer makes a scoffing sound. "Leanne has enough going on with helping her aunt recover and settling in, plus getting ready for the wedding."

"How fancy of a wedding do you think they're planning?" Atticus asks. "I think Victoria's right about encouraging Patti to return to the compound. Whether she stays at Fergus Lodge or another home, there's no way she can make three hundred miles, not with those little kids before winter anyway."

"Well, this isn't our problem," Jennifer says. "We have enough on our plates just getting ourselves back to the ranch. With all the delays, we'll be pushing hard to make it before the snow."

What has come over my friend? She's always the first to offer a helping hand to anyone and makes a point of living by the famous Golden Rule from Jesus' Sermon on the Mount. Jennifer's even kind to people when they don't deserve it. Her invitation for my sons and me to move to her ranch is a perfect example of this.

The strength she's shown with the death of her son Asher is also part of her deep belief system. Not just beliefs. *She lives it.*

Until today, I haven't seen her be deliberately insensitive. Maybe she's still angry about Ledger Hyde pulling a gun on Atticus, her remaining twin boy. That would make sense. I close my eyes as the pain in my head becomes more intense. We were sidetracked by Patti, and I never did get any pain medication.

"Part of me wonders . . . " Kimba taps her hand to her mouth before turning to Rey. "You don't think Ledger Hyde would do something crazy, do you?"

"Ha!" Atticus snorts. "He's *absolutely* crazy."

"Crazy enough to get revenge against Mosher for banishing them?"

"One man against their armed security? It'd be a suicide mission." Rey shakes his head. "He'd realize that."

"Would he?" Kimba raises her eyebrows.

As our group begins to break up, each going back to what they were doing, I remind Jennifer about the meds.

"Oh, Victoria, give me just a minute. I had the tea water heating on the stove earlier. It probably boiled dry after all that ruckus."

"What was that about?" I lift my eyebrows at her as I meet her eyes.

"Humph. Who knows?"

"No, Jennifer. I don't mean about Patti and Ledger. I mean you. Why were you so . . . " I lift my hands.

"I don't know what you mean." Her voice is abrupt, almost harsh. "I'll get the tea. Do you want the willow bark now, or wait until you can have a swallow of tea to wash away the bitterness?"

I purse my lips. "Now's fine. My headache's ratcheted up several notches in the last few minutes."

"No doubt." She works the zipper on the little fanny pack she wears. She suggested I carry the meds on my own, but my brain is so foggy I'm concerned I'll forget when I had my last dose.

Daniela Reynolds made a point about the overdose symptoms being something we'd want to avoid—stomach cramps and internal bleeding, plus the possibility of increasing the pain in my head. It's better to have Jennifer help.

She opens a well-used plastic zipper bag and fishes out a piece of the tree.

A couple months ago, we stayed at a house while two people in our group recovered after falling in a creek. That's when we harvested the willow by taking a couple small limbs and stripping the inner bark away with a pocketknife. We dried the strips near the woodstove to use for tea or chomping on.

Kimba also added some to a small bottle of vodka we found in an empty home and put it in the bottom of her pack to brew. She waited several weeks before declaring the willow bark tincture was ready to use.

I'd never heard of a tincture, but Kimba said it was something she learned about while living at the ski lodge. The medical team was transitioning from store-bought meds to things they could grow or wildcraft. Tinctures became an important part of their medicine cabinet.

Although we had a basic knowledge of herbs for health, Daniela Reynolds seems to know everything. Her title of master herbalist did sound a little pompous, but it's certainly something needed in today's world.

Jon would've called her a hippy-dippy. Anyone who looked for alternatives to conventional medicine—or conventional anything for that matter—was a hippy in his mind.

"While you chew, I'll get you a cup of tea." Jennifer plops the dried bark in my hand. "Don't choke on it. Remember, it seems to swell as you work it."

"Right."

I lean back on my comfy perch: a sleeping bag we found in a home outside of Roundup, Montana, along with a few blankets and a camping pad. Even though it's the middle of June, Jennifer started a small fire in the metal ring. Its mild warmth is welcome, and the smoke might help with the bugs that always seem to appear as the day advances toward night.

I stretch my back, doing my best not to move my arm. The headache seems to be increasing in intensity, and I'm starting to feel an overall ache. We walked such a short distance today; I can't imagine how I'd feel if we'd gone the usual ten miles we strive for on traveling days.

A shiver runs through me. I lift my good hand toward the fire. When I do, I get a new ache, starting at my lower back and wrapping around to my stomach.

Jennifer marches toward me with an insulated coffee mug. She gives me a smile, which quickly falters. "What's wrong?"

"Oh . . . nothing. I'm just achy, probably from the walk."

"Your face is flushed." She sets the mug on the ground and puts the back of her hand to my forehead. "You feel warm."

My entire body shudders. "I . . . I'm freezing."

<p style="text-align:center">~~~~~</p>

"She has a fever." The voice is soft and full of concern.

My eyes flutter several times as I will them to open.

"You're okay, Victoria. Just sleep. That's what you need right now."

I mumble something unintelligible, even to me, and allow myself to drift back into the abyss.

"Victoria, I need you to sit up a little bit. We need to get some tea in you."

"Mmm." I pull myself from the fog and allow them to gently move me. "Time'zit?" I ask.

"Almost bedtime. Here, now sip from the cup."

I take a tentative drink of the lukewarm beverage. It's sweet, not like the usual tea we have. "Honey?" When no one answers, I open my eyes.

Jennifer's unsmiling face greets me. "Hey," she says in a soft voice.

"Where'd you find honey?" My voice is hoarse, barely coherent.

She tilts her head to the side. "Honey? The camp host brought it over. They have a hive. Does your throat hurt?"

"N-no." As I speak, I reevaluate. "Maybe? I feel . . . awful."

"Achy?"

"Terrible. Bad. Just . . . just bad. What's wrong with me?"

"We think maybe the flu. Or . . . " Her voice fades away as she looks toward the ground.

"Or?"

72

"You might have an infection."

My eyes go wide. "How? Where?"

Jennifer lifts a shoulder. "We checked the cut on the back of your head. It's fine, not red or swollen. No pus . . . nothing. And we checked your arm to see if something's been rubbing and left an ulcer of some sort."

My uninjured hand goes to my sling. "And?"

"Nothing. We didn't fully undo the splint, but there's no sign of broken skin. No blood. We can't find anything pointing to infection. Except you're suddenly running a high fever and seem totally zonked out."

"I feel zonked out."

She helps me drink more of the sweetened tea. "Think you can get your feet under you and make it to the tent?"

I lift my head slightly to look at the tent. The distance isn't far, maybe fifteen feet, but my brain translates it as much farther. Can I make it?

"We'll help you," Jennifer assures me. "Before we do, how about something to eat? We made stew."

I manage a few bites before asking Jennifer to help me to my tent.

Chapter 12

Fergus Peak Lodge
Tuesday, June 16, After Breakfast

Sadie

Yesterday, the day after we found him, was Gray Nelson's funeral. Mom, Sebastian, and I didn't go. We'd never met him and didn't want to leave Aunt Karla home alone. Aunt Karla, who had been friends with Nelson's wife before she died of cancer a year or two before the EMP, also stayed home, too exhausted after her trek to the stables when she gave Loomer a piece of her mind.

A smile creeps across my face as I remember how fiery she was. Boy! I can see where my mom gets it. Grandma Jackie, Aunt Karla's younger sister, wasn't like that. She was much more subdued. In some ways, she was very much like our friend Jennifer—always looking for the good in people.

Donnie attended the funeral at Aunt Karla's insistence, not only because he'd met the man on several occasions but also to apologize to Randy Loomer. While everyone agrees Loomer was out of line, punching him in the nose was excessive. At least that's what Mom and Aunt Karla say.

I think Donnie was right to do it. The guy was a total creep.

After Sebastian suggested teaching the other children some of the self-defense things we know, we asked our aunt about it. She thought it was a great idea. We had our first class after supper last night. I thought Mom would be the instructor, but she insisted it should be Sebastian and me. "The children can relate to you," she said.

We didn't do too much, just some conditioning and then basic escapes. One of the girls, a redhead a few years older than Sebastian, came up to me afterward. She said she was really happy about the class, especially with Mr. Nelson dying and a crazy murderer on the loose.

Crazy murderer.

Loomer and Jack think Ledger Hyde is responsible, but I don't know. Something about it just doesn't seem right.

"You didn't do it right, Sadie," Sebastian says.

"What?" I look up from the bread I'm kneading. We're in the shiny stainless-steel kitchen of the lodge, mixing up batches of bread dough to cook outside over the fire.

"You taught the escape wrong last night." He peers at me from his perch on a stool, his batch of dough neglected.

"Less talk, more work. We're never going to get these ready in time for supper if you don't get with it."

"We just finished breakfast," he grumbles.

"Yeah, well, bread takes a while. There's still another batch for us both to do. And you have school soon, so hurry up."

He puts his hands back in the dough. "Why isn't anyone helping us with these?"

"Mom said she'd be back."

"That was . . . that was hours ago."

"Humph. More like ten minutes, squirt."

"I don't know why she needed to talk to Donnie anyway. What do you think that's about?"

"Dunno. What didn't I do right?"

"The cross-grab armbar. You forgot to show them to hack the elbow." He lifts one dough-crusted hand in a karate chop motion.

"Oh, that. I was going to, but Ms. Reynolds was staring at me . . . scowling. I figured we could save it for when she's not there."

He gives me a look, which looks much older than his eight years, before turning back to his work. The rhythmic pounding of the dough being turned fills the room. I take in a deep breath and inhale the yeasty aroma.

Sourdough.

Whoever had kitchen duty last night mixed it up so it could rise overnight. Now we'll knead it and let it rise again, then shape it into loaves after lunch and bake it by the fire later this afternoon. Mom says it's good it's summer because the heat of the day helps the bread rise. During winter, we'll need to find a warmer spot for it.

I have no idea how she knows this, since I can't remember her ever making bread at home. Here, breadmaking is an assigned duty, and the three of us have it today. This bread will go with our supper and tomorrow's meals. We'll start another batch before bed, and whoever's on duty tomorrow will repeat the process.

Aunt Karla says we're very blessed last year's wheat crops, both winter and spring, along with barley, were planted and growing well before the EMP. Several of the local farms raised cash cereal crops, which became survival food for them.

Without any combines or large machinery, the harvest took the entire community weeks to accomplish, and the threshing, separating the wheat seed from the straw, took several more weeks. But it kept them all fed well.

Apparently, Ledger Hyde was one of the farmers whose entire field went to feeding the community.

Now that he's gone, they're still working his fields, and someone's even living in his house. Finding out the man was driven not only from his home but also from his farm, it makes more sense he'd snap. I still don't like him—he held a gun on me and Atticus, after all—but I know how people can do crazy things. Look at my mom, she wasn't herself for a long time.

Just as I finish this thought, the dining room door swings open with a squeal. I lift my head and meet my mom's shining eyes. Her cheeks are lightly flushed, and she has a ginormous smile.

"Something good?" I ask.

"What's that?" Her voice is light and airy.

"You look . . . happy."

Her smile increases in size. "We set a date."

"For what, Mom?" Sebastian's face is scrunched up in a question.

"The wedding."

My brother's smile quickly matches my mom's. "That's good! When?"

"A week from Sunday. The man who set Victoria's arm, Chuck, he'll be the preacher. And he's even going to do a full church service before the wedding."

"A full church service?" My eyebrows shoot up my forehead.

"Isn't it wonderful? We'll have church on the front lawn, and then walk to the gazebo for the wedding ceremony followed by lunch on the patio. It'll all be so . . . so proper."

I can't help but grin at my mom's excitement. "Sounds good. What'll you wear?"

"I'll find something. And, Sadie, I want you to be my maid of honor. Sebastian will be Donnie's best man."

"Really?" Sebastian gushes. "I'm the best man? Shouldn't I be the best *boy*?"

Mom lets out a hearty laugh. "Best man, best boy . . . whichever you want. You'll be standing up with Donnie, and Sadie will be with me. It's going to be so perfect! And Donnie and I are going into Lewistown on Saturday. They have their biggest trading day then. We're going to look for . . . " Her hands cover her mouth in a show of excitement.

"For what?" I ask.

"Wedding rings. We're going to find wedding rings."

I give her a smile. It's nice seeing her so happy, so in love. As gruff and difficult as Donnie was when we first met him, he really is the one for her. "That's great, Mom. It'll be fun to go into town."

"Are you sure?" Sebastian asks.

Mom turns in his direction. "Sure?"

"About town. They didn't . . . I don't think they like us much, the people that live here. Remember what they said?"

"Oh, that. People talk about things they don't know. Obviously, we know this community isn't a cult."

Sebastian's face goes dark. "I don't know, Mom. Maybe . . . maybe they know more than we do."

Chapter 13

Lewistown, Montana
Wednesday, June 17, Late Morning

Victoria

Yesterday's a blur of tossing and turning and being too hot and then too cold. I didn't even come out of the tent. And out of fear whatever's wrong with me may spread through our small group, Jennifer's stuck as my sole caregiver. My illness is still a mystery. While I undoubtedly have a fever, there's no cough, runny nose, upset stomach, or any of that nasty stuff.

Today is better. The last hour or so, I've started feeling closer to normal. Not great—still exhausted and achy—but I don't have the chills or the sweats. We're still taking precautions to prevent the spread, but I'm out of the tent and sitting on my comfy perch of blankets near the firepit.

I've just finished a cup of broth and am considering a nap—big goals for the day. Jennifer's at the outhouse. I'm embarrassed to say her main reason for going is so she can dump the toilet bucket the camp hosts gave us, which I've been using in the tent.

Before Leanne and her children reached their aunt's home, I shared this tent with Jennifer. Thankfully, she's now using Leanne's. I can't imagine being sick and trying to share such a small space. Then add the bucket . . . *yuck*.

As I'm watching for Jennifer to exit the little building, movement near the entrance of the campground catches my eye. It's two men on horseback. One of the men has a second horse tied to a lead rope. The ponied horse has a bag or something over it. Maybe he's being used as a pack horse?

The men make their way to the camp host. Once they reach the travel trailer, the man without the pack horse dismounts and raps smartly on the door. Out of the corner of my eye, I see Jennifer stepping from the outhouse. About the same time, the camp host husband, Charlie, responds to the knock.

Jennifer's pace slows as she nears the camp trailer. At this distance, I can't hear the conversation.

Charlie drops his head and gives it a shake. The horseman motions toward his friend, then starts moving in that direction with Charlie.

Jennifer has now fully stopped, only steps from the tidy front yard of the camp hosts, the toilet bucket dangling from her fingers by the wire handle.

As the men reach the horses, the one still mounted says something and motions to the ponied horse behind him. With the horses in the way, and his head slightly bent, I'm unable to see Charlie's face and can't determine exactly what's going on.

Jennifer, though, must have a perfect view. She drops the bucket and moves her hands to her face.

I realize I'm not the only one watching. Atticus and Rey stride quickly in Jennifer's direction.

Charlie steps away from the horses and calls out to Jennifer, "Everything's okay. Um, well, it'll be fine."

She gives a nod as Atticus reaches her. He swoops up the bucket with one hand and offers the other to his mother. She shakes her head and points toward the horses. Atticus briefly looks in that direction and then nods, again motioning for Jennifer to take his hand.

Rey continues past them and heads toward Charlie. "Need any help?" he calls out, his voice carrying across the campground.

Charlie makes a motion with his hands and then puts a finger to his lips.

Rey nods and keeps walking toward the men. When he reaches them, there's a quick talk—maybe introductions—and the second man gets off the horse. He holds the reins while Rey and the other two remove the bundle from the pack horse.

Part of the material covering the bundle slides off, and a bare foot pokes out.

My hands go to my mouth. I look toward Patti Hyde's camp.

The three men heft the body off the horse and carry it a few feet, then gently lay it on the ground. Within a minute, the two men are back on their horses and riding away.

Brett appears by my campsite, standing on the other side of the fire. "Mom, did you hear what Jennifer said?"

"No, I'm sorry. Was she talking to me?" I keep my eyes on Rey and Charlie.

"She heard what they said. It's Ledger Hyde—the body."

I bite the inside of my mouth. I think I knew it was Hyde as soon as I saw the foot. Who else could it be?

"It's good his wife will have answers," Brett says.

"Definitely. Although, it won't be the answer she wanted."

"Better than thinking he ran out on her."

I give my son a sad smile. "Better, yes. But also final. With not knowing for sure, she'd still have hope."

"She'll be able to make plans now, figure out what she's going to do. It's not like she can live here in a tent forever."

Rey lifts a hand in our direction. He shows two fingers and then raises his other hand to show one finger. I don't know what his gestures mean, but it seems Atticus and Kimba do.

Kimba tells her children to stay put, then she and Atticus head over to him. Charlie says something to Rey before turning toward his camp trailer.

For many minutes, Rey, Kimba, and Atticus stand near the covered body of Ledger Hyde, talking quietly with their heads close together.

"Do you think we'll help bury him?" Jameson asks as he sits next to me.

"Don't get too close, honey. I may be contagious, and you don't want whatever I have."

He dutifully slides a yard or so away. "You look better."

"I feel better. Tired, but not so out of it."

"Jennifer says it'll still be a few days before you feel like going anywhere."

"She's right, unfortunately. I can't even imagine . . . " I lift my good hand in surrender. "I know every day we're stuck here just zaps our supplies a little more. I'm . . . I'm sorry."

Brett squats. "It's not your fault you're sick, or that you were hurt. I shouldn't have insisted you go hunting with us. If anything— "

"Dude." Jameson puts a hand on his arm. "I thought you got over the whole guilt thing? It was an accident."

Brett lifts a shoulder. "Anyway, Atticus and Axel said the wild game numbers should increase once we get past a place they call Eddie's Corner. The towns will be spread out again, which should help."

"There's the other camp host." Jameson points to the woman exiting the camp trailer, with Charlie on her heels.

When she reaches Rey and the others, she kneels by the body as she crosses herself, then bows her head and places her hands together in a prayer motion. Her husband and Rey smoothly remove their hats. Atticus fumbles with his but finally gets it off.

After the short prayer, the woman stands, says something to her husband, and starts toward Patti's tent.

Charlie lifts his hands before turning to Rey.

With a nod, Rey, Atticus, and Kimba walk back to our campsites.

Chapter 14

Lewistown, Montana
Wednesday, June 17, Early Evening

Victoria

With her head held high and her back straight, Patti Ledger stands by her husband's grave. The camp host woman, Lauren, holds the baby while the older child sits at Patti's feet and runs a toy car through the dirt.

Our group, the host couple, and others at the campground worked together to dig Ledger's grave. There's little fanfare during the solemn service Charlie leads.

I join them and sit several feet away in a folding chair. I'm feeling better, not really well enough to walk again, but we need to get going. I thought we'd be at the Dosen ranch by now. Before leaving the ski lodge, we painstakingly mapped out our journey, plugging in the distances between stops where members of our traveling group would break off to be reunited with their loved ones.

Four hundred miles. By car, it'd be no problem. On foot, that's a different story. With snow on the ground and young children in our group when we left, our goal was six miles a day. Now, with eight-year-old Naomi being the only child and the ground clear, the goal is double.

I'm beginning to think it'd be best if my sons and I stayed here. Not here at this campground, but in Lewistown. We could stay with Leanne at her aunt's place while I heal from my injuries. Jennifer and her sons can get back to their ranch and get everything done before winter, and we could head up there next spring.

Last winter was one of the coldest and snowiest on record. Will this year be the same? Many believe the nuclear fallout from the ground detonations on both coasts are to blame for the terrible weather. Some think the extra rain we've seen this spring is also due to changes in atmospheric conditions.

While the excess snow over the winter made things difficult, and the spring rains have made traveling miserable, Jennifer keeps saying what a blessing both have been. They'll have good grass for their cattle—the herd they hope to find flourishing in the care of their hired man.

They left their ranch just over a year ago to check out colleges Atticus and Asher were considering. They made a family adventure of it, loading up their large SUV and inviting Nina, Jennifer's sister who lived in the mother-in-law cottage on their ranch, to join them. The attacks happened while they were still almost six hundred miles from home.

With their SUV running on fumes, they parked it a few miles outside of Thermopolis, Wyoming, just exiting the Wind River Canyon at a boat launch parking lot known as the Wedding of the Waters, where the Wind River becomes the Bighorn River. They'd been fortunate to make it as far as they had with the packed roads, fuel shortages, and cyberattacks bringing travel to a near standstill.

Atticus and his dad walked into Thermopolis, praying they'd find fuel to make it a little farther up the road. They didn't.

After spending the night with their vehicle and making plans to walk the rest of the way, they set out. Jennifer's husband fell into a ravine north of Thermopolis, before they reached the town of Meeteetse. He later died from his injuries. It was there they met the Hoffmanns.

"Mom? You okay?" Jameson lays a hand on my shoulder.

I blink my eyes several times.

He furrows his brow. "The funeral's over. We're going to start covering his . . . um, Mr. Hyde."

"Yes, I'm sorry, I was . . . " I give a slight shake of my head.

"Let me walk you back to camp so you can rest again."

I glance at Patti Hyde. She's still standing by the grave as Rey and Atticus begin shoveling dirt.

Jameson offers me his hand, and I heft myself from the chair. Having only one good arm and being weak from illness makes the simple movement difficult. My body's so heavy, I swear I've gained fifty pounds of pure blubber.

I'm quickly out of breath, needing to pause partway just to rest. On impulse, I ask Jameson what he thinks about going back to Leanne's aunt's place.

He scrunches his face. "Why would you want to do that?"

"Because . . ." I motion to my arm.

"I thought you said Jack Mosher was a chauvinistic pig?"

I let out a snort of laughter. "I believe the word I used was misogynistic."

"Is there a difference? He doesn't want women to help with security, just to do the cooking and cleaning. Isn't that a problem for you? I mean, with the way Dad was . . ."

"Well, maybe. But Donnie and Leanne thought they might do things a little differently since they're slightly separated from the main community. I'm positive Leanne plans to have her handgun nearby in case she needs it. And she made it sound like her aunt might have weapons stashed somewhere. They just don't flaunt them like we're so used to seeing."

"Or Jack Mosher is like Dad and knows that, by keeping people unarmed, he has control."

I close my eyes. That was part of my husband's scheme. When he convinced the Bakerville council to pass an edict preventing people from being armed in public, his end plan was to enact a hostile takeover. He almost succeeded, but he didn't count on people ignoring the rules and carrying their weapons concealed. When it was over, Jon and most of his cohorts were among the dead. And our lives changed forever. My sons and I were branded as outcasts in the community.

"I don't think it's a good idea." Jameson's head moves back and forth like it's on a swivel. "Besides, with Asher dead, they'll need us more than ever. Atticus said, even with all of us, we'll have a hard time running the ranch."

"Maybe so. But we don't even know what to expect when we get there. Their hired man—do you remember his name?"

Jameson lifts a shoulder. "Scott, maybe?"

"We don't even know if he's still there, if he's been caring for things or— "

"Or if someone came in and rustled all the cattle."

"Rustled, huh?" I smile at my son.

"Isn't that what it's called? Stealing cattle—rustling cattle?"

"Yes, I just like the way you said it. You sound like an old-time cowboy."

"We will be cowboys—riding horses and fixing fences, all the stuff needed to take care of a ranch. Atticus will teach us."

"You almost sound excited about it."

"I am . . . I guess."

My heart soars. Jameson has been so surly since his dad died—long before even. The life we lived prior to the attacks was stressful. We never knew what mood Jon would be in, or what little thing may set him off. Jameson tried hard to please his dad, to get encouragement and congratulations from him. The atta boys were few and far between, while the condemnations were plentiful. It was a difficult way to live.

I give him a little smile. "With my injury and illness, I'm holding up the group. They've said many times how much we'll need to do before winter."

"They all feel bad for you. No one talks about you holding us up."

"Jennifer has been . . . odd. The way she's acted a few times . . ."

"Humph." We start moving again. "That's not about you. She doesn't like Patti Hyde."

"Doesn't like her? She doesn't even know Patti, does she?" I scrunch up my forehead, trying to recall the interactions between the two. I've been out of it the last couple days, but I think Patti has only been around the one time.

Jameson lowers his voice. "Atticus says she has a few prejudices."

"No, she doesn't." My words come out in a rush. Jennifer's kind and loving to everyone, usually excessively so. She makes a huge deal about living the way Jesus lived and other drivel.

Don't get me wrong, I'm grateful for the way she is. She was able to forgive me for the death of her sister at the hands of my husband, and offer us a new life because of those extreme beliefs. But it's rather odd, and often annoying, to have her quoting Bible verses about loving one another.

Jameson lifts his shoulder. "According to Atticus, she does. I didn't get details. He and Axel were embarrassed by the way she acted and the things she said. Even today, she made a remark or two. I didn't hear it, but Atticus whispered not to say stuff like that."

As we reach the camp, Jameson helps me get in a comfortable position by the fire. I'm still not convinced we should continue on to

Great Falls, but Jameson makes a good point about us being needed—assuming my arm works as it should after it heals.

If it doesn't, I won't be doing Jennifer any favors. She needs someone strong and healthy who can help not only with the ranch work but all the household stuff too. Not someone physically challenged.

If my arm doesn't heal right, will they even want us to stay?

Chapter 15

Lewistown, Montana
Thursday, June 18, Midafternoon

Victoria

"Victoria?" Kimba's voice is soft as she summons me from the other side of the tent wall.

"Yes?"

"Did I wake you?"

"No, I was just thinking about coming out. My nap was wonderful, but this tent's getting hot."

The fabric shudders as she starts to work the zipper. The movement suddenly stops. "Uh, are you decent?"

I let out a laugh. "As decent as can be expected. My hair's a dirty, disgusting mess, but I'm fully clothed if that's what you're asking."

She finishes with the zipper, giving me a brilliant smile as the flap opens. As usual, her blond hair is shiny and smooth, her bright blue eyes and perfect features not requiring any makeup to still look stunning. She and her daughters are natural beauties. Even her husband and son are excessively gorgeous. They could all model for any international agency and make big bucks starring as the all-American family.

I awkwardly run a hand through my scraggly hair. "Anything exciting happening?"

"We're having a group meeting. There's something we need to talk about."

"All right. Give me a minute to wiggle out of this tent."

"Need a hand?"

"No, I'm fine."

"Do you need the bucket?"

"Mercy, no. I'm walking to the outhouse. That bucket— " I scrunch up my nose.

She responds with a light laugh. "I'll walk over with you. Rey's still rounding up Axel and Nate. They're out with the traps and slingshot."

Kimba walks me to the outhouse, making sure I'm steady on my feet. I've been fever free for almost two days, since the day Ledger Hyde's body was brought back and buried. I'm still tired, but I'm essentially on the mend.

Last night, I grandly announced it's time to start traveling again. After my talk with Jameson, where I suggested we stay in Lewistown, he went to his brother. They came to me together, pleading their case to continue on. They insist we're needed at the ranch and I'll heal good as new. Everyone's willing to wait for me to get well enough for walking.

When we return from the outhouse, our group's gathered around the firepit. Thanks to the warmth of the day, we let the fire burn out.

Thirteen-year-old Nate is sitting on the ground with his arms crossed, a sour look on his face.

"What's up, bud?" his mom asks as we step near them.

"I broke my sling shot."

"The rubber?"

"Yeah. And my replacement piece—the one we got out of the bike tire at that one house—it was too rotted. The stupid thing snapped when I tried to use it. I thought we had another one, but no one seems to know where it is."

"I think it was with the stuff we left behind in Roundup." Atticus lifts his hands.

"We wouldn't have left it," Nate insists. "Everyone knew I needed it."

"Well," Kimba says in a patient voice, "I'm sure if it was left behind, it was by mistake. We'll ask Charlie if he has any tubing or knows where we can find some."

"Could probably get some at the trade station set up at the courthouse," Rey says, clapping his solemn son on the shoulder. "We can check tomorrow. We're going to see if they have any new stuff we need."

"Why'd you call us back anyway?" Nate asks, his bottom lip still pushed out.

Jennifer pats the ground next to her.

I gently sit, being careful not to move my arm too much. It's sore and aches deep in the bone.

Before we left the camp by Mosher's compound, Daniela Reynolds undid the wrapping and put some salve on my arm and then put it back together. She gave me a container of the same stuff to use once I take off the bandage and splints, but that won't be for several weeks. I'd love to rip it off right now and massage the healing lotion in. Anything to stop this ache.

Kimba squats on the ground near her son. "Patti Hyde stopped me earlier."

I swear I feel Jennifer's body stiffen next to me. She lifts her chin slightly. "And?"

"She asked if they could travel with us."

"No. No way." Jennifer shakes her head.

With wide eyes, Atticus shoots his mom a look.

"I mean . . . " Jennifer starts. "With the babies, we'd . . . it's already so late."

"Mom, I'm sure we can figure out something to make it easy with the babies," Atticus says.

"Really? Like what?" Jennifer crosses her arms.

"Patti has a two-child stroller," Kimba says. "And also fabric carriers for each child and a wagon. She's offering to share her supplies, says she's fairly well stocked and— "

Jennifer shakes her head. "It isn't a good idea."

Atticus looks directly at his mom. "For I was hungry and you gave Me something to eat, I was thirsty and you gave Me something to drink, I was a stranger and you invited Me in . . . "

"Please." Jennifer puts up her hand. "You don't need to quote scripture to me."

"I think maybe I do, Mom. You seem to have forgotten verses you've been living your life by."

"Fine." She lifts her hands. "If you all want to be saddled with two crying babies—babies who won't know when they need to be quiet, who might put us in danger—then by all means, let's invite them to join us."

"What's this really about?" Kimba asks, her voice soft. "Because it seems to be about more than just traveling with the young children."

Jennifer pops to her feet. "Do what you want. Invite her to travel with us. Whatever."

Kimba moves next to Jennifer and gently drops a hand on her shoulder. "Let's discuss this. If it's truly a problem, please tell us why."

"Mom doesn't like Indians," Axel blurts out.

Jennifer's head spins toward her son.

"I mean, Native Americans," Axel whispers.

"It's not . . . it's not like that," Jennifer stutters.

Atticus stands next to his mom. "Tell them."

Jennifer gives a slight shake of her head. "I'm not prejudiced. It's just— " She puts a hand to her mouth.

"You want me to . . . " Atticus lifts a hand toward his mom.

Jennifer gives a slight nod and then sinks to the ground next to me. She stares at her knees as she says, "I'll tell the story, Atticus. After all, it's my issue, not yours. But thank you. Thank you for offering to make it easier on me."

Atticus squats next to her.

She gives him a tight smile before lifting her chin. "Maybe there's some truth to what Axel said, even though hearing it makes me feel . . . terrible. The thing is, Patti reminds me of someone—someone from long ago."

"I take it this person wasn't a friend?" Kimba gives Jennifer a half smile.

With a scoff, Jennifer says, "Hardly. She was . . . she was my dad's lover. They had a child together while he was still married to my mom, then two more kids later, after he left us."

"And she was from the Flathead Reservation?" I ask. "You grew up in Montana?"

"I'm from Missoula." Jennifer nods. "It's not far from the Rez. Anyway, she was Kootenai."

"But she's not the same person, right?" Nicole Hoffmann asks, confusion painting her voice.

Jennifer sighs. "Of course not. I just . . . she reminds me of her. Look, I know it's not logical."

I shake my head. "When we were in Pryor, at Chief Plenty Coups, on the Crow Reservation— "

"I didn't have an issue with them," Jennifer says hurriedly. "It's not quite the way Axel made it sound. I'm not a . . . a bigot."

I raise my eyebrows. The things she's saying, they don't sound at all like the Jennifer I've come to know over these past several months.

She's made such a point of trying to live her life like Jesus, to *show* the love of Jesus, this ugliness is not fitting.

She reminds me of my dead husband. He'd spout off all kinds of God stuff when we'd go to church each week, but once we were out of that building, he didn't live it. He said terrible things about the preacher, the other church members, people in town, and complete ethnic or religious groups. Jon was truly a bigot, a racist, and more. He was not a good person.

Jennifer, though, this is a surprise. I tilt my head toward her. "So, it's not all Indigenous people you have a problem with, just ones who remind you of the woman your dad abandoned your family for?"

She drops her gaze and shakes her head. "I've tried to overcome this. I've asked God many times to take this burden from me. I thought . . . until I saw *her*, I thought it was gone."

"Is anyone else opposed to Patti and her children joining us?" Rey looks around our small group.

His seventeen-year-old daughter, Nicole, and his son, Nate, both shake their heads. His youngest daughter, Naomi, says, "I'll help with the babies. I like babies."

Brett and Jameson look to each other and give a shrug. Brett speaks for them, saying they're okay with it. I nod my agreement.

Atticus and Axel both look at their mom. In a soft voice, Atticus says, "I won't strand a new widow with two young children when we can help."

"We won't be stranding them," Jennifer insists. "They've lived in Lewistown for years. Mosher will take them back."

"About that," Kimba says. "I asked Patti why she doesn't return. She said it isn't safe for single women."

"Isn't safe for single women?" I echo.

Kimba lifts a shoulder. "That's what she said. I pressed her for details, but she clammed up. She's insistent on going to St. Ignatius, whether she travels with us or alone. She can be a help to us. Daniela Reynolds took her under her wing while they were neighbors. Patti knows some of the herbal stuff and even has a book with hand-drawn pictures Daniela made to help with foraging wild things."

My hand goes to my broken arm.

Kimba notices my movement and gives me a nod. "We've been blessed so far, to find the right people at the right time. But none of us know much about medicine, and we know even less about natural medicines. That's not all, Patti says they planned for this—her and her husband."

"In what way?" I ask.

Kimba raises her eyebrows and moves her head forward. In a low voice, she says, "The have caches."

"Caches?" Nate repeats. "Like they buried stuff for later?"

Kimba lifts a shoulder. "Seems so."

"That's so cool!" her son says. "But . . . why?"

"Preppers?" Atticus wonders.

"I asked. She said her husband wanted to make sure they had a plan in place for all kinds of scenarios."

"Humph." Jennifer shakes her head. "Would have to be him. No way any— "

"Anyway . . . " Atticus stands. "Like I said, whether she can offer supplies or not, I'm not okay with ignoring their need. I say we take a vote. Majority rules."

Jennifer reacts as if she's been slapped. Her voice comes out tight. "I guess we know how that'll go. You all just do what you want. But remember my words, I have experience with the inhabitants of the reservation. And if she's from there, you can bet she's just like them. We'll want to sleep with one eye open."

Jennifer lifts herself to her feet. In her haste, she loses her balance. Atticus steadies her, but she yanks her arm away and shoots him a look before stomping off in the direction of the trees at the edge of the campground.

"Wow," Jameson says under his breath.

"I'm . . . I'm sorry." Atticus shakes his head. "You all know my mom isn't— "

"She's never like that." Axel jumps in. "Other than where the Flathead Reservation is concerned."

"All because her dad left her mom?" Nicole asks.

Atticus and Axel look at each other. Atticus gives a barely perceptible shake of his head, then drops a hand on his brother's shoulder. "Let's vote."

Chapter 16

Fergus Peak Lodge
Saturday, June 20, After Breakfast

Sadie

"Sadie, is this a weed or one of the plants?" Sebastian points a dirt-crusted fingernail at a scraggly stem.

I lean in his direction. "Mom would probably say a plant since it doesn't look very good. The weeds always grow hearty." I shake my head. "But I don't know. Better leave it until Ms. Reynolds comes around again to check on us."

"I'm glad we don't have school today. Do you miss going to school?" My brother lifts an eyebrow at me.

"You know Mom and Aunt Karla gave me all those books to read, right?"

"You love to read. It's not like it's hard for you."

I flick my head in agreement. He's right. I do love to read. But some of the stuff they've picked out for me aren't things I'd choose. They're educational so I can keep learning.

We work in silence for many minutes before Sebastian asks, "How come we didn't have a garden at home?"

"Mom was gone too much. Everyone was busy."

"We're busy now."

"Um, yeah, but it's a different busy. Way different."

"I like it. I mean, I miss the way things used to be—when we had TV and computers. But this is nice. I'm glad we're here. I don't . . . " He shakes his head. "Sometimes I'm still nervous about being here. Especially after . . . " He tilts his head toward the rest of the compound.

"Yeah." I nod. *Especially with Gray Nelson's death.* There's still no real answer to who killed him, but the speculation about it being Ledger Hyde continues.

The only one who seems to disagree is Aunt Karla. Any time it's brought up, she insists Ledger would never hurt anyone, saying he was a vital part of the community and even had special training with some kind of search and rescue group to help people.

Even Ms. Reynolds says his medical knowledge was useful, that he was a healer not a murderer. Seems she became very good friends with his wife.

Ms. Reynolds wasn't a close neighbor before everything happened. She lived in Fergus County but near another town. I'm not sure exactly what happened, but there was an attack of some kind and Ms. Reynolds was in hiding for several weeks.

Jack and a group of men went scouting and found the ruined town. They later found her, the only person left alive.

Her house had been pillaged, and she was a mess. They brought her here, and Aunt Karla nursed her back to health. When Ms. Reynolds was better, she had Jack take her back to her home to salvage what they could from her stash of natural medicines. They also dug up starts from her herb garden and brought them here.

The special herb garden is tended only by Ms. Reynolds. The rest of us can work in the food gardens, but she says the medicinals need special care.

Mom and Donnie left before daylight this morning, riding Gordie and Legend into Lewistown. Jack showed up here yesterday. He and Donnie were talking about the trip into town, but when Mom said she was excited to go, Jack got a weird look.

"Why's that?" Jack asked.

"Just the whole thing. It'll be fun."

He blinked a few times. "You didn't tell her, Karla?"

"She's an adult who can make her own decisions."

"Tell me what?" Mom asks.

Jack ran a hand through his full beard. "Only the men do the trading."

Mom's laugh was loud. "You can't be serious. Why in the world is that?"

"It's our way." He lifted his hands. "A way to protect the women here, to keep others from knowing about them."

"Others?" Mom mimicked, then shook her head. "That explains a lot, why the entire town thinks you're running a cult."

Jack lifted a hand. "Let them think what they want. Some of these women . . . you've heard the stories?"

"Now, Jack," Aunt Karla said. "Leanne is well aware of the— " she cleared her throat " —the difficulties women have encountered since the troubles started. She knows what can happen."

Jack's ears turned crimson. "I'm sorry. I didn't . . . look, it's best if you stay here. Tell her, Donnie."

"Tell her what? Leanne has a mind of her own. And truth be told, I'd like my fiancée with me while we find things for our wedding. You can't really expect me to come home with the correct doodads, can you?"

Mom's eyes were fiery as she crossed her arms, daring Jack to say anything further.

With a huff and a puff, he muttered, "Never could tell her to do anything."

Sebastian pushes on my arm, bringing me back to the present. "What's happening there?"

"Where?" I ask, looking around the garden.

"The rabbit, just outside the fence. Is it . . . rubbing its back in the dirt?"

I smile at the furry creature as it spins round and round. Then, when its face comes into view, my smile freezes. "Um, I don't know. Something's not right."

"Is it . . . " Sebastian's voice becomes a whisper. "Is it dying?"

I answer with a slow nod. "I think it is."

He gets to his feet. "We need to help it."

"No!" I grab his leg. "We don't know what's wrong with it. It could be contagious."

"You think it has that blood disease?"

I shake my head. "I don't know what's wrong with it. But we can't risk getting sick, or getting the caged rabbits sick." I look around our little farm. The chickens are out, running about and eating bugs. The small goat herd is in one of the paddocks, near the edge of the trees. Can whatever's wrong with the rabbits spread to the rest of our livestock?

"We need to tell Aunt Karla," Sebastian says.

"Tell Aunt Karla what?" Ms. Reynolds asks, causing me to jump.

"Look." I point to the rabbit. He's stopped spinning and is now just giving the occasional twitch.

"It's dying," Sebastian whispers.

Ms. Reynolds closes her eyes and lets out a long breath. "We found one a few days ago out in the forest. I was hoping they wouldn't get this close to our farm."

"What should we do with it?" I ask.

"Bury it. We don't want whatever it has to spread. Karla and I were talking about moving the rabbit pens inside. I think we should. Are you two almost finished here? You can help me."

Ms. Reynolds takes care of burying the rabbit while Sebastian and I quickly finish with the garden. Then, after consulting Aunt Karla and making final plans for moving the rabbits, we walk with Ms. Reynolds to a shed beyond the stables.

"We've gone through this shed, taking usable items out. It's mostly junk left behind." Ms. Reynolds works the padlock on the door. "Now, if I can just find the right key . . . " The fourth key on the large ring releases the lock. "There we go."

A plume of dust escapes the hot, dry building. It's decent size, large enough to hold a car with room to spare.

"You want to put rabbits in here?" Sebastian shakes his head.

"We'll clean it up. It'll be a good place to try this stacking method I read about."

"Stacking what?" I ask, looking around the dirty space. The four small windows are covered with cobwebs, and there's a heavy layer of dirt on everything.

"Chickens and rabbits. We'll move the rabbit cages in and let the chickens live here too. Some of them, anyway."

I shake my head. "Why?"

"The rabbits and chickens will have a symbiotic relationship. The rabbit droppings will fall through the bottom of the cages. You know how the chickens love to dig underneath?"

I lift a shoulder. "I guess."

"They'll do the same thing. Right now, it only happens in the summer because the chickens are locked up separately during the winter. If they live with the rabbits, they'll be able to dig all winter long. And I think it'll stay warmer. Last year, we had trouble keeping the rabbits warm and lost a few. Chickens too. This will be much better. I wish I'd read about this sooner."

"What do we do first?" Sebastian asks. "Clean?"

"Yep. We'll empty it out, then scrub it down. Then maybe take the doors off and make some type of screen doors for summer. Karla has rolls of screening in another storage shed. That'd help cool the space."

Sebastian wrinkles his forehead. "Will it be safe? Won't the screen door let whatever the wild rabbits have inside?"

"Good question. I don't think so. I think, as long as we don't carry the disease in with us and they don't share water or food, it should be okay."

She opens the screened windows. "I hope this works. There's a lot we can do to increase our food supply if we're smart about it. I've tried to tell Jack about some of the things I've read, but he's an old rancher from an old ranching family. Hard to convince to make changes."

We spend the rest of the day working on the shed, only stopping to eat and take water breaks.

"Well, I guess that's enough for today." Ms. Reynolds looks around the now clean space. "You two are hard workers."

Sebastian points to the piles of stuff now stacked outside. "What will we do with that stuff?"

"Next time Jack is here, he can look it over and see what they need at other homesteads. Then we'll find places for whatever's left. Tomorrow, we'll move the rabbit cages. I suppose Donnie will come in handy for that."

I force myself not to smile. She was adamantly opposed to Donnie moving here with the women and children, insisting this is to be a male-free refuge for them.

We have just enough time before dinner to lead a short martial arts lesson. I'm completely surprised when Ms. Reynolds says she'd like to join us. I even show the follow-up for the armbar.

Sebastian makes sure to tell everyone it's important so, if a person was hurting us, we could stop them. "Don't quit until the threat is eliminated." He makes eye contact with each of the children and the few women taking the class. "You have to keep fighting."

Ms. Reynolds surprises me again by giving several slow nods after my brother makes his point.

~~~~~
~~~~~

We're sitting on the patio after supper. It's hot and muggy and feels like rain. Sebastian and the other children are running around on the lawn, playing and laughing, enjoying being kids.

Aunt Karla and Ms. Reynolds are both working on mending. I'm trying to crochet. It's not something I know how to do, but both of them said I should learn. I'm using a length of the ugliest green yarn I've ever seen, crocheting a long chain to learn the process.

"There's your mom." Ms. Reynolds points with her chin. "I was beginning to think they wouldn't make it back tonight."

"Should I go help them unsaddle?" I ask my aunt.

"We've got it," Brooke says, nudging Cassie. The two women put down what they were working on and quickly head to the stables.

It's about twenty minutes later before Mom and Donnie walk toward the main patio, hand in hand.

"How was it, dear?" Aunt Karla asks.

"Fantastic." My mom is beaming. "I found a dress. And we— " She looks shyly toward Donnie. "We found rings."

"Don't know if I'll wear mine much," Donnie says. "Might be dangerous with working and riding Gordie. But it's a matched set, so we got 'em both."

Sebastian bounces from foot to foot. "Can I see?"

"Yup. And remember, as my best man, you'll be in charge of holding your mom's ring for me on the wedding day."

"Really? That's cool."

Donnie pulls a tiny box out of his pocket and lifts the lid off.

Sebastian nods. "Looks good. Wanna see, Sadie?"

Moving the box toward me, Donnie bends slightly so I don't need to stand.

"Aren't they lovely?" Mom's voice is dreamy.

They're both wide gold bands etched with hearts. They are pretty. Practical too. No diamond or any other gem. "Very pretty. What about your dress?" I look from my mom to Donnie. "Did you let him see it?"

"She wouldn't!" Donnie chuckles. "Said I have to wait. She didn't even let me shop with her."

Mom giggles. *Actually giggles.* "I want it to be a surprise."

"You traded the jewelry and things?" Aunt Karla asks.

Mom nods. "And the magazines. You were right about those."

We collected jewelry and other trinkets as we traveled. For much of the time we were on the road, jewels had no value. People traded for food, bullets, guns—things to keep us alive.

But now things seem to be improving. With the military clearing Interstate 90 around Billings, and the Air Force in control of Great Falls, trinkets now hold some value.

Aunt Karla sent a few tattered magazines. I thought those were a strange trade item, but she insisted they'd be popular, maybe even more so than the jewelry. At first, I thought it was because people wanted to read, but Mom said they'd want toilet paper.

Here at the lodge—in this entire community, in fact—we use cloth toilet paper. While on the road, we used whatever we could find. A magazine would've been amazing.

Mom and Donnie both take a seat at the table.

Donnie leans back in his chair, taking the front legs off the ground. "We heard something interesting today. Ledger Hyde was found dead."

Both Aunt Karla and Ms. Reynolds put their hands to their mouths. The other women and children near the patio also react, with several questions thrown at Donnie. How and when are the ones I hear most.

Donnie tells what he knows. He was found dead a day or two after Nelson was killed, and based on the condition of the body, he'd been dead a few days. It looked like his skull was fractured.

"What about his wife?" Aunt Karla asks.

"Heard she's moved on and is trying to get to her folks' place before winter."

My aunt releases a loud breath. "I wish she would've come here."

"Me too," Ms. Reynolds says. "Patti's a wonderful girl."

With the rumors I've heard about how she and her husband were driven out, I doubt she'd feel very welcome—even if Aunt Karla and Ms. Reynolds liked her. The rest of the community is super judgy.

Donnie scratches his arm. "Mosher says that finding out Hyde is dead strengthens his theory that he's responsible for Gray Nelson's death."

Mom shakes her head. "Still sounds like a stretch to me."

"Why?" I ask. "How does Hyde being dead help?"

"Seems Hyde had a few wounds to his hands—cuts. That's not what killed him. Like I said, he hit his head. But since Nelson was killed with a knife, Mosher thinks the cuts could've happened during the attack. Then he fell and clobbered himself trying to get away."

I slowly nod. I hope Jack's right. Ever since we found the body, I feel like I need to constantly look over my shoulder. "So that's it then? Mystery solved?"

Mom lifts a shoulder. "As far as Jack and the rest of the protectors are concerned."

Donnie clears his throat. "That's a wide swath you're painting."

She reaches for his hand. "Except my fiancé, of course. He's as skeptical as I am that Gray Nelson's killer has been found."

Chapter 17

Fifteen Miles West of Lewistown, Montana
Monday, June 22, Late Morning

Victoria

The squeak of the stroller wheel combines with the pounding of our feet, the cadence producing an out-of-tune melody. Last night, Atticus liberally greased the wheel with vegetable oil. It helped silence the noise until about an hour ago. Now it's beginning to annoy me.

After voting to allow Patti and her children—LJ, her almost three-year-old son, and her six-month-old daughter, Trish—to join us, we stayed at the Lewistown campground another couple of days to allow me more recovery time while they gathered and organized supplies.

Leaving yesterday morning, I felt strong, ready for the trip. Now I'm forcing myself to keep going, counting my steps and watching the highway mile markers. We stop at each one for water and a brief—*way too brief*—rest. Any minute, we should see another marker.

I need it. My body's on autopilot, with only the annoying melody keeping me in the present. As bothersome as it is, it gives me something else to focus on rather than how rotten I feel.

"There it is, Mom." Jameson points to the marker. "You ready to stop?"

Not trusting my voice to sound any better than the awful stroller wheel, I give a nod.

"Let's have lunch," Kimba says. "Lunch and a long break. Victoria looks like she could use a nap."

"We're never going to get home at this rate," Jennifer groans. She quickly drops her gaze before muttering, "I'm sorry, Victoria. That was . . . unkind." She pulls back her shoulders and gives me a half smile. "Of course, you need your rest. We probably should've stayed another day or two at the campground so you could regain your strength."

Without any discussion, Patti immediately sets things up for lunch. After we told her she could join us, she had Atticus and Brett go with her to a cache not far from the campground. It had a second, much smaller tent, emergency blankets, and packages of food, including wheat, corn, rice, and barley.

Those items, combined with things she'd brought from the rundown house they were staying in, really increased our supplies. A surprisingly large amount of dried meat and dried spinach and other greens from the garden, along with a partial container of vegetable oil, were very welcome.

With Patti's husband pulling a gun on Atticus and Sadie for hunting on the creek near his house, I expected them to be starving. Patti says, when they were kicked out of Jack Mosher's community a few months earlier, they knew it was coming. They'd already started storing food and other supplies in various caches outside of the compound. And the farther away caches, like the one near the Lewistown campground, had been established well before the EMP.

Nicole and Naomi play with Patti's children while she reheats the cornmeal mush she made at breakfast. I watch as she chops some dried venison into it and then adds a hearty spoon of vegetable shortening. "Bear tallow would be better," she says, giving me a smile. "But I didn't want to dig it out of my bag."

"Bear tallow?" I scrunch my eyebrows together. "Bear fat?"

"Exactly." She smiles. "Rendered fat."

"When . . . where'd you get that?"

"Ledger and a couple of the others went bear hunting in the spring, before . . . anyway, have you had bear before?"

I give a slight shake of my head.

"I have some dried. We'll plan on having it soon. Right now, I want to use up this deer since it's the oldest."

"I didn't know there were bear here." I nervously look around.

She lifts a shoulder. "Here and there. In the mountains mainly. They see them at the lodge fairly regularly."

"Are they grizzlies?"

"Black bear. But there'll be grizzlies where you're going, right?"

I close my eyes. I already know this. Jennifer told me they have bears, wolves, and mountain lions, just like we had in Bakerville. Bears were so common in our region of Wyoming, a grizzly once went through the Dairy Queen drive-through in Cody, just south of where we lived. And in another small community, a fall corn maze was closed for several weeks due to a sow in the maze.

"The water is hot. Do you know which tea you're supposed to have?"

Jennifer strides toward us. "I'll take care of Victoria's medicine."

Patti gives her a slight smile. "Of course." Although Patti pretends not to notice, it's no secret Jennifer doesn't like her.

I've tried several times to talk with my friend, to let her know I'm happy to listen if she wants to talk. Last night, she told me to give it a rest before storming off. She's barely spoken to me today.

I wanted to go to her this morning and tell her I was sorry. But she's been such a jerk, I'm now more angry than sorry. Whatever her problem is, it's her problem. I suppose I shouldn't be surprised.

Jon was the same. He pretended to be all holy, pious even, when we'd go to church on Sunday. No one knew how he really was. They had no idea the way he talked to me or to his children. The way he treated us . . . he was a fake.

I thought Jennifer was authentic, that she was truly trying to live like Jesus with the way she always spouts on about it. But maybe this is the true Jennifer and the rest of it was fake.

Jennifer doesn't even smile or meet my eyes when she hands me my mug. "Nettle, in case you're wondering."

"Yes, thanks."

"Maybe it'll perk you up. Let's see if we can get another five miles in today. I can't bear it if we don't make it as far as yesterday."

I dip my chin. "I'll do my best."

Chapter 18

Fifteen Miles West of Lewistown, Montana
Monday, June 22, Evening

Victoria

Every bit of my body aches. Although I pushed myself to keep going, I had to call for a halt when we made six miles. There was still plenty of travel time left, but not for me.

Stretched out on my sleeping mat by the small fire, I'm enjoying the heat it's putting off. It may be late June, but there's a chill in the air. We're well off the highway, behind a small dune, camped along a small, tree-lined creek. If I had the energy, I'd gush over how beautiful it is.

"Storm's coming." Atticus points to the mountains in the distance.

Gazing at the beautiful cotton candy sky, I stifle a sigh. It rained while we were camped in Lewistown, both by Mosher's compound and the city campground, but it's been dry since we started walking—the way we all prefer it. Slogging through the rain is miserable.

"Maybe just a short one?"

He makes a face. "We'll see."

After dinner—more of Patti's dried meat cooked in barley to make a stew—we're sitting around the fire when the sky lights up in the distance, far enough away the thunder isn't audible.

"Maybe it'll go around us," Jameson says.

"Don't bet on it," Atticus responds. "Good thing we got those extra tarps in Lewistown. And Patti's tent." He motions to the tiny backpacking tent, which was part of Patti's cache and is now being used by Axel. The brothers were sharing a tent, but with both of them being so large, it makes sense for each to have their own.

I shake my head. While the tent is great, decent quality and brand new, the tarps are a different story. They aren't even really tarps but rather vinyl advertising banners. One announces the grand opening of an Irish pub, and the other touts a real estate company.

"You think we need to put them out?" Kimba asks. "Which tents are the worst of the lot?"

"Humph," Rey scoffs. "They've all seen better days."

"We better cover Victoria's tent," Jennifer says. "We don't want her getting sick again."

"I don't think my tent has any leaks. It stayed dry during the last thunderstorm. Wasn't yours leaking, Atticus?"

"We put some duct tape on it," Axel answers. "Good as new."

There's a spattering of laughter.

Rey stretches out his legs. "Well, it sounds like we're all set then. I guess all that's left is assigning watch schedule."

"I'll take watch tonight," Patti volunteers.

"What about your children?" Rey asks.

"I told her I'd watch them," Nicole says. "I'll stay in her tent."

Unlike the rest of us, who have tiny little backpacking tents, Patti's is a spacious six-man tent. Because of its size, it's divided between her backpack and the one her husband had.

Brett now carries Ledger's pack; his was falling apart and wasn't a good long-distance pack but more of a book bag. There were one or two sentimental items of Ledger's Patti moved into her own bag, but she offered everything else to our group.

Patti's wagon has been very helpful too. It allowed us to barter in Lewistown for a few additional things we thought we'd need. And the tarps will undoubtedly be necessary at a future point.

"Okay, that'll work." Rey gives Patti a nod. "You want first watch or last?"

"I'm fine with either."

"How about last watch with me?" Kimba asks, giving the young woman a smile. "We'll watch the sunrise together."

"Sure, sounds good."

After Rey hands out the rest of the watch schedule, they begin discussing other things. I stare into the fire, letting my thoughts drift as their voices carry around me. Even before I broke my arm, I wasn't a regular on watch. When a third person is needed, I'm added. But because I don't use firearms, I'm not part of the two-person teams. I bite my lip, thinking about my aversion to guns.

My daddy made sure both my sister and I could handle rifles, taking us and our mom target shooting and hunting on a regular basis. He even said we were naturals, nicknaming me Sharpshooter and my sister Deadeye. Naturals or not, we were not only comfortable with targets but rarely missed when we went deer hunting.

When I went away to college, I rarely had an opportunity to practice shooting. That was fine. It wasn't a city thing to do. Many things I'd done in the country weren't city appropriate. During my first year at school, I truly felt like a proverbial fish out of water.

Mama and Daddy had been so happy, so proud when I was not only accepted to a four-year college, but also when the scholarships and grants covered the costs without me needing any student loans.

I'll tell you, though, putting in for those scholarships was almost a full-time job. I'm so grateful my guidance counselor gave me the help I needed to find and pursue financial aid.

I only wish my older sister would've done the same. She, too, had left home when she graduated, moving into the city. Not for school but for work. She soon fell into what my parents referred to as *the wrong crowd*. She started drinking and partying, then moved on to harder things. She came home for my high school graduation looking like a train wreck.

I was in my second year of college when her body was found in an alley.

The next year, my parents were killed in a car accident.

I already knew Jon but not well. It was about a month later, when I was mourning my folks, that we became close friends. We didn't start a serious relationship until our final year. Then we quickly married. Too quickly.

After we moved to Wyoming, Jon became interested in guns and shooting. I asked him if he'd take me along, but he kept putting me off, telling me it was a guy thing. I finally nagged him enough he gave in.

It was me, him, and four of his friends. They had a variety of rifles and handguns they were shooting. Jon gave me a "lesson" on how a .30-30 rifle worked. I listened carefully while he gave his spiel, not mentioning I'd shot an almost identical one more times than I could remember. Even though Jon and I were a good couple then, I knew better than to interrupt. We may have been happy, but it was happiness with rules.

When my first shot hit the target dead center, the bullseye, his friends all hooted and hollered. Jon gave me a reluctant "good job," following with "beginner's luck" before grabbing a new gun for me to try. And so it went. He deemed each rifle he handed off to me as "more difficult."

At first, he'd give me a quick lesson on usage, but as my accuracy continued, he stopped talking and just handed me the guns. As the weapons changed, so did the distance from the target. I whispered to Jon I was fine, that I'd had enough shooting for one day, but he insisted I continue.

One of his friends must have noticed what was happening because he offered to take me to a different target and let me practice some more advanced shooting. Jon spun on him, practically frothing at the mouth as he accused his friend of trying to get me alone. It was bad. The other men quickly made excuses to leave.

As they packed up, I started walking to the car.

"Where do you think you're going?" Jon demanded. "We're not done here."

After they left, taking most of the guns with them, Jon pulled out a new one he'd bought so he could go elk hunting in the fall. As he handed it to me, he sneered, "You'll have finally met your match with this one."

Part of me wanted to flub the shot and confirm his assumption that I wasn't up to the task. I couldn't do it. It would've been unfaithful to the things my daddy taught me about firearms.

After my shot was done, catching the upper right corner of the center target, Jon growled, "Bet you can't do it again."

I gave him a nod and lined up for my shot. Right as I was about to pull the trigger, he kicked me in the leg and yelled something awful. My shot went wide—dangerously wide. I spun on him, demanding to know what he was thinking. Did he not realize guns weren't something to mess around with?

He grabbed me by the hair, pulling my face close to his. "Don't you ever talk to me like that again. I'll do what I want when I want."

That was the last time I even thought about shooting a gun. Something changed in me. Even hearing gunshots in a movie caused me to cringe. I couldn't even watch action films without trembling.

Jon only went elk hunting one time. I'm not exactly sure what happened, but I heard from the wife of a man in his hunting group that Jon's gun-safety procedures were lacking. Seems he kept pointing the muzzle willy-nilly. One guy called him out on it, and they almost came to blows.

When we moved up to Bakerville a few years ago, Jon wanted to teach the boys how to shoot. I watched from the window, astounded by his carelessness with the muzzle and him teaching Brett and Jameson incorrectly. I wanted to talk to Jon about it and tell him if he wasn't going to teach the boys gun safety, then he couldn't teach them about guns at all. But I knew it'd be worse if I said anything.

The next time he wanted to take the boys shooting, I managed to come up with an excuse as to why they couldn't go. After that, Brett started making his own excuses. Jameson would excitedly agree, striving to get any sort of recognition from his dad. Jon shut him down and threw a fit about how it was both boys or neither. Whatever Jon could do to cause dissention between his sons, he did.

I'd started ax throwing a few months before our move to Bakerville, when my friends and I took a weekend trip to Cody. Something about the precision needed took me back to those times with my daddy when he was training my sister and me with the rifles.

And axes are quiet, no loud percussion causing me to jump. I enjoyed ax throwing so much, I thought it'd be great to have my own throwing alley. Moving another half hour north of Prospect put me even farther from the place I'd gone in Cody. Convincing Jon I needed a throwing lane took a little doing, but it did eventually happen.

I was no longer getting together for lunches or weekends away with my friends by then. Truly, I'm surprised it didn't end before our move. Each time I told Jon about a getaway, I expected him to put the kibosh on it. But thinking back, I realize why he didn't—because I made sure the boys were staying with friends, so Jon had free rein of the house to do whatever he wished.

With the boys and I isolated in the tiny town of Bakerville, it was Jon who was now off gallivanting around. Still working in Prospect, he'd often blame the weather for needing to stay in town. And he was always away at conferences for a few days or a couple of weeks.

We were in Bakerville about eighteen months before the terrorist attacks started. In those months, I went deep into a dark hole. So deep I couldn't pull myself out. My girlfriends from Prospect reached out to me, calling and inviting me to lunch or just wanting to chat on the phone. I stopped taking the calls. I stayed off social media for fear they'd see I was on and try to chat with me.

I was at my lowest, or so I thought, the day I discovered the car wouldn't start after the EMP. The coordinated terrorist attacks had been going on for over a week. The loss of life was terrible, but none of it was happening to us—not until the cyberattacks took out the power, banking, internet, and pretty much everything else. Since fuel was one of the things affected by the attacks, Jon was stuck at home.

Thankfully, he spent most of his time hiding out in his office, not even sleeping in our room. One day, my phone was completely dead. I tried to charge it in the car, but the car didn't start. Jon called me all kinds of names, telling me how stupid I was. I tried to not look too smug when he couldn't get it to turn over either.

There was no apology, not that I expected one. After throwing a fit for a good hour, he rode Brett's mountain bike to a neighbor's house. He got a crash course in electromagnetic pulses and the damage they could do.

It was probably also when Jon started planning and plotting how he could get his name in the history books.

Before the attacks, he was running for county commissioner. It was a steppingstone to his real goal of becoming governor and then moving to a national posting. While I don't think he believed he could be president, not realistically anyway, he did want more than just state service. Governor would give him the exposure he needed.

When the world changed in the blink of an eye, those plans were shattered, or put on hold indefinitely. It didn't stop him.

Fred Lassiter, a creepy guy who worked as a jailer for Prospector County, showed up at our house later with his equally creepy friend Jackson, and the three of them stowed away in Jon's office for hours. Over the next several days, others went in and out, too, or Jon went to them.

When Bakerville elected a town council to get us through the crisis, Jon was nominated by Lassiter, and he was voted in. Jon often said he was the only one on the council with a lick of sense. Judge Avery, a long-retired circuit court judge, was put in charge, giving Jon plenty of terrible things to say. While Judge Avery was always pleasant with Jon, I know he didn't think much of my husband. They'd had several run-ins through the years.

"Would you like a cup of chamomile before bed?" Jennifer's question quickly brings me back to the present.

I tilt my head before giving it a slight shake. "I'll pass tonight. As exhausted as I am, I doubt I'll have any trouble falling asleep."

"Keep in mind, in addition to helping you relax, chamomile's also said to have anti-inflammatory properties. It might help with those body aches."

"Good point. Maybe it'll be a cup of magic elixir and will leave me feeling fit as a fiddle."

She gives a tight smile. "We can only hope."

I nod my agreement.

Kimba chimes in, saying she'd love a cup; her muscles are also tight and achy tonight. I give her a smile, doubting her athletic body has felt a muscle strain or even a twinge of pain since we started this trek. I do appreciate her attempt to make me feel less like a failure and the reason why we're making such poor mileage.

As we sit around sipping tea, Jameson points a finger at Patti. "What'd you do to get voted off the island?"

I sputter mid-sip and barely avoid spitting out the warm liquid. "Jameson!"

"What?" He shrugs. "Isn't that pretty much what happened?"

A smile plays on the corner of Patti's mouth. "That's how Ledger and I referred to it too. I guess we didn't play the game as well as we should've."

"We heard you stole something. Or your husband did."

I drop my head at Jameson's choice of words. Jack Mosher implied Ledger stole, but it doesn't need to be brought up like this.

Patti lifts a shoulder. "Not exactly. Randy Loomer saw my husband digging a cache. He was burying our things, but it turned into a big deal, and we were accused of not sharing with others. Or I should say not sharing *enough*. We'd set up a few caches before, at the end of summer, just so we'd have something put aside." She lifts her hands. "We thought it was smart. Ledger was always like that. He was, um . . . *cautious* for years."

"He was a prepper?" Kimba asks.

Patti screws up her lips. "I guess prepper would be a fair label. Our community did well over the winter, really banded together to survive. By the time the weather started to improve, the entire community had heard about the president's announcements. We had a big party. Many thought the troubles were coming to an end. Like flipping a light switch, things would return to normal."

"We thought so too," Jameson says. "Where we lived, some people stopped working."

"Same." Patti nods. "But Jack Mosher was cautious. He supported the celebration, though he made it clear we'd still have a long road until our world was back to normal. There were many who fought the rationing and stopped being smart with supplies."

"Your story is— " Jennifer stabs a finger in Patti's direction. "You're telling us you were kicked out of the community for burying your *own* supplies?"

"That's correct. Uh, part of it anyway."

"And the other part?" Jennifer crosses her arms and raises her eyebrows.

"That's a little more complicated."

"Oh, I'm sure it is." Jennifer's voice is harsh.

Kimba rests a hand on Patti's arm. "Whenever you're ready to share, we'll listen."

Patti dips her head. "I'd best get the children ready for bed."

Nicole stands. "I'll help."

Chapter 19

Fifteen Miles West of Lewistown, Montana
Monday, June 22, Night

Victoria

My tent shakes, jolting me from near sleep. I pull the sleeping bag up higher as big, fat raindrops *plop-plop* on the roof. Atticus was right, as usual. As I settle, another stronger gust rattles the nylon fabric. *Great.*

A rainstorm is bad enough, add in the wind rustling my tent all night, and I'll be lucky to get any sleep. The splatter starts beating a faster tempo. I let out a long breath. At the end of my exhale, the sky lights up like day and is followed by a crack of thunder a second later. One of Patti's young children screams.

The storm seems to respond to the frightened child, intensifying with another flash and boom. The rain hits harder and faster. As I shiver inside my sleeping bag, the pounding escalates, switching from rain to hail.

I pull the bag over my head, hoping the thin-walled tents are enough to protect from the bombardment of ice pellets. I wish Brett and Jameson were with me, then I'd know they're okay.

The cries and screams of Patti's children, barely audible through the storm, sound after each boom of thunder. I pull the bag tighter over my head, holding it in place with my good hand. The ground shakes as the roar increases, sounding like a freight train barreling down on us.

Now it isn't just the children crying and screaming; I'm adding my own cries. The tent flaps fill with air and then the walls come in on me. When it opens up again, I go with it, lifting from the ground.

I'm weightless. Suspended in the air. Flying. Twisting and turning as the nylon tent wraps around me.

Something jabs my side. Then my leg. I scream out in pain.

I'm slammed to the ground. Fabric's tangled around my face, my arms, my feet. The ground still shakes. The noise is almost deafening.

Please, God. Please. Let my children be okay. Let everyone be okay.

Wrapped tight in the fabric, with the flashes of lightning and crashes of thunder, I'm shaking. Crying. *Pleading.*

Movement entangles me more. I let out a yelp of pain as something pokes into me. With my face covered and my body aching, I lose all track of time. My senses begin to numb.

Finally, the clamor begins to lessen, and the pellets pounding on my collapsed tent change their cadence. I squeeze my eyes tight and try to focus.

I hurt everywhere.

My broken arm is excruciating, my back aches . . . my leg, my side. As the hail turns to rain and the noise diminishes, I once again hear the cries of children and adults.

"Kimba? Naomi?" Rey's distraught voice calls. "Babe, are you okay?"

"We're okay," Kimba responds. "Nate? Is he with you? What about Nicole?"

There's a pause. "Nate? Nate! Where are you?"

"Rey? What's happening?" Kimba calls. "I can't find a way out of this stupid tent."

"Mommy, here!" Naomi yells.

I move my feet, trying to untangle them. Pain shoots up my right leg. I groan in agony.

There's more talking outside. Axel asks Jennifer if she's okay. I think she answers, but she's so quiet I can't make out her response.

I strain my ears, hoping to hear my sons. I gingerly move again, trying to untangle myself without causing pain. I attempt to roll on my side, but the fabric constricts and wraps me like a burrito.

I hear a wail in the distance. Is one of our people hurt? I listen for it to come again.

"Mom?" Brett's voice is hesitant.

"Brett! Oh! Where's your brother?"

"Here, Mom," Jameson answers. "We're both here."

"Thank you, God," I whisper. In a louder voice, I ask, "Can you get me out of here?"

"Give us a minute. You're pretty wrapped up," Brett says.

"Is everyone okay?" I ask.

"We . . . we're not sure."

As my sons work to free me, they talk to me in soft tones, letting me know what they're doing and urging me to protect my broken arm.

"It's not just the arm. I think one of the poles might have cut my leg. My side too." I don't say it aloud, but I'm very grateful I don't keep my ax in the tent with me, instead choosing to stash it in my backpack. If I had it with me, I may be in real trouble.

There's a murmur of concern from one of the boys, which is drowned out by cries from Patti's children. They're much closer now. Other cries are louder too. I'm listening, trying to determine who all is crying.

The tent shudders, pulling tighter and digging the pole deeper into my side. "Wait! Stop! The pole."

Finally, after they decide to work from the top down, my face is free. I gasp in the fresh air. The mist of rain dampens my face as the sky lights up in the distance. "Let me look at you," I demand. "Are you hurt? Jameson, is that blood?"

He wipes the back of his hand across his mouth. "A branch caught me. It doesn't really hurt."

"Brett?"

"I'm okay, not injured."

With my head uncovered, the crying and sobs are completely clear. "Everyone else? Are they just . . . scared?"

"The children, um, Patti's children, yes. Her tent's still standing."

"I heard Kimba and Naomi—Rey too. What about Jennifer?"

"Tangled up like you. But I think they almost have her out."

"Is she hurt?"

"Maybe, I don't really know. Atticus and Axel are helping her. Now let's try and get this off your arms. Tell me if anything hurts."

"Nicole? Nate?"

"Nicole was in with Patti. She's fine," Jameson says.

I hold my breath as they tug on the nylon.

Brett lets out a sigh. "We need to cut it."

"No," I say. "I need a tent."

"I don't see any way this will ever be used again. It's a mess. And in the dark like this, I can't sort out what to do."

"Cut it," Jameson agrees.

A flashlight bobs in the distance. A second illuminates Axel's face as he helps free his mom. We only have two lights since batteries are scarce.

"Maybe Rey can help? If he brings over the flashlight, you can salvage the tent."

"Rey's . . ." Brett lets out a sigh. "Nate's tent was tossed around like yours. They're working on getting him out."

"Is he hurt?"

"He's not talking." Jameson's voice is quiet. "He might have got knocked out."

Even in the darkness, I catch the look Brett sends his younger brother.

"Brett?" My voice is cautious.

He lets out a sigh. "Our tent moved too. But instead of flipping and twisting, it just sort of . . ."

"Scooted," Jameson adds.

"Yeah. It still collapsed, but we weren't tangled. We got out without much trouble. Nate's tent was near ours. He's . . ." Brett puts a hand on my shoulder. "I don't think he's alive."

"*Nooo . . .*" I groan out the word.

Jameson moves a little closer to me. His voice is quiet. "We went to help him. Nate's arm was out."

"He didn't have a pulse," Brett whispers. "We told Rey. He and Kimba are there now. Nicole's with them, but Naomi's in Patti's tent. They're getting Nate out. Maybe we were wrong?"

Not Nate.

I close my eyes and allow them to fill with tears.

He's so young, only thirteen, less than a year younger than Jameson. Nate's made a point of helping me whenever possible. I know he feels some guilt and thinks it's his fault I slipped. He isn't just helpful to me, but to everyone. He and his slingshot have fed us many nights. And while he occasionally has a bout of teenage angst, it's usually because he's limited in what he can do.

Tears run into my ears.

"You want me to use my bandanna?" Jameson asks. "To wipe your eyes?"

I nod my response. He takes care of cleaning me up, even drying my ears, but it doesn't help much since the tears continue. A rip of fabric lets me know Brett resorted to using the knife. I let out a breath as my left arm comes free. The tightness around my injured right arm lessens.

"Here, Mom." Jameson stuffs the bandanna in my uninjured hand.

I dab my eyes. "Careful with the other arm. It's hurting."

The fabric makes another tearing sound, followed by an exclamation from Brett.

"What is it?" I ask.

"The tent pole . . . I mean *poles*. One's stuck in your side. The other's in your leg."

I let out a snort. "Of course they are."

"Is it bad?" Jameson asks.

"I can't tell. They're busted off, so it's hard to know how deep they go. I don't want to just yank them out."

With the fabric loose, the adrenaline drains from me. I'm suddenly exhausted. Scared. Sad. I close my eyes. "Whatever you think is best."

"Jameson, can you get a fire going? Right here near Mom. She's starting to shiver."

The drizzly rain has stopped. I'm not even sure I noticed when it stopped misting my face. I feel Jameson move.

"First," Brett says, "go grab some blankets from our tent. We need to cover her up better."

I want to ask my young son to check on Nate, to find out if he's . . .

I gulp back another sob. I let Jameson go without voicing my request.

"Is Jennifer loose?" My voice is high pitched and reedy.

Brett lifts his head. "Looks like it. She's sitting near the trees—or what's left of them. I think, when daylight comes, we aren't going to recognize this place anymore.

"I think it was a tornado."

"Yeah. Seems so. Billings had a tornado several years ago. We learned about it in school, along with the bad tornado in Wright, Wyoming."

I give a slight bob of my head as I remember the Wright tornado. Two died and at least a dozen were injured. A group from our church went to help with cleanup. I thought we should join them, but Jon had too much work. And me going without him certainly wasn't an option.

Jameson returns and hands a blanket to his brother. "I have one of those crinkly blankets in my backpack. You think we need it?"

"Let's start with this. If the rain returns, we'll use the emergency blanket to help keep these dry. Those things are good to hold in body heat, but they won't warm her up, and I think she needs to be warmed up more than anything."

"Did you . . . any updates on Nate?"

Jameson sighs. "They got him out. I didn't ask, but with the way Kimba was holding him, with Rey and Nicole squatting beside her . . . I think we were right."

"Poor Kimba," I mutter.

"I'll g-get the fire going." Jameson's voice is wobbly.

"Make it a big one," Brett says. "We're going to need it."

Chapter 20

Fifteen Miles West of Lewistown, Montana
Monday, June 22, Night

Victoria

Once the fire is going, Atticus and Axel help their mom hobble toward it.

"Are you injured?" I ask Jennifer.

"Bumps and bruises," she says, wincing as she speaks.

"Hopefully," Atticus adds. "Her knee is swollen, and her back hurts. How are you, Victoria?"

"Fine," I answer quickly.

Brett cocks his head at me.

I give a slight shake of my head and mouth, *later.*

With Jennifer reclining by the fire and covered with blankets, Atticus looks at his brother. "I'm going to where Nate is."

Hearing the sadness in Atticus's voice causes a sob to catch in my throat.

"See if you can convince them to come near the fire," Jennifer says. "I'm worried about Kimba becoming shocky from the . . . the loss."

"Is Naomi with them?" I ask.

"She's still in with Patti," Brett answers. "Sounds like the babies have gone back to sleep. Maybe Naomi too."

"Must be nice to be able to sleep," Jennifer scoffs.

"Patti's awake. Jameson spoke to her a few minutes ago."

"Humph."

Brett goes with Axel and Atticus to see what they can do to help the Hoffmann family. Jameson stays close to Jennifer and me, asking if we need anything.

"Can you put the kettle on to boil?" Jennifer asks.

"If I can find it. Things aren't where we left them."

He grabs a limb from the pile he has near the fire, set close enough to dry out a little. How he even managed to find dry tinder and wood is a mystery. He places one end of the limb into the flames until it catches.

"Please be careful," I say, realizing he plans to use it as a torch.

The bob of his head is illuminated by the blaze. When he determines it's adequately burning, he sets off to where our campfire was the night before, a dozen feet from where we're at now, the glow of his torch marking his path.

A few odd noises come from Jennifer. It takes me a couple seconds to realize she's crying. I wish I was close enough to reach her hand. Listening to her sounds of distress have my eyes filling up all over again.

I blink rapidly, forcing away the tears. I don't want to be a crying mess if Kimba comes over. I want to be strong for her so she can grieve as she needs.

Asher's death a few weeks ago was terrible. He was such a wonderful young man. Like his twin, Atticus, he was an important part of our group. Where Atticus took on a leadership role, though, Asher went out of his way to be helpful to all of us. If he saw something that needed done, he did it. No muss, no fuss. He just did what needed doing.

I'll always be so grateful for the way he reached out to my sons when they were hurting, when things were so low for us, and how he convinced his mom and brothers to give us another chance.

Nate was just a child and was so much like Asher in many ways. He never hesitated to provide food for our group. He was often the one who started our fires and was always willing to set up camp. He was quiet and thoughtful. Loving, especially where his family was concerned.

Even with all the devastation around us, the Hoffmanns believed they were on a mission. They wanted to help rebuild our country. Nate mentioned many times how important it was to stand up for what's right.

Losing his life like this, in the middle of nowhere during a freak windstorm, is just wrong.

Movement by the fire catches my eye. Jameson's back, setting the kettle near the flames. "You want me to go after your pack, Jennifer, and get the bag of herbs?"

"Please."

As Jameson disappears, I hear a rattle from Patti's tent. She steps out and quietly glides toward the fire. "Naomi's sleeping. Do you know . . . " She lifts her hands.

"We think . . . " My voice catches.

"They're coming this way," Jennifer says softly.

I swallow hard before turning my head. Rey is carrying Nate; Kimba's by his side holding her son's hand. Axel has an arm around Nicole, while Atticus and Brett walk by their side.

As they step near the fire, I avert my eyes.

"We couldn't leave him alone." Kimba's voice is low and rough.

"I have a sheet," Brett says. "Should I get it for you?"

Rey's nod is barely perceptible. My son scurries away in the direction of his collapsed tent. Rey motions with his head to Kimba, who gingerly sits near the fire. The way she's moving makes me think she may be injured.

Once she's down, Rey plants a kiss on his son's forehead, then hands him to his mom. She, too, drops a kiss, this one landing on Nate's cheek. I avert my eyes, unable to bear the heartbreaking scene.

"Naomi?" Kimba's voice is weak and strained.

"Asleep," Patti answers. "I can get her if you'd like."

"Let her sleep." Rey sighs. "Nothing's gained by waking her. Nate will still be— " Rey chokes up.

A whimper escapes Nicole.

I glance back at the grieving family to see Rey put an arm around his oldest daughter's shoulder, allowing her to melt into him.

When Brett returns with the sheet, Kimba gives him a watery smile. "Thank you. It'll be his shroud."

The crack of the fire is the only sound as Rey takes the sheet and spreads it on the ground. He gently takes Nate from Kimba, then wraps the cloth around him.

"Don't cover his face. I can't . . . I want to look at his sweet face a little longer." Kimba's voice is quiet.

Rey bobs his head before moving a lock of hair from Nate's forehead. He spends several long moments gazing at his son before picking him up and returning him to Kimba.

"Rey? Axel?" Brett steps near the grieving man. "Can I use one of the flashlights? My mom's hurt."

Rey fishes the flashlight from his vest pocket. "Is it serious?"

I want to say I'll be fine, but Jameson blurts out, "Her tent poles are stuck in her."

"Victoria," Jennifer gasps. "Why didn't you say something?"

"Rey?" Kimba's voice is small. "Will you hold our baby? I'll check Victoria."

"No, no," I urge. "Please just let Brett. Please, you all stay together."

"And you stay put, Mom," Atticus warns Jennifer. "I'll give Brett a hand."

Brett kneels next to me, then turns on the light and directs it to the right side of my body.

"Ouch," Atticus says. "The one in the stomach doesn't look like it's in too far, but the leg . . . I don't know."

"It's not really my stomach. More my side, below the ribs I think."

"Does it hurt?"

"When I move. Otherwise, no."

Patti peers from behind the boys. "Can you shine the light at the base? Let's see how much blood there is."

"Hard to tell with her shirt in the way."

"I think you need to slit the fabric. The pants too."

I shake my head. "I don't have anything else to wear to bed."

"No choice," Patti insists. "We need to get a better look, can't just go yanking out those broken poles."

"She's probably right." Jennifer's tone is reluctant. "The poles could be acting as a stopper, keeping you from bleeding out."

"You're saying if we take the poles out of her, she could bleed to death?" Jameson's voice is tight, barely controlled.

Patti's eyes meet mine. "That isn't something we want to find out. I'll be as careful as I can with your clothes. Your yoga pants may end up being yoga shorts, but we'll make it work."

"Just one leg will be shorts. The other we'll leave long." Brett gives me a wink.

"Ha. Wouldn't that be the perfect apocalypse fashion statement?" I flutter my hand at my son. Guilt quickly comes over me. It feels wrong to be joking about anything with the death of Nate Hoffmann so fresh.

Atticus says he has a pair of heavy-duty scissors in his backpack.

"We may need those," Patti agrees. "I have a small sewing kit in my things, which has a seem ripper and scissors. I'll grab it."

She disappears into her tent while Atticus goes to his collapsed tent.

When Patti returns and starts cutting the fabric of my T-shirt, tears sting my eyes. I know it's stupid to cry over clothing when Rey and Kimba are mourning the loss of their son just feet away.

I have so little. And at the moment I don't even know where my things are. My backpack was sitting outside my tent, wrapped in a piece of heavy plastic. My tennis shoes were tied to the pack and my hiking boots were sitting next to it. For all I know, my bag blew somewhere to never be found again. She could be cutting into the only clothing I own. I let out a groan.

And my glasses. Where are my glasses? I'd tucked them inside a storage pocket of the tent.

"Brett, when it's daylight, can you try and find my glasses? They were in the tent."

"I'll look for them."

I'm sure I'm not the only one who's missing things, since all of us keep our bags outside the small tents. Patti's is the only one large enough to stash her possessions inside.

Atticus is still making plenty of noise and the occasional audible exclamation as he looks for his scissors. Is his pack missing too?

Brett lets out a gasp.

"That bad, huh?" I turn my head to look, but my broken arm hinders my view.

"There's quite a lot of bruising," Patti answers. "And it goes through."

"Goes through?"

"You were skewered, Mom," Jameson says. "Like a shish kabob. It goes in one side and pokes out the other. That's why we thought it wasn't bad. We were just seeing part of it."

"Is it just taking a small bit of skin?" Jennifer asks.

"Yes," Patti replies. "It's maybe an inch along the side."

I let out a breath. A year ago, an inch was a layer of fat. Now, with the forced rations and exercise, I have little fat anywhere. That inch could be going through something vital.

What's around there? Gall bladder? Liver? A kidney? I had my appendix removed in junior high; I think it'd be lower anyway. What about my intestines? Could I have perforated that? *Ewww.*

"Let's look at your leg before we do anything with this." Patti gives me a half smile.

"I finally found my pack. It was in the creek," Atticus says. "Things are everywhere."

Rey lets out a loud exhale. "We'd better check and make sure we haven't lost anything else. With the rain, the creek is probably swollen."

"Victoria's was in the creek too. I grabbed it but didn't see any others."

Relief surges through me. I haven't lost everything.

"But it's a good idea to do a better search," Atticus continues. "Let me give you the scissors. Do you need a knife?"

"I have one. With what I'm seeing, I think we need to wait until daylight."

"The leg too?" I ask.

She tilts her head. "I think we can pull them both out, but there could be blood—lots of it. And I'd feel better if we had more light. Jennifer, what do you think?"

Outlined by the glow of the fire, Jennifer's face first registers shock, then annoyance. "Why are you asking me? You're the one examining her, pretending like you have a clue about anything medical."

Patti nods. "It's true, I don't know much. I worked as a CNA before I was married. Emptying bed pans and giving baths isn't quite the same as helping someone who's been impaled."

"Impaled?" My voice comes out in a shaky gasp.

"Well . . ." She lifts a shoulder. "That does sound a little extreme. Pierced?"

Jameson shakes his head. "Like I said, skewered."

"We'll need to dig Nate's grave once the sun comes up." Kimba's voice is vacant, faraway sounding.

Rey reaches a hand toward her. She lifts her fingers slightly, allowing his to intertwine while their hands rest on Nate.

I close my eyes. "If you think waiting is best, let's do it."

"Try and sleep," Patti says, resting a hand on my shoulder. "Your body has been through a lot in the past several days."

"Do you want some tea first?" Jennifer asks. "The water should be hot. Maybe chamomile and lavender together?"

"I'm not sure about sitting up to drink it."

"I'll help you, Mom," Jameson says.

Brett reaches for my hand. "And I'll go check the creek, look for our stuff."

"Let's go," Atticus says. "Axel, can you stay and help Mom with tea?"

Axel answers with a nod, then Jennifer gives him instructions. She asks Kimba's family if they'd like some, but they all decline.

"Do you want to try to sleep?" Kimba asks Nicole.

"I . . . I'm not sure I could."

"We'll find blankets and set you up by the fire," Brett offers.

She gives a weak nod. "Yeah, okay."

"Kimba? Are you warm enough?" Axel asks.

She lifts a shoulder. "I'm fine."

After Jameson spoons the lukewarm liquid into my mouth, I settle back and close my eyes, trying not to move—to not make the impalement worse.

Chapter 21

Fifteen Miles West of Lewistown, Montana
Tuesday, June 23, Morning

Victoria

My eyes flutter open. A band of light is on the horizon. Birds sing in the trees. I shift my body and let out a gasp. The pain of the night before washes over me—being thrown around in the tent, stabbed by the poles. *Nate Hoffmann.* My eyes fill.

"Can I get you anything, Victoria?" Patti's voice is quiet.

"My boys?"

She motions with her hand. "Asleep."

"Have you slept?"

"I wanted to stay on watch. I'm one of the few uninjured in some way. Atticus, after he and Brett gathered everything up, he's been patrolling."

"Kimba?"

"Still with Nate. Nicole's sleeping, but the parents are still awake." She stares off in the distance. "It's going to be a beautiful sunrise."

I close my eyes and listen to the birds.

After a minute, Patti says, "But I will sing of Your strength, in the morning I will sing of Your love; for You are my fortress, my refuge in times of trouble."

I crinkle my forehead. "Is that . . . from the Bible?"

"Psalms." She nods.

"Are you a Christian?" I whisper.

Patti responds with a weak smile as she dips her head. "You?"

"I . . . I'm supposed to be."

She tilts her head and raises her eyebrow. "Supposed to be?"

"Well . . . it's a long story."

"Have you accepted Jesus as your Lord and Savior?"

"I used to go to church almost every Sunday. My husband took us, the boys and me."

"And?"

"And what? I know what it means to be a good person."

"Sure, it's good to be good. But whose standard of goodness do we use?"

I shake my head and receive an instant jolt of pain. I let out a groan.

"What hurts?" she asks, immediately scooting closer.

"My head, maybe my neck."

"Doesn't surprise me with the way you were tossed around. Here." She delves into a pocket and produces a small tin container. "I gave a couple of these to Jennifer last night. You were already asleep. It's just ibuprofen."

She helps me drink water to swallow the pills, then looks back at the eastern skyline. "It won't be long until we have enough light to figure things out. I've been thinking, we should be ready to cauterize the wounds."

"Cauterize." I say the word, but the meaning is slow to come to me. In a rush, I realize what she wants to do. "Burn? You want to burn me?"

"We should be ready in case it's needed."

"Will that . . . will it work?"

"Maybe? I also remember reading from somewhere—some fiction book I think, so it may or may not be accurate—about putting sugar on a wound to help stop bleeding and prevent infection. I also have a little yarrow. It's in the book Daniela made me as helping with infection. It grows wild around here, so we may be able to find more."

"Honey helps with infection."

"Yes, that too."

"We have the honey from Lauren at the Lewistown camp. We don't have sugar."

"I have some sugar."

My eyes shoot to the top of my forehead. "You seem to have a lot of things we haven't seen in ages."

"My Ledger." She shrugs. "He always said he wanted to make sure LJ, Trish, and I had everything we needed. There were times, as I was tripping over things he'd bought and not yet found places for, I thought he was going overboard. He was that way before we'd met too. As a single man, he didn't worry about having stuff everywhere, but it drove me crazy."

"He was older than you?"

"Fifteen years."

Fifteen years? Yikes. Almost a lifetime. I paste a smile on my face. "And how'd you meet?"

"Through friends. I'd moved to Missoula, much to my parents dismay." Her nose gives a slight twitch. "He was in town for the Cowboy Ball."

"The Cowboy Ball?"

"He went to college in Missoula, was on the rodeo team and did some saddle bronc and bull riding. But he excelled at team roping. The Cowboy Ball is their annual fundraising event, and he always went back for it. Even after we were married, we went. He knew Jack Mosher from college. That's why he lived in Lewistown. Jack convinced him it was the best place on earth."

"Oh? I didn't realize . . . "

She lifts a shoulder. "They'd been friends for years."

Fine way to treat a friend. "Had Ledger been married before?"

"No, he said he was always too busy to settle down. He kept rodeoing after college. He and his team roping partner went pro but couldn't quite make it. He was able to buy the house with his earnings, so it wasn't a total bust. He started a construction business, did some farming and ranching, became a farrier, hunted, fished, really had a full life."

"And then he met you."

Her smile turns shy. "We were good together."

"What happened with Mosher?"

Her face turns hard. "Mosher was fine. He has everyone's best interest at heart. His main fault is he's too trusting."

"Really?"

"You know Chuck and Daniela delivered Trish?"

"Chuck? The guy that set my arm? I never really understood his . . . is he some kind of doctor?"

"Nah. Just an old rancher. But I did hear some rumors about him. Heard he'd gone to veterinarian school. Someone else said he was a medic in the Army. I asked him about it after Trish was born, but he said something like 'rumors are rumors.' Whatever he meant by that.

We're getting enough daylight now. I'm going to look in on my children and Naomi, then maybe see if one of your sons can help me."

"About the, uh, cauterizing . . . how will you do it?"

"I think we should use a couple of the big Bowie knives, get them hot in the fire and have them at the ready."

My stomach churns. "I hope you don't have to do it."

"I'm praying we won't need to.".

Chapter 22

Fifteen Miles West of Lewistown, Montana
Wednesday, June 24, Late Afternoon

Victoria

Yesterday was a blur. God didn't hear Patti's prayers—or didn't *listen* to them. She and Brett were able to get the pole out of my side without much blood; the pain wasn't even too intense.

My leg was a different story.

She gave me a warning. The pain was instant. I let out a scream and heard her say, "It's out. Put pressure on it."

"It's bleeding through!" Brett said.

"You have to stop the bleeding!" Jennifer yelled.

There was more intense pain—*agony*—and an awful smell. I'm sure I screamed again before everything went black.

When I woke up, it was late morning. The first sound I heard was quiet sobbing. While I was out, they'd buried Nate. His sisters were sitting together, rocking back and forth, crying. Jameson helped me get some water and two more of Patti's pills. The pain was intense. I either fell asleep or passed out—not sure I could tell the difference.

Today isn't much better. I'm awake at the moment, in massive pain.

Jennifer's also a mess. The swelling in her knee has increased, and the pain in her back wraps around her entire body. She has the knee elevated, and her sons keep alternating cold cloths soaked in the creek with cloths warmed by the fire. She's trying to reduce the pain by not moving.

Patti has kept her on a variety of herbal teas. She only has a few ibuprofen left and is keeping them in case one of us can't handle the pain with herbs alone.

I'll admit, I'd kill for a narcotic, something to dull the pain enough and usher me into a deep, healing sleep. I wish we'd saved a few from the ones Jack gave us.

Patti made a potion out of wild lettuce. She mashed it up and combined it with a little of the vodka Kimba's been hoarding. She let it steep for several hours before giving me a teaspoon or so. I don't know if it was the vodka or the wild lettuce, but there was some relief.

Everything here is a mess. I know about tornadoes from living in St. Louis and believe that's what it was based on the path of destruction. While not common here, as Brett said, they do happen. Patti mentioned there was a tornado years ago in Lewistown that did several hundred thousand dollars' worth of damage.

"Victoria?" Atticus says. "You ready for more tea? You want to sit up a little?"

Atticus helps me into a somewhat reclined position. He puts the cup to my lips and gently tilts it. As soon as it hits my tongue, I know something isn't right with it.

"That good, huh?"

"Awful."

"Does it need more honey?"

"It needs to be dumped out. What is it?"

"Ginger and garlic."

"Why?"

Atticus lifts a shoulder. "It's from Patti's herb book." He wrinkles his nose in thought. "She says this should be anti-inflammatory and anti-sickness. Or something like that. The garlic kills bacteria."

"Do I need bacteria killed?" As soon as the words are out of my mouth, I remember the concern of infection. Those tent poles could've introduced all sorts of nasties. Patti slathered honey on my side before bandaging it; I don't know about the leg since I passed out. "Never mind. Give me another swig of the stuff."

After giving me another drink, his voice drops to a whisper. "Patti thinks my mom may have broken a couple ribs."

I close my eyes and give a slight shake of my head. "What can we do for her?"

"Not much, just hope it heals without hurting any of her internal organs. Mom says she doesn't agree and thinks she just twisted her back." His eyes meet mine. "She says Patti doesn't know what she's talking about."

I lift my eyebrows. "She may be right. The girl admits she was only a CNA. How many broken ribs has she seen?"

"A few when she worked in a nursing home. I guess it happens with the elderly? And she and her husband were both CERT trained and part of . . . some organization I can't remember that helps during emergencies."

"I don't know what CERT is."

"Community Emergency Response . . . something. It's a disaster preparedness training team. Oh, Team. Community Emergency Response Team."

"Ah, I do know about it. I think we had it in Prospect. The search and rescue group had training like that. We had people get lost in the mountains all the time."

He gives a solemn nod. "Probably about the same kind of stuff. She may know what cracked rib symptoms are. But Mom won't let her examine her to make sure."

"What kind of exam?"

"Check for bruising, touch the spots to see if the pain increases."

"Why don't you examine her?"

He makes a scoffing sound. "She won't let me either. She can't bear the idea of Patti being right."

I have another drink of tea, which is starting to not taste as awful. Maybe it killed my taste buds? "What is it with your mom and Patti?"

He glances to where Jennifer is lying on the ground, apparently asleep. "You know how her dad left their family for a lady from the Kootenai tribe?"

"Yes, but that still seems— "

"Yeah. What Mom didn't say was the woman killed my grandpa and then herself."

My eyes go wide. I shake my head. "Didn't your mom say they had children?"

"The kids were at a neighbor's house. Seems my grandpa had quite the roving eye. She, her name was Jane, thought he was having an affair. Caught him with the woman and . . . " He lifts a hand. "She shot him."

"What about the woman he was with?"

"She wasn't harmed. Jane shot him and then turned the gun on herself."

I feel my brow furrow as I try to sort this out. What an awful tale. "Your mom doesn't like Patti because a woman named Jane killed her dad?"

"Weird, huh?"

"What about your mom's *treat others the way you want to be treated* thing?"

"I guess it doesn't apply to Kootenai who look like Jane. Not in Mom's eyes anyway."

"And you?"

He looks at the cup. "I'm praying Mom can sort this out. This is a . . . a thorn in her flesh."

I finish the tea in silence. Before he leaves, Atticus says, "We're going to need to move you and Mom into Patti's tent. We'll see some rain before the day is done."

I'm sure my face registers terror at the thought of another storm.

He purses his lips. "I think it'll just be rain. Nothing . . . bad."

"What about everyone else?"

"We've already put up the tarps and set up the undamaged tents." He motions to the line of fabric. The vinyl sign announces the grand opening of an Irish Pub and is showing off a bowl of stew.

"Will the tarps be enough?'

"They'll have to be. Brett and Jameson's tent is standing too. The poles were busted, but we're using limbs. My tent is okay, other than another hole we taped up. The rest . . . " He shakes his head. "Oh, and Jameson found your glasses."

"Broken?"

"They're fine, just like they were before."

I can't help but smile. Not being able to see is a scary sensation. Even though the taped-together pair sit weird and make the progressions slightly off, they're better than being without any corrective lenses. I shudder to think what it'll be like in the future as my vision changes and the mended pair is no longer enough. Or when the tape job no longer holds.

When it's time to move to the tent, I break out in a sweat just thinking about how much it's going to hurt.

Brett suggests they carry me, but Patti wants me to walk. "Even a little movement will help. I'm concerned you and Jennifer could end up with new troubles from being in the same position too long."

"You mean like bedsores?" I ask, remembering Robyn Sorensen. She was traveling with us originally and fell in a creek and hit her head. Either being underwater or the knock on the head caused serious issues. Bedsores were a big concern while we were caring for her.

Patti bobs her head. "That or a UTI. Even pneumonia."

"Pneumonia," Jennifer scoffs from her bed by the fire. "That doesn't even make any sense."

Patti lifts a hand. "Immobility can cause a whole host of problems, and with your back hurting the way it is, we need to make sure you're taking deep breaths and moving the air around."

"Especially if you have a broken rib," Atticus says.

Jennifer makes a face and gives him a less than kind look.

"True." Patti nods.

"My knee hurts too much to walk," Jennifer whines.

"You can lean on me, Mom," Atticus offers. "Let's take a short walk around camp while Axel moves your bedding into the tent."

Jennifer lets out a noisy breath. "Fine."

"You too, Mom." Brett rests a hand on my arm. "We'll hobble behind them, and Jameson will move your things."

Getting up is painful—not as bad as I expected, but bad enough. Once I'm up, the world tilts. Brett, who's taller than me and much stronger, holds me steady.

Atticus has his mom up and encourages her to take a deep breath. She winces and then coughs.

The entire thing strikes me as funny and causes me to snort out a laugh. "Look at us, Jennifer. We're like a couple of women in a nursing home."

She gives me a weak smile. "There's some truth to that."

Once our beds are made, our sons help us inside. Even though Patti's tent is much larger than what I've been sleeping in for the past several months, it's still a tent and requires me to stoop through the doorway. Pain shoots through my side.

The tent is tight with Patti and her young children in with us. There was quite the brouhaha from Jennifer when she was told she'd be staying with Patti. Kimba snapped at her and said she was being ridiculous. Jennifer quickly dropped her gaze and gave a reluctant nod.

Having buried her son only yesterday, Kimba's doing as well as can be expected. I've noticed she's trying to take his death in a similar manner to how Jennifer took Asher's. She's said she'll see him again in Heaven and wonders if he's rejoicing with Jesus.

Jennifer said she wishes she could do more to help Kimba and her family while they grieve. I also believe Nate's death is bringing back all the emotions of losing Asher less than a month ago.

And while she hides it well, Patti is also mourning the recent loss of her husband.

We're a mess.

As a group, we've hit rock bottom. Settling into my stinky sleeping bag and blankets, I wonder how we can get past this. Maybe Jennifer and I need to heal enough so we can return to Lewistown. We could move in with Leanne and her family for now, for the winter maybe, then start again next spring.

As if reading my mind, Patti kneels beside me. "This too shall pass."

"What does that even mean? Really? Do you think we'll suddenly get over all this . . . this loss?"

"We fix our eyes not on what is seen," Jennifer says in a hollow, distant voice, "but on what is unseen, since what is seen is temporary, but what is unseen is eternal."

Patti nods. "It's not easy to accept the message Paul gives us in Second Corinthians."

I glance to Jennifer.

For the first time I can recall since she's been around Patti, her face is relaxed. "None of us like to be reminded it's our weakness, our humanity, that most shows God's power. His love."

The two women share a small smile. Then, as if suddenly realizing who she's speaking with, Jennifer abruptly turns her head.

Patti's face falls before she turns back to me. "Your friends will get through this, and you'll get through it, with God's help."

Chapter 23

Fergus Peak Lodge
Thursday, June 25, After Lunch

Sadie

"It's finally starting to feel like summer." Mom wipes the back of her hand against her forehead. "All this rain we've had, I know the gardens and crops need it, but I was beginning to feel like we'd float away."

Sebastian pokes the needle into the buttonhole. "I'm glad we finished the rabbit shed."

"Mostly finished," I say. "We still need to bring in more ground cover."

"Yeah, but Daniela said we should wait until the forest dries out a bit. What'd she call it?"

"Duff," Aunt Karla says. "We'll rake the forest floor to get bedding for the chicken and rabbit house."

"Then we'll move the chickens in, and they'll all be friends."

"Only some of the chickens, remember?" Aunt Karla smiles. "We're going to leave the young roosters in the pen they're already using and divide the rest of the flock in half. It's a smart thing to do."

Sebastian gives her a look of understanding. "If a predator attacks, we'll have backup chickens."

Mom chuckles. "I guess that's one way to put it. Kind of like not putting all our eggs in one basket."

I roll my eyes, but my brother starts laughing. Losing control of his needle, he catches his finger. "Ouch!" He puts the finger in his mouth.

Aunt Karla peers at him over her reading glasses. "Got to pay attention when you're working with sharp objects. Now go wash your hands, make sure the bleeding has stopped before returning to your project."

He plops the shirt he's working on to the side. "How much more mending do we have to do?"

Aunt Karla motions to the box by her feet. "All this that Jack brought."

When Mom and everyone went to town on Saturday, Jack found someone trading old, worn-out clothes. With the size of our community, he figured we could probably find enough usable items. Somehow, repairing the stuff fell on Aunt Karla, who enlisted help from me, my mom, and my brother.

Sebastian and I only do the simple stuff, like buttons, seam repairs, and patches. Mom and Aunt Karla can do more. Although Mom's sewing with us, she isn't working on the community clothing. Not at the moment anyway. She's taking in her wedding dress.

In the mornings, while Sebastian's in school, Mom and I have been working on the rabbit house with Ms. Reynolds, who told Mom yesterday she may as well call her Daniela since it seems we're staying. The woman even gave Mom something resembling a smile.

When we first met Daniela, I thought she was close to my Aunt Karla's age, but I've discovered she's almost a decade younger. She told me she recently turned fifty-five and has never been married. "Men are a bother I never needed. I've had a plenty fine life on my own."

While we worked on the rabbit house, Donnie spent time getting the little cabin up the creek put together. The four of us will move there after the wedding—a few days after anyway.

Aunt Karla wants my brother and I to stay with her so Mom and Donnie can have the place to themselves for a couple days. Donnie said it was a good idea so he can get it ready for us. I smiled and pretended like that was exactly what was meant.

Anyway, they'll stay at the unfinished cabin alone for a few days. Even though we still call it unfinished, it's getting closer to completed. They found some needed materials last weekend in town.

Several houses in Lewistown have been torn down, and the insulation and pieces of sheetrock were offered to anyone who could use them, even some lumber, though most is being used as firewood.

Donnie also found a guy with a woodstove. He'll go back to town the week after the wedding to get it since Mosher's wagon was full of the other supplies and trades.

I'll admit, I was less than happy when Mom said we'd live in the tiny cabin. I want to live in the lodge and have one of the nice, finished rooms. Mom insists us taking an unoccupied space will be the least disruptive.

I know she's right. And even though the cabin isn't terribly large, it'll beat living out of a tent.

Before the attacks and EMP, the cabin was only at the shell stage, fully enclosed with windows and doors but nothing more. No walls, no insulation, no fixtures.

The small bedroom, part of the design Aunt Karla had in mind, is just large enough for a queen-size bed and a small table on each side. The area planned as a kitchenette now has a loft, which will be my bedroom. It's large enough for a full-sized mattress and a row of shelves. Underneath is a twin bed for Sebastian and a closet for us to share.

The bathroom, like everything else, wasn't even close to completion. Donnie built a compost toilet and added a shelf for a water pitcher and plastic dishpan. No shower or tub.

For bathing, we'll go to the lodge, where Aunt Karla has a bathtub with a solar shower contraption. Daily showers are a thing of the past anyway. It's more likely we'll use the dishpan and a washcloth for sponge baths, just like we've done for the last year.

"You working with us on the rabbit house tonight or with Donnie?" I ask my mom.

"Wherever I'm most needed." She answers with a shy smile.

"I'll admit," Aunt Karla says, leaning forward in her recliner, "I'm jealous over the work you all get to do. As soon as this ankle stops aching, I'm going to get my hands dirty again . . . working in the garden, building things. Not just sitting around sewing and doing other handwork."

"It all needs done, Auntie," Mom says. "And we definitely want your ankle healed enough so you don't injure it again."

Aunt Karla tilts her head. "I suppose."

A loud knock on the patio door causes me to jump. Sebastian, on his way back from washing his hands at the sink, cranes his neck to look out. "It's the guy Donnie punched in the nose."

Mom furrows her brow. "Mr. Loomer?"

"Yeah, I guess."

Setting her dress aside, Mom stands. "Please try and remember your manners, Sebastian."

"But he was— "

Mom lifts a hand before turning slightly toward Aunt Karla. "Should I invite him in?"

She closes her eyes and lets out a long breath through her nose before waving her hand. "Go ahead."

Mom's cordial when she opens the door, just like Aunt Karla is with her greeting.

As soon as the pleasantries are out of the way, Aunt Karla asks, "What can I do for you, Randy?"

With his ballcap in his hand, he twists the fabric. "Thought we might have a talk." He looks at Mom. "Privately."

Mom's eyes travel to Aunt Karla.

With a smile I'm positive is phony, she leans forward in her chair. "Let's sit on the patio. I could do with a little sunshine."

I jump to my feet to help my aunt, who promptly waves me off.

"I can walk the twelve feet necessary."

Randy goes out first, not even waiting to make sure my aunt makes it.

When she exits, she leaves the door slightly ajar.

Sebastian sinks back into the couch and picks up his sewing.

Mom's eyes meet mine, her eyebrows nearly all the way up to her hairline. Without verbalizing it, we both move to the patio door and stand behind the curtains.

With Mom on one side of the door and me on the other, she moves her finger to her lips while motioning at my brother. His mouth is in an *O*, then he gives a nod and scurries next to me.

Aunt Karla's in the lounger with her injured leg up. Her other leg is off to the side, her foot solid on the ground. "Please." She motions to the other chairs.

Randy perches on the edge of a regular chair before clearing his throat. He plops his hat on his head and then takes it off again, twisting it between his hands before again clearing his throat. Then he launches into a long, drawn-out apology.

Aunt Karla listens politely, nodding occasionally, as she allows him to finish. When it's clear he's wrapping it up, I realize his apology wasn't much—the kind of apology I might give to my mom, not because I was sorry I did something but because I was sorry she caught me. An apology that was expected rather than heartfelt.

Really, he never said he was sorry for anything. Instead, he was shifting things around to make it seem like he was a victim. He was wrongly accused, and things just got out of hand.

With a tight jaw, Mom turns to me and shakes her head.

Aunt Karla lifts a hand. With the perfectly fake smile still on her face, she says, "That's fine, Randy. Just so we're clear, you understand the women and children here are under my care? Samantha is special to me. I won't have you hurting her."

He narrows his eyes. "With respect, Karla, Samantha's an adult. I'm pretty sure she can do what she wants."

Her voice is controlled, almost gentle. "To a point, yes. But the rules we've established will be followed. You and Samantha are free to . . . visit. But not in the rooms."

"Of course. But you can't stop her from coming to my place or us meeting elsewhere."

"Randy, dear, I wouldn't stop her. Like you said, she's an adult—a *young* adult. What is she, a dozen years your junior?"

"Something like that," he mutters. In a stronger voice, he says, "Age doesn't matter much anymore, not that it did before. Plenty of men marry younger women. Shoot, even women marry younger men. Even you could— "

"Thank you, Randy. And I appreciate your . . . *apology*. I'm sure my niece will be happy to know you don't plan to make any future inappropriate remarks directed toward her."

A man's voice says, "You better believe he won't." Donnie comes around the corner, positioning himself next to Aunt Karla's lounger.

Randy smirks at Donnie. "You can have her, bud. She's a little too old for me anyway."

Donnie takes a step forward, fire shooting from his eyes.

Aunt Karla raises a hand and taps Donnie on the wrist. "Funny thing, Randy. My niece is right around your age, you know."

He makes a noise of disbelief before seeming to catch himself. "Maybe so. Donnie's a lucky man. She's a fine-looking woman. A little skinny, but that's to be expected after all the walking."

Donnie gives him a hard look. "You should stop talking now."

"Yeah, okay." Randy plops his hat on his head. "Thanks for your time, Karla. I'm going to visit with Samantha while I'm here. You know where she is?"

Aunt Karla's voice is tight. "Probably at the firepit near the creek. She had laundry to do."

He tips his hat at her before slinking away.

"What a pompous— "

Aunt Karla raises a hand to silence Donnie. "You can come out now, Leanne. You too, Sadie."

Mom and I bust out laughing before pushing the door open.

Sebastian bounces out first. "It wasn't my idea."

"I'm sure. Yet here you are." She motions to the foot of her lounge chair.

Once he's seated, Mom takes the other lounge chair and I sit where Randy Loomer was.

Donnie's still standing, stiff and unyielding. "I heard his so-called apology."

"I know you did." Aunt Karla smiles. "I saw you peeking around the corner. How'd you know he was here?"

"I didn't. I came to see if Leanne was available, wanted her opinion on something. I'm glad I showed up. Randy Loomer is trouble."

Chapter 24

Fifteen Miles West of Lewistown, Montana
Monday, June 20, Sunrise

Victoria

It's been three weeks since Nate died. Jennifer and I are finally able to begin our walk again. The decision to keep going wasn't easy. Until yesterday, I was still leaning toward returning to Lewistown. As bad as things have been so far, I fear they may get worse.

I've been having terrible dreams about disasters and death. In the dreams, I'm running away, calling for Jameson and Brett to run faster. Something's chasing us, but what, I'm never sure. Sometimes it growls like a wild animal, other times it rumbles like a freight train, others I swear a man is laughing.

Taunting us.

The man's voice sounds very much like my dead husband's. Could these awful dreams be a premonition of things to come?

I used to think Atticus and his weather predictions were premonitions, but he insists he just looks at the sky and the way the air feels. There's nothing supernatural about it.

And Sebastian used to say things like, "I know we'll get to Aunt Karla's place because God told me." When we did get to Lewistown, he acted all weird about staying at his aunt's lodge. But then he seemed fine with it. Whatever was bothering him must have been eased by seeing the actual home they'd live in or meeting his great-aunt.

Did God talk to Sebastian? Seems rather far-fetched. I mean, really, who wouldn't want to *think* God was speaking directly to them. It could certainly make a young boy feel special to believe he had a direct line to the Almighty.

"Ready to go?" Brett hands me my cane.

"As ready as I'll ever be." Crafted by my sons during the first thunderstorm after Nate's death, the smoothness of the cane's handle is almost like a loving caress.

While the storm wasn't violent like the one before, it was long lasting and gave us two full days of drizzle before sunny skies returned. Trapped in the tent, I started to spiral. The nylon walls felt like they were closing in.

That's when the nightmares started.

The first was so bad I woke up screaming, waking the babies and the entire camp. Rey was on watch at the time and was there in an instant. He thought we were under attack.

After the rain stopped and the ground dried out, we all moved outside to sleep, allowing Patti's dank tent to air out a few days. In the open air, the nightmares continued.

The weather hasn't been our friend. More rain a few days later caused the creek to swell and forced us to move farther away. The last few days have been clear and dry.

The inflammation in Jennifer's knee has finally subsided. Like me, she's sporting a new cane made by her sons.

With a lump in my stomach the size of Montana, we're continuing west toward the Dosen ranch and our new life.

"Want to race?" Jennifer rests a hand on my shoulder as she leans heavily on her cane.

"I'm more turtle than hare. I'll happily let you win." As I talk, my pants slip lower on my hips. With a sigh, I ask Jennifer to hold my cane while I put myself together. I cinch my belt to the last notch. Camping in one spot for so long has taken a toll on our food supply.

During our time here, we've seen very little wildlife. Jameson has taken over plinking birds with the slingshot, but he doesn't have Nate's prowess.

From our camp, hidden from the road, we've seen others walking the highway. I don't know if the increased traffic was part of the issue, but we're getting desperate for meat. With the help of Patti's picture book, we were able to forage a few things: wild mustard, onions, chives, curly dock, and a few others.

The wild weeds, our dried meat, and the things from Patti's cache have barely sustained us. Since we weren't walking, we all agreed it made sense to ration.

My eyes travel to Kimba. She spends her days working out and practicing her fighting moves, expending as much energy as if we were walking. Where I'm looking scrawny, she is sculpted. Most of the rest have been working out and staying in shape, too, but they don't look like Kimba. She's even started weightlifting by hefting around limbs and a boulder she found along the creek. The rationing affected her little, if any.

There was a discussion about sending Brett and Axel back to Lewistown for more supplies, but we already know what they have to offer and what we have to trade. It wouldn't be worth the effort.

Patti has a cache a few days walk from here. She offered to go ahead and get it, bring it back so we'd have it. If we were staying here a few more days, we'd seriously need to consider it.

I'm not the only one getting scrawny. Jennifer's injuries have really taken a toll. She admits to being considerably overweight before the terrorist attacks, but with her height being only a couple of inches below six feet, she carried her weight well.

When I met Jennifer last summer, I considered her big boned. Now those bones jut out and her skin hangs from her frame. Her swollen knee and likely cracked ribs—she did finally agree to let Patti take a look; she had bruising and tenderness to the touch—left her with little appetite regardless of our food rationing. It got to the point her sons were forcing her to eat.

Part of me wonders if it was really a lack of appetite, or if Jennifer was on the verge of giving up. Since the death of Asher, she seems less and less like the Jennifer I knew. Patti joining us showed me a different side of her, one I didn't like much. Her injuries took even more of her away, replacing her with someone I barely recognize.

Surprisingly, it was Patti's baby, Trish, and to a lesser degree little LJ, who brought Jennifer around. Jennifer was reclining against a log the boys had carved to resemble a backrest, when the little girl wiggled her way toward her. She tried to shoo the baby away but soon gave in to the insistent little thing, eventually cuddling her and talking to her. When Trish fell asleep, Jennifer also leaned back and closed her eyes.

The next day, the baby did the same thing, with her older brother also trying to get close to Jennifer. With the children taking so readily to Jennifer, things began to change. The harsh looks and muttered comments directed at Patti lessened. I wouldn't say they're friends, not yet, but they are almost friendly. Once in a while, I'll still catch a narrowing of the eyes, but Jennifer seems to have realized her father's death had nothing to do with Patti.

Our extended stay where Nate lost his life has done little to help ease the Hoffmann family's pain. They're all still in deep mourning and often sit by Nate's grave.

I overheard Kimba tell her husband she'd be happy to stay here, to not leave their son. But she'll do what they agreed to; she'll get the Dosen family home. Maybe someday, if things get back to normal, they can return here and set up a proper headstone for their child.

We've only gone a couple of miles when we see buildings in the distance. In this flat area of Montana, the landscape stretches forever. Our goal today is modest: the outskirts of the small town of Moore, Montana. The day after the storm swept through, Atticus suggested he walk into the town and see if we could find a doctor to help me and his mom. Estimating we were less than seven miles away, we considered the idea.

It was Jennifer who said it'd be a waste of time. She's driven this highway enough, going from Great Falls to Billings, to know the size of the town. It only had a couple hundred people, with many Hutterites and Amish in the area.

She thought we were actually nearby the Hutterite colony featured on the National Geographic channel a few years ago. They may be able to provide us with some medical help, but being a closed community, it was a risk. Returning to Lewistown, less than fifteen miles to the east, might've been the best choice.

Thankfully, it never came to that. With the herbs Ms. Reynolds gave us and Patti's knowledge, we're as well as can be expected. I still hesitate in my decision to continue west with the group. But seeing those buildings gives me a lift.

Maybe we'll be okay. Maybe we're on the right path.

I remember being in church once, sitting in the pew and wishing the long-winded preacher would wrap up so we could get on with Jon's obligatory hand pumping and schmoozing before going out to breakfast. The preacher stopped his spewing, took a deep breath, and said something that still sticks with me. "Keep doing the things you know God has directed you to do until He tells you to do something else."

Since I hadn't been paying attention up to that point, the sentence was out of context, but it made sense. Not that I'd ever really asked

God what I was supposed to be doing, not then anyway. But now it's different.

I didn't pray and ask God if we should leave the ski lodge and go to Montana with Jennifer and her family.

No, I jumped at that chance—to start a new life where we could live without the shadow of what Jon did. Although things were tense between Jennifer and I since Jon was responsible for her sister's death, our boys got along great.

Well . . . mostly.

Jameson was surly with everyone after his dad's death, before even. But Brett and the three brothers were easy friends. There was no need to pray and ask for guidance; I knew it was right. Besides, even though I regularly attended church, my relationship with God didn't extend beyond those walls.

I didn't pray—*we* didn't pray. We didn't read the Bible or acknowledge God in any way outside of the church building on Sundays, unless Jon was giving a campaign speech or otherwise trying to impress people. If they knew how he really was, they wouldn't want him as county commissioner.

Prayer and Bible reading wasn't part of my life then, but it has been since we began this journey. Before we left the ski lodge, we had several planning meetings. Each meeting started and ended with prayer. I thought it was a little over the top.

On the road, Kimba, Jennifer, Rey, or PJ Cameron—who traveled with us as far as Billings—would read a Bible passage while we packed up or ate breakfast and then someone would pray. There was also the whole praying before meals thing and impromptu petitions when we'd find ourselves in some sort of peril. Pray, pray, pray. I'd never heard so many prayers in my life!

But since Nate's death, we've had little praying and little Bible reading. Atticus read a few passages, but it was lackluster to say the least. I'm told Rey read from the Bible at the funeral, but I was out of it and not there, and I don't know the details. What I do know is nothing is like it was before.

Even Jennifer, who's always happy to spout off a verse, is staying quiet. The spiritual leaders of our group are silent.

Patti does her own thing. She tells her children stories from the Bible, prays with them before bed, and reminds them to thank God for their food, as meager as it is.

"I think, with being this close to town, it's time to make a decision." Rey's voice jars me from my thoughts. "It's midafternoon. We've gone a good distance for our first day in so long, especially considering . . . " He raises a hand while lifting a shoulder. "Should we approach the town or find a campsite?"

Kimba glances around. "Doesn't matter. Another mile or two, who cares?"

"A house would be nice." Jennifer looks around the bare land.

"Let's just stop," Kimba grumbles. "This is fine. There isn't a good hiding place since it's so flat, but there's water." She motions to the creek alongside the road.

"We'll put some distance between us and the road." Rey gives his wife a tight smile. "It'll do."

We set up our two remaining tents—Patti's and the Dosen boys'—a couple hundred yards from the highway. My son's tent needs branches or limbs to make it work. We chose not to bring the long branches we were using, and this pancake-flat land is devoid of trees.

We stretch the tarps out on the ground to sleep under the stars. Jameson and Axel take off with Nate's slingshot and to set up a box trap in hopes of providing dinner.

With the heat of late June, we don't bother with a fire. Good thing. In this area of the high plains, wood is scarce. Should the boys miraculously return with some sort of game, we have a few pieces of wood tucked in the wagon from the last camp, and we'll twist prairie grass. Someone suggested we look for cow patties to burn since pioneer's used to burn buffalo chips, but we haven't seen any cows since we left Lewistown.

I close my eyes. Again, the feeling of trepidation washes over me. Mosher's compound had cattle, goats, chickens, and more. They'd even been smart and trapped wild rabbits, grouse, turkeys, and who knows what else to raise in captivity.

My eyes are closed and I'm almost asleep when there's a hoop and a holler. I jolt up, feeling a slight catch in my side as I do. At least the arm didn't hurt from the movement. "What's happening?"

With a rare smile, Rey points in the distance. "Looks like they got something."

Squinting, I can plainly see each boy holding up a bird by a leg. "Two somethings!"

"Let's get the fire going," Rey says. "We're eating good tonight."

I glance at Kimba in time to see her wiping at her eyes. With a slight, asymmetrical smile, she gives a nod.

"We got 'em." Jameson's smile is as wide and beautiful as the Montana sky. "Found a bunch of rocks to set up the trap. It didn't take long. One went in, and I nailed the second with the slingshot. We left the trap in case another happens to stroll by."

Our dinner of roasted pheasant is amazing. The bones are, of course, put on the fire to begin the breakfast broth. After they've boiled about an hour, Jennifer and Patti work with the hot bones to remove the last bits of meat.

"We'll combine it with some of the rice and use the broth to make something like a congee," Patti says. "I'll put the rice on to soak now so it won't take long to cook in the morning."

"How are we doing on rice?" I ask, dreading the answer.

"Close to three cups left. I'll use half for breakfast. We have about the same amount of barley and corn, and a little more wheat."

"Where's the next cache?" Rey asks.

"The other side of Eddie's Corner, not far past the Amish store."

"And you're sure you can find it?"

She dips her chin. "I can find it. It's fairly new. We set it up when I was pregnant with Trish. There's a second one about five miles farther that we had in place before LJ was born."

"Why are they so close together?" I ask.

"Ledger." She shrugs. "In case one is empty, we'd have the other without needing to go too much farther. There isn't a lot in them. We set them up for either two or four people."

"It'll help. Anything will help."

Chapter 25

A Mile or so East of Moore, Montana
Monday, July 20, After Dark

Victoria

"Mom!" Brett's voice is a harsh whisper. "Mom, wake up."

"Mmm." I will myself to respond. Did I wake him again? I remember screaming and gunfire. I must have had another bad dream. "Sorry, another nightmare."

"No. It's not. Wake up!"

I open my eyes. The shooting continues. "What— "

He puts a finger to his lips. "It's nearby. We're moving to the rock outcropping by where they found the pheasants."

It's a new moon, not even visible, giving us only the starlight to see by. Even in the darkness, I make out movement. Patti's tent is being taken down.

"The other tent's already collapsed." Brett has my good elbow and is urging me to my feet. "Jameson's taking a load of blankets. We'll get you safe and then I'll make sure you have your bedding."

My mouth is a tight line as I nod my agreement.

Stumbling through the dark, using my cane for balance, is harrowing. If it weren't for Brett, I would've gone splat more than once.

After a couple minutes, Jameson meets us. "I'll go for her sleeping bag."

"Help Mom the rest of the way. Then stay hidden," Brett says. "I'll get our stuff and help the others. Are the babies already over there?"

"Nicole and Naomi are with them. Patti went back to camp."

"Are we packing everything?" I ask.

"We'll see," Brett answers. "The main goal is to get the tents on the ground. It's so dark, that should be enough for them to not be seen."

"Where're the shooters?"

"Not sure. Rey thinks maybe in the town, or maybe between here and there. You know how sound can travel funny."

Jameson helps me the rest of the way to the rocks, which, even in the dark, are obviously not much concealment. "This is it?"

"Better than nothing. Farmland, ya know. There's another grouping a few yards away where Jennifer is. It's smaller than this bunch."

"Great," I mutter.

The Hoffmann girls are up against a large boulder with Patti's babies in their arms. Jameson helps me sit next to them.

"Where will you be?" I ask.

"Here, with you."

I huddle next to Naomi as Jameson puts a scratchy blanket across my lap. Within a few minutes, more of our group arrives.

Kimba leans toward Nicole. "If things go bad, I'll need you to take care of your sister and Patti's children. Axel says there's a stream or something farther south, they saw a line of trees earlier. Jameson, do you know where it is? You'll help her."

"I know where it is. I'll need to help my mom."

"No," I say too abruptly. "You'll go with the others. Kimba will help me."

"But— "

"Jameson, no arguing. Nicole will need your help."

"That's the meeting spot," Kimba adds. "Everyone knows to go there."

"Fine," he huffs. "But you'd better make sure my mom is okay. She can't . . . she's been through too much."

I rest my hand on his arm. "We all have, honey. We all have."

While we huddle close behind the rocks, Kimba and Rey keep watch. Atticus, Axel, and Jennifer are at the smaller group of boulders about fifty feet away. The shooting has mostly stopped by the time we're all hunkered down. There's still the occasional scream, sounding haunted as it carries across the darkness. A scream is usually followed by a single gunshot.

After a while, Kimba urges her children to sleep. "You too, Victoria. We'll keep watch."

Chapter 26

A Mile or so East or Moore, Montana
Tuesday, July 21, Daylight

Victoria

I adjust my position only to get poked in the back. Opening an eye, I take in the area. The middle of the night move to hide behind the rocks comes back in a rush. What'll we do with daylight here? Continue on our course and hope we don't run into the shooters?

"Hey, Mom," Jameson says, meeting my eyes. "You sleep good?"

"I slept *well.*" I raise my eyebrows at him.

He bobs his head.

"Did you sleep *well?*" I ask, trying to make my point. Then I wonder why I even care. We're hiding behind rocks, in fear for our lives, and I'm nitpicking his grammar? I offer him a smile and reach for his hand.

"I helped with watch, slept a little."

I glance around. The Hoffmann girls and Patti's children are still asleep. Their parents are nowhere in sight. Neither is Brett or the Dosens. "Where is everyone?"

"Rey and Atticus left a while ago. They wanted to find the . . . uh, the problem and be in position before daylight."

I take in a deep breath. "Is that smart? Safe?"

He cocks his head. "Otherwise, we'd be stuck here waiting and wondering."

He's right. They were right to go. "Brett? Kimba?"

"Gathering water. We may be here awhile. I'm not sure when Rey and Atticus will be back."

Or if they'll come back.

It's midafternoon when Atticus and Rey return to our hideout. Kimba was a wreck all day, nervous and wringing her hands. Since Nate's death, the calm and confident woman has faltered. She's often spacey and jumpy, and even making decisions is hard for her. She snaps at us and is often grumbling or complaining—nothing like the Kimba who left the ski lodge.

My mind knows it's part of the grieving process, but it's difficult to see her this way. And it scares me. We've come to rely on her quick thinking and even manner to keep us safe.

Rey's obviously grieving, too, but he still seems sharp. With him, he's more edgy. Before, he was easygoing and somewhat upbeat. Now he has less patience—toward Kimba and also with others. He's even snapped at me a few times.

But the worst is watching how their interactions with each other have changed. A wedge has come between them. Gone are the loving glances and obvious teamwork. Instead, there are rough words and crossed arms. Their marriage is deteriorating before our eyes.

"What was it?" Jennifer asks as soon as they reach us. We're all clustered together around the largest group of boulders, using them for shade on this hot day.

Rey shakes his head. "Raiders. They hit the town. It was like what happened to the people left in Bakerville—a massacre."

My hand goes to my mouth. Not everyone who lived in our little community of Bakerville chose to move to the ski lodge last fall. Those who stayed behind were attacked and most of their supplies taken. Only five children, who were in an unexpected place, survived.

"Survivors?" Kimba asks.

Atticus looks at his boots. "None. We waited until the pillagers left. It was . . . bad."

There's several minutes of silence.

"Did you bury them?" Jameson asks.

"Too many."

"We'll stay here tonight," Rey says. "Start up again tomorrow."

"You're sure it's safe?" Kimba asks.

"From the raiders? Probably. They got in their trucks and headed off."

"Which way?"

"West."

"The same way we're going."

"Eddie's Corner is a junction," Patti says. "They could go south there."

"Or not. We may run into them again."

Rey lifts his hands. "There's no way of knowing. We did see others walking on the highway an hour or so after the raiders left."

"That's right." Atticus bobs his head. "If they ran into the raiders, they survived it."

"It's possible they're only targeting large populations and not walkers." Rey reaches for his wife's hand.

She hesitates before intertwining her fingers with his. "I guess we don't have a choice. We need to get Jennifer and Victoria home."

She doesn't say *before anything else happens*, but it's certainly implied.

Chapter 27

A Mile or so East of Moore Montana
Friday, June 23, Midmorning

Victoria

The caches were exactly where Patti thought. We found the first one yesterday, just past a burned-out shell of a building, which Patti says used to be the Amish store. It held five-gallon buckets of rice and lentils sealed in mylar bags, vacuum-sealed coconut flakes, almonds still in the shell, oatmeal, and several small bags of spices, hard candies, water purifying tablets, a handgun, ammo, and more.

We all got a good laugh when Patti said we needed to turn on Treasure Road to find the cache. It truly was a treasure.

The second cache is buried less than five miles up the road and is what we're looking for now. Patti tried a few different spots last night, thinking it was there, only to end up empty handed.

"I'm sorry." She shakes her head. "I was sure I knew the landmarks. Plus, the stake Ledger pounded in, the top's tinged in blue. I don't know why I can't find it."

"Let's give it a little longer, see what you can come up with," Rey says.

Patti has my sons, the Dosen boys, and all the Hoffmanns helping her look while Jennifer and I sit and rest, playing with the babies.

After another fifteen minutes or so, Axel lets out a whoop. "Patti! C'mere. I think I found it."

This treasure has a dozen freeze-dried meals, a #10 can of freeze-dried chicken, and a vacuum-sealed bag of oatmeal. And food isn't the only thing in this stockpile. They stashed shoes, clothing, blankets, and backpacks, along with a 12-gauge shotgun with shells. It feels like Christmas and my birthday all wrapped in one. Patti sharing these things will help us get home.

"We stashed two more between here and Great Falls." She hugs her little girl close. "More backpacking meals and miscellaneous things. One has a handgun and ammo in it, too, plus more clothes and other goods."

"What about beyond there?" Atticus asks. "Do you have these all the way to St. Ignatius?"

She lifts a shoulder. "Here and there. We left a few things with friends. I'm not sure . . . " She shakes her head.

"Will you be able to get home?"

"Oh yes, we'll absolutely get home."

Jennifer, who's holding little LJ, cuddles him closer. "It's still over two hundred miles from Great Falls. It's already late July."

Patti gives her a nod. "I'm hopeful the Air Force has some sort of transportation figured out and we can catch a ride."

"They weren't taking civilians, not when we were in Billings anyway. I wouldn't count on hitching a ride with them. I just don't know how you'll make it on foot before the cold and snow hits."

Patti smiles. "If it gets too late, we'll stay at our friends' homes, the ones keeping our things. God knows my needs. I don't know what'll happen tomorrow, but He does."

Kimba lets out a loud sigh. "I wish God knew my needs. I just . . . how do I . . . " Her hands go to her face as she dissolves in tears. Her husband and daughters go to her, and the four of them cling to each other as they cry.

Chapter 28

Fergus Peak Lodge
Sunday, June 28, Midmorning

Sadie

"Do you think it's too loose, Sadie?" Mom pulls at the waistline of the dress.

"Not too loose. It looks good."

"There isn't enough of it to wear my— " she lifts both eyebrows " —my gift from Kimba."

The small pistol Kimba gave Mom has been a regular part of her daily clothing. Even with the weather warming up, she wears the tank top holster with a light fabric shirt or T-shirt over the top, rinsing it out every few days as needed and letting it dry overnight.

But she's right about this sundress having entirely the wrong cut for tucking a gun under her armpit.

"Guess I don't really need it for my wedding." She tucks the tank top holster and pistol in a drawer. "Besides, Donnie and your aunt will both be armed, along with any of the patrollers who show up."

"Aunt Karla?"

Mom blinks at me several times.

"I mean . . . " I stutter over my words. "Of course, you're talking about Aunt Karla, but I didn't know she . . . " I shake my head.

"You've never noticed she always has her purse hanging off her? She has more in there than just a lipstick." She gives me a wink. "You heard her tell us how she's able to take care of everyone here? She doesn't just pray they'll be okay. She ensures it. And the handgun isn't the only thing. There're guns locked away in several places."

"Does Daniela know?"

Mom chuffs. "I doubt it. You know how she is." Her bright red lips go in a tight line. "I look like a clown in all this." She motions to her face. "Donnie won't even recognize me."

I raise my eyebrows at her. She's not wrong. Even though she used to wear makeup every day before the world fell apart, it now looks odd.

She lets out a sigh. "At least the weather's near perfect. The rain and wind—I'm ready for some sunshine."

"Isn't it supposed to be good luck if it rains on your wedding day?"

"Good luck?" Mom wrinkles her nose.

I let out a soft sigh. "You know what I mean." *Ugh.* She can be so annoying sometimes with this whole God thing.

She reaches for my hand. "God has given us a beautiful day. He's led us here to start a new life. He's given me a love for Donnie—something I never thought I'd have again. And I believe all is happening according to His will and plan."

"I know, Mom. I know you believe it."

Her eyes rest on mine for a moment. "You look beautiful."

I dip my head in thanks.

"Sometimes it's hard to see God's hand in things, especially with all that's happened. My prayer for you, baby girl, is you, too, can see His wonders—can *believe* His wonders. Not just get hung up on the bad stuff."

My voice is small when I respond. "I'll try, Mom."

"Well, I guess that's about it." Mom's eyebrows knit together.

"Are you ready? You look . . . " I lift my hand. "Nervous?"

Her face relaxes as she lets out a laugh. "I shouldn't be. It's silly." The worried look returns. "I think . . . can you get me a fresh washcloth? I'm wiping all this gunk off my face. Don't know what I was thinking putting all this on."

She dabs her cheeks and then her eyelids, removing the color from both. She leaves the mascara and eyeliner in place before moving on to her lips and taking the red away. When she's finished, her lips are a muted red, stained from the pigment.

"You want some gloss?" I ask, pointing to a sparkly tube.

"I think just the balm, the stuff Daniela makes."

With Mom now satisfied with her face, saying she looks more like herself, she says she's just about ready to go outside for the church service.

I step out of Aunt Karla's bedroom in front of Mom.

"Are you ready to see her?"

Sebastian tilts his head and tries to look around me. I step to the side. "Ta-da!"

"Oh! Don't you look lovely!" Aunt Karla gushes. "Both of you."

Mom does look amazing. The dress is a creamy white with a random floral print in pinks, reds, blues, and more. On her feet are bright red peep-toe wedges, almost the same shade she originally had on her lips.

I'm wearing a flowy pale pink dress with white ballerina flats. My hair's piled at the nape of my neck in sort of a messy bun.

Aunt Karla, who's now using a cane instead of crutches, is also wearing a light pink dress. I glance at the messenger bag she's wearing.

Sebastian is also dressed to impress, wearing a button-up shirt and slacks with his everyday tennis shoes.

"Looks like the entire town is here." Sebastian points out the window. "Are you ready?"

Chuck, the man who set Victoria's arm, is leading the church service. Dressed in western jeans, boots, and a cowboy-cut vest, he looks the part of a country preacher.

The sermon reminds me of something from Easter Sunday. He talks about Jesus' ministry on earth and how He was arrested after fake allegations, then sentenced to death. Growing up in church, I'd heard it all before. Today it seems different.

It *feels* different.

I don't know if being outside, hearing birds sing in the background as I enjoy the beautiful landscape, makes it seem more real. But as Chuck speaks, I feel a tug at my heart. Especially when he talks about how Jesus personally took the punishment for his own sin.

Then Chuck points to people in the audience—the congregation—and says Jesus died for them. When his eyes rest on mine, he gives a very slight nod before saying, "For you, too, Sadie Monroe."

Tears slip from my eyes.

Mom's hand reaches for mine. She gives it a squeeze.

I can feel her staring at me. I keep my face forward. I know enough to understand I'm in an emotionally charged situation. As soon as this is over and the crowd disperses, I'll come back to my senses.

To logic.

God and Jesus are fine. I totally understand believing can help people through terrible things. I'm just not sure it's for me.

When the preaching wraps up, many people are teary eyed.

Jack Mosher moves to the front and shakes Chuck's hand. He then turns to the rest of us with a kind smile on his face. "I know we've all heard Chuck speak before, but I must say, today was something special."

There's a chorus of amens and other agreements throughout the group.

When it's quiet again, he continues with, "We've heard the rumors the townspeople have spread about us. How we're a cult, a bunch of fanatics. Well, I think if they listened to Chuck just now and saw how charismatic he is, the cult rumor might have some bearing." He releases a nervous laugh.

"But seriously, you'll all get a chance to hear him again shortly. In about half an hour— " He looks to Mom and Donnie, who are both nodding. "Good, yes. Half an hour at the gazebo, that's where the wedding ceremony will be. We'll meet back on the patio for lunch."

I glance around the audience and wonder how many will actually walk down for the ceremony. We've only been in this community a few short weeks. Will they join us for the vows or choose to stay here and wait for the meal?

I mean, I get not passing up food. I'm sure that's why the bulk of them made the walk to the lodge. Not for the preaching or the ceremony, but for the almost lavish meal and a chance to get together—for the party.

People are mingling and many offer Mom and Donnie their best wishes and a lifetime of happiness. Even Randy Loomer gives Donnie a cordial nod and mumbles congratulations. I'm sure he was prompted by Samantha, who's on his arm and is gushing over how great my mom looks and how exciting it is to have a wedding.

Like most of us, Samantha's wearing a dress with cowboy boots on her feet. Poking out the top of her boot is a knife. Over the last few days, after we had one of our self-defense classes on defending against a knife attack, I've noticed she's taken to wearing a knife on her belt, a fixed-blade similar to mine.

I subconsciously touch my own waist. Like my mom leaving her little pistol behind, I also left my knife. I should've thought of wearing boots like Samantha's. I'll definitely remember that the next time I dress up.

The day Jack and Randy showed up here, after we found Gray Nelson's body, Samantha seemed almost embarrassed to admit her association with the man. Today, she's holding her head high and acting like a proper girlfriend, hanging on his arm and his every word. I still don't get the attraction. It's not like Randy's some kind of catch.

To make things easier for Aunt Karla, Donnie found a wheelchair somewhere. When Mom whispers it's about time to head to the gazebo, he tells her he'll see her soon, he's going to push Aunt Karla. Mom watches as he walks away, the smile on her face of adoring admiration.

She turns to me and is about to say something when Jack appears by her side. "Hey, Leanne. You look . . . you look amazing."

Mom nods her thanks.

"I think . . . Donnie's a lucky man."

"Thank you. I'm feeling pretty blessed myself."

His eyes dart to me and then back to Mom. "Um, do you have a minute?"

"Now? I'm just . . . it's time." She motions in the direction of the gazebo.

"This won't take long."

Mom shakes her head and then turns to Sebastian and me. "Wait for me so we can walk together."

Jack walks a dozen feet away with Mom following. When he stops, she crosses her arms and gives him a questioning look. At first, she has a slight smile on her face, then her smile fades. She shakes her head and turns away.

Jack reaches out and grabs her by the arm.

She stares at his hand while he appears to plead with her. Finally, she shakes his hand loose and marches toward us.

"Let's go," she mutters as she keeps walking.

"What was that about?" I ask.

She stops and drops her head. "Of all the days—that Jack Mosher. He's just as infuriating now as he was when we were young."

"And?"

Shooting Jack a look, she puts her head near mine. "He said he's realized he never should've let me go. All those years ago, he . . . he made a mistake. He wants me back! Can you believe that? *On my wedding day.*"

I glance toward Jack. He's still in the same spot, staring at the ground, his feet shifting.

"Why'd you two break up in the first place?"

She lets out a sigh. "We were young. Too young. And things . . . happened. Things that changed how I felt about him."

"Did you love him?" Sebastian asks.

Mom smiles at my brother. "I thought so at the time. But now I know it wasn't real love. Not like I had with your dad. And not like I have with Donnie."

"Okay, then let's go. Donnie will be waiting for you."

"Good idea," Mom says, pulling my brother into a hug. "Ready, Sadie?"

"Are you?" I ask, taking another peek toward Jack.

"Definitely."

The wedding is beautiful. Joy and love shine on Mom's and Donnie's faces. My heart swells and tears again sting my eyes. I'm happy for my mom, happy she's found this man to share her life with, happy she's found peace and comfort in God. I may think differently than she does, but it's good to see her this way.

Mosher isn't at the ceremony, and when we go back to the patio for the meal, he isn't there either. If he likes my mom that much, talking to her before today might have been smart—but not minutes before her wedding.

The meal is great, with a fresh beef roast cooked in a pit along with fresh greens and other items from the community gardens. It's set up as a potluck, and people brought whatever they wished. There's lots of laughter and even music, compliments of a group of men with guitars and a harmonica. They aren't particularly good but aren't terrible either.

By late afternoon, the beautiful weather shifts and a breeze blows. Everyone except those of us living at the lodge head out to get their chores done before the wind gets much worse or rain begins. Many from our group disperse to take care of their responsibilities, but our small family has the day off. We sit on the patio and play a few games of cards before having leftovers for dinner.

After eating, Aunt Karla says, "The children will be fine. Go on."

She doesn't tell Mom that, after the ceremony, she sent me, Daniela, and several others to the tiny cabin with candles, fresh flowers, snacks for this evening, and breakfast for the morning. She wanted to make it as special as possible for them.

Mom hugs Sebastian and me, telling us to have a good night. I want to tell her how happy I am for her, but my eyes fill up and the words stick in my throat. She seems to understand as she pulls me into another embrace.

After they leave, Aunt Karla suggests another round of cards, this time in her apartment where Sebastian and I will stay a few more days, giving private time for the newlyweds.

Newlyweds! It's strange to think of my mom as married again. And to think of Donnie as my stepdad. He made it clear he doesn't expect me to call him *Dad* and that *Donnie* is just fine.

Sebastian, though, who doesn't remember our dad at all, seemed disappointed when Donnie said that. Picking up on it, Donnie added, "Unless you want to call me Dad, then that's okay too."

We stay up later than we should, playing everything from Rummy, to Go Fish, to Crazy Eights, laughing and having a fabulous time. When we finally call it a night, I can barely keep my eyes open. Expecting sleep to come easy, I stretch out on the sofa. Sebastian's in the recliner, already snoring.

I don't know if it's the noise he's making or the excitement of the day, but I find myself tossing and turning. After fluffing my pillow, I settle in again, counting backward from one hundred as I slowly breathe in and out.

I'm just about asleep when someone bangs on the door connected to the lodge. "Karla! Karla! Wake up! There's a fire!"

Chapter 29

Fergus Peak Lodge
Sunday, June 28, After Dark

Sadie

I bolt out of bed. "Sebastian! There's a fire!"

"Huh?" he responds, his voice heavy with sleep.

The banging returns. "Get up!" I run for the door and fling it open.

Samantha's face is colorless, her eyes frantic. "The . . . the honeymoon cabin . . . it's on fire!"

Aunt Karla, now out of bed and by my side, lets out a gasp. "What? How?"

With a shake of her head, the frightened woman says, "They're trying to put it out. We need more help."

"Leanne? Is she . . . " Aunt Karla's hand goes to her mouth.

My heart sinks to my toes. *Is my mom okay?* I turn to Aunt Karla. "I'll go. You . . . will you keep Sebastian safe?"

With her lips in a harsh line, Aunt Karla nods. "And we'll be praying."

"Grab a bucket or something. Maybe some towels." Samantha calls over her shoulder. "I'm getting more help."

I slide into my shoes, barely taking time to do the laces properly, then quickly grab a gallon-size bucket and a couple of towels.

"Put on a sweatshirt," Aunt Karla commands. "Protect your arms. Sebastian, get dressed in case the fire shifts and we have to leave in a hurry."

I grab a sweater, stuffing it on top of the towels in the bucket, then rush out the patio door. As I round the corner of the lodge, the flames are easily in view.

My breath catches in my chest.

The fire looks huge! The entire cabin must be—Mom!

I take off at a run, the bucket banging against my leg. There're several women rushing toward the flames. Many carry buckets, some have cooking pots, and others have blankets or towels.

"Has anyone gone for help?" I ask the wrangler Brooke.

"Cassie. She took her horse. We have to stop it. Keep it from spreading. This wind . . . it's swirling in all directions."

"What happened?"

"You mean how'd it start?"

I nod in the dark.

Even though she can't see my response, she answers, "Don't know. Candles, maybe?"

Candles. We set a lot of them in the cabin to try and make it romantic for Mom and Donnie. But they were all in holders or containers. They should've been safe.

The glow from the fire is huge. The cabin's a good distance from the lodge, but the wind is crazy. Anything could happen. I'm breathing hard when we reach the gazebo. The cabin's completely engulfed. My eyes scan the surrounding area, looking for my mom. For Donnie.

"She's here!" Daniela calls to me. "Sadie! Your mom is here."

I let out a cry of relief and start to run toward her.

Brooke grabs my arm. "Give me your bucket."

I keep the sweatshirt and hand the rest off to Brooke.

Mom is near the gazebo, laying on her side with Daniela squatting next to her.

"Mom?"

"She's breathing. It's . . . it's ragged, but she's doing it." Daniella's rubbing Mom's back.

I glance toward the burning cabin. "Donnie?"

She bites her lip as Mom lets out a hacking cough.

"There you go." Daniela's eyes briefly meet mine. She gives a slight shake of her head. "We found your mom on the ground, outside the window. They're . . . Donnie wasn't with her."

A whimper escapes my mom. She lifts her head to look at me, and I get my first look at her. Her face is black, covered in soot, obviously burned. Her lips are blistered.

I let out a gasp. "Should we . . . what do we do?"

"I sent someone after the stretcher, then we'll take her to the lodge."

"Should I help with the fire?" I ache to stay with my mom.

"All they can do now is keep it from spreading. I doubt you'll be much help."

"How is she?" Jack asks as he strides toward us.

My brows knit together. "You're here? Already?"

"I was out . . . walking. I ran into Cassie as she was on her way for help. More are on their way."

"There's the stretcher." Daniela motions with her chin to the makeshift stretcher—a bunch of boards put together.

"You two take one end," Jack says. "I'll take the other."

Daniela raises a hand. "You stay here and direct our people. They need you. We've got this. Is Chuck on his way? I'll need his help."

"I'm sure he is. I'll send him to you." Jack looks at Mom. "Leanne?"

She lifts a hand. The back is blistered and burned.

"Okay. I'll . . . I'll check on you soon."

"Donnie— " Mom croaks out his name. "Find . . . him." She starts coughing again.

Jack gives a slight nod, then turns toward the fire and begins barking out orders.

Daniela takes the end of the stretcher with Mom's head, while the other lady and I take the feet; it's heavy and awkward.

Mom cries out in pain many times. We stop often so Daniela can check her and so we can rest.

When we're close to the lodge, the other woman asks, "Where are we taking her?"

"The dining room. I want her on the longest table. As soon as we get there, Sadie, go grab your aunt. I'll need her help."

Inside the dining room, Daniela asks the woman to light the lanterns.

I tell Mom I'll be right back. When she doesn't respond, I look to Daniela.

"Passed out. Probably for the best."

"She's . . . her breathing's okay?"

"Go get your aunt."

I go through the kitchen and the hallway, then shove open the solid wood door. Aunt Karla and Sebastian both jump to their feet.

"Where's Mom?" my brother looks past me.

"Hurt." I turn to Aunt Karla. "Daniela says she needs you."

"What about me?" Sebastian hustles toward the door.

I shake my head.

"Come along, Sebastian," Aunt Karla says. "You can sit out of the way. Better than sitting alone."

"What about Donnie?" Sebastian tugs at my arm.

"I don't know where he is. They were still looking for him. The fire . . . it's bad."

In the well-lit dining room, Mom looks even worse than she did before. Sebastian lets out a cry. I motion for him to sit at a table in the corner.

"Bring him over for a moment," Daniela says. "Let your mom hear his voice. Yours too."

While Sebastian and I tell Mom she'll be okay, Daniela and Aunt Karla make a treatment plan. I'm half listening as Daniela says the burns are probably first and second degree—except the palm of her right hand; it looks like third degree. Of larger concern is smoke inhalation.

I tilt my head to get a look at Mom's hands, but they're covered with a thin blanket.

The front door opens with a creak, and Chuck slides in. He takes a quick look at Mom and shakes his head.

Without opening her eyes, Mom has another coughing attack.

"Turn her on her side," Chuck says. "Step back, kids."

There's a flurry of activity while he and Daniela help Mom as she coughs. Something black and slimy comes out.

Sebastian looks at me with wide eyes.

"Um, if you don't need my help, I should take my brother back to the apartment, don't you think?"

Daniela looks to Chuck. "I thought I might need her help. But with you here— "

"Yeah. Leanne, we're going to have your children wait in the apartment. We'll get you feeling better and then they can visit."

Mom mutters a response I can't make out.

"Go ahead, dear," Aunt Karla says, her eyelashes heavy with tears. "We'll take care of her."

Sebastian and I sit together on the couch. He cries while I hold him, rocking him.

"Pray with me, Sadie."

I nod my agreement.

"You start," he whispers.

I clear my throat. Praying is not my strong suit. Does God even hear my prayers? I mean, if I'm not one of His children, why would He listen to me?

"Dear God," I start with a stutter. "You know about our mom. You know she . . . she loves You now. She needs Your help. She doesn't— " I swallow hard, trying to compose myself. "And Donnie. He loves You too. He says You have a lot of work still to do with him. But I know he really believes in You, in Your Son. I hope . . . please let them find him. Let him be okay."

I squeeze Sebastian's hand. He squeezes back. "Father God, help my mom. Take care of Donnie. Please don't let anyone else be hurt by the fire. We could really use some rain. Please. Amen."

Sebastian wipes his nose on his sleeve. We sit and cry until he gets the hiccups and then eventually falls asleep. With him leaning against me, I put my head back on the couch. A rustle of wind followed by a splattering sound against the French patio doors causes me to bolt upright. I stare at the glass.

A slight smile forms on my lips. *Rain.* That'll help get the fire out and prevent it from spreading. It's probably too late—I squeeze my eyes shut as a vice grip goes around my heart. Mom's already hurt. And Donnie . . . I hate to think . . .

Biting my lip, I stare out into the darkness. My words come out in a whisper. "Please, God. Please. Please don't take her away. We need her. Our mom is everything to us. Please. Help us."

"I am with you."

I turn my head, looking for the voice.

I'm alone. My eyes go wide. I shake my head and let out a nervous laugh. That was . . . weird. I close my eyes as a comfort washes over me, covering me like a blanket. I let out a long breath.

Did God just speak to me? No, that can't happen. Not in today's time, if it ever could.

By the time Aunt Karla opens the apartment door, my arm's numb from Sebastian leaning against it. There hasn't been any more weird voices, which I've decided was just the wind going through the room in an eerie way.

"Is she— " I shake my head. "Is my mom okay?"

Aunt Karla hobbles across the room and sinks into her recliner. "She's holding her own. It's raining now, hard and strong. They're going to get the fire out."

"Do you . . . Donnie?"

"Nothing yet. I'm afraid . . . we should be prepared for the worst."

I give a slight nod. When he wasn't with Mom, when they didn't find him in those first few minutes, what else could be expected?

"Can I see her?" I ask.

She dips her head. "She's asking for you. Your brother, too, but let's leave him to sleep."

"Does he *need* to see her?"

The corners of her mouth lift ever so slightly. "I don't think so. Daniela and Chuck think she's going to make it as long as— " She lets out a loud sigh. "We must worry about infection, of course."

"The burns?"

"Those and her lungs. Pneumonia."

I shake my head. "No. She almost died from pneumonia before."

"I know. We'll do everything we can to keep her from getting it again. Daniela's already using her herbs."

"Do they have antibiotics? Just give them to her now."

"We'll do what's necessary. I'll stay with your brother. Go visit your mom."

My pace is slow. I want to see my mom, but I'm also scared to. She looked so bad before. Will she look any better now?

The swinging door squeaks as I step from the kitchen. Chuck lifts his head. "Good. Your brother?"

"Sleeping."

He nods. "Leanne, your little girl's here."

Mom's quiet, her voice rough, but I'm sure she says, "Baby girl."

I rush to her. "I'm here, Mom. I'm here."

She's still lying on her side, her face now covered in some kind of goop and a thin layer of gauze. Some of her hair is missing. How did I not notice that before?

I lift my eyes to Chuck. He's doing something with a syringe at Mom's arm. Daniela is at Mom's feet.

"What's that?"

"Subcutaneous hydration," Chuck answers.

Subcutaneous . . . I know the word from my books—under the skin.

"We're injecting saline water to try and rehydrate her," Daniela says.

"Why don't you just use an IV?"

"Don't have any." Chuck looks at me, his bushy eyebrows close together. "We do this for dogs and cats. It should work."

I turn back to my mom. "Does it hurt, Mom?"

She gives a slight shake of her head. "Donnie?"

Chuck answers. "As soon as I'm finished here, I'll see what I can find out."

Her voice is a gravelly whisper. "I'm afraid— "

I helplessly stand by, not sure what I can do to comfort her. With her burns, I'm afraid to touch her. Neither Daniela nor Chuck say anything.

I reach for a chair behind me and pull it close. Mom's hand is heavily bandaged. Her arm is goopy and lightly wrapped like her face.

When she starts coughing, Chuck stops with the syringe, setting it on the table nearby, and begins to clap Mom on the back. "Might want to scoot back." He lifts his chin at me.

I slide the chair back just as more of the gross black stuff dribbles out of Mom's mouth.

When the coughing fit finishes, Daniela says, "I think I've done enough for now. Probably time to steam her again. I'll get it ready."

"Okay, Leanne." Chuck gives my mom a weary smile. "We're going to sit you up again and use some of Daniela's voodoo on you."

"Really, Mr. Rice?" Daniela puts a hand on her hip and narrows her eyes.

Chuck gives her a wink. "You ready, Leanne? Let's get you sitting up."

"Can I help?" I ask.

"You can stay with her. We're making a steam tent."

"With thyme," Daniela adds. "But first, she needs to drink." She steps over with a coffee mug.

"What is it?" Mom croaks out the question.

"Same as before, marshmallow root and slippery elm. I'm glad I've been hoarding this. I thought we might need it if a bad virus swept through. Never thought . . . Sadie, you help her sip while I get the steam ready. In fact, let's put you under the tent with your mom. She can keep sipping while steaming."

As Daniela turns back to the fireplace where she has a stockpot of water heating, the front door opens.

Jack steps in, rain dripping from his cowboy hat.

Mom lifts her head toward Jack. Her shoulders sag. "My husband?"

"I'm sorry, Leanne. We . . . we got the fire out. He was still inside, by the window. I'm— " He shakes his head. "I'm truly sorry for your loss."

Chapter 30

Belt, Montana Rest Area
Thursday, July 30, Late Afternoon

Victoria

"Won't be long now." Atticus rubs his hands together. "This rest area's only twenty miles from Great Falls."

"A little *over* twenty," Jennifer corrects. "Another three days."

He tilts his head to the side. "We've been making great time."

Following the massacre in Moore, we've had zero issues. We made it to this old car and truck rest stop, now set up as a campground, in better time than I could've hoped.

Jennifer and I are both healed enough we're rarely using our canes. The day before yesterday, we accessed another of Patti's caches. The next one, according to her, is just a mile or so past this rest area.

"Can I help you with this?" Jennifer motions to Patti.

"It's almost ready. I'm just steaming it, then we'll add some spices."

In the cooking pot is a batch of lentil sprouts. Patti started soaking lentils and then sprouting them when we found her first cache. She soaks the lentils overnight in a pot, drains them the next morning and moves them to a pillowcase, then rinses the legumes several times a day. After a few days, they're soft with tiny tails and are almost like a vegetable.

With today's batch, she's cooking half of them and will add taco seasoning from her cache. The other half she moved to a jug and doused with vinegar; she said it'll be a salad for lunch tomorrow.

Some of the seeds they stashed, which I thought were for growing in a garden, are for sprouting. She has a batch of radish sprouts going, which she says will be ready tomorrow to add to the lentil salad. Fresh greens as we hike! It's almost unbelievable. I'm very thankful for Patti and her caches.

Jennifer no longer makes faces or noises directed at Patti. She isn't overtly friendly, but she's no longer cruel. And she's incredibly loving toward the children, to the point LJ started calling her *granny*. When Patti tried to correct him, Jennifer waved it off and said he could call her whatever he wishes.

Unless I'm way off base on the things I'm seeing, Atticus may wish for Jennifer to really be LJ's granny. I've seen the looks Atticus gives Patti, the way he seems to hang on her every word, how he's super helpful to her and more.

As a widow for only a month, and five years older than Atticus, Patti doesn't return the interest. He's respectful of her recent loss and isn't at all inappropriate.

Atticus has taken a stronger stance on being the spiritual leader of our group. This, too, I think is related to his soft spot toward Patti. He's witnessed her praying and sharing stories with her children. Rey and Kimba, still too overwhelmed with their own grief to resume their leadership roles, are happy to let him lead.

Rey's still in charge regarding security measures, but he does increasingly rely on Atticus with Kimba unable to think on her feet and make quick decisions. I hope she'll be able to return to the strength she previously had before much longer.

Once we reach the Dosen ranch, the Hoffmanns intend to continue on, backtracking to Eddie's Junction, near the decimated town of Moore, and heading south to Bozeman. I suspect, being so close to Nate's grave, they'll stop there first.

Once they connect with their friends in Bozeman, they plan to return to Billings. Although the excitement of helping with the rebuilding efforts has faded for them, Kimba now says they'll probably do what they can in Billings over the winter, but then she wants to go back to their home in Denver. She says she desperately needs to return to their abandoned condo to retrieve photo albums and family pictures.

While Rey has a family photo in his wallet, she only had pictures on her phone—which was fried by the EMP along with so much else. I understand the need to have photographs of her son. When we packed up our house last fall, a few pictures were something I made sure we took along, though the number I packed then is considerably more than what I have now.

I only have the most recent school photos of the boys and a picture of the four of us together. After Jon attacked our community, I considered cutting him out of everything he was in. I didn't do it. Now I'm happy to have this one pic of us together, looking happy on the surface. Even though we weren't. We were terribly good at faking the happy family. I do wish I had a wedding photo, something from a time we truly were happy—before things so drastically changed.

When we left, his loss and everything leading up to it was just too raw. One of the women at the lodge told me she'd keep the photos in the storage house and, if I returned, they'd be there for me. How long she'll keep them, we didn't discuss. I really have no intentions of returning.

How could I?

This journey has been more difficult than I could've ever imagined. I just want to get to the ranch and start fresh—start our new life.

Chapter 31

Two Miles East of Great Falls, Montana
Sunday, August 2, Early Afternoon

Victoria

"We're fine," Rey says in a low voice. "This is just like every other checkpoint we've run into."

I take in a deep breath. Rey may say it's the same, but the military vehicles and half dozen armed and uniformed Airmen make it feel considerably different. The roadblock is set up a couple of miles from Great Falls, at a crossroads with a large housing complex just beyond. Malmstrom Air Force Base, located on the edge of Great Falls, is within view.

We knew we were getting close, not only because of the mile markers and road signs on Highway 89, but because of the increase in walkers, vehicles, and even helicopters. The first one we saw was while we were still camped at the rest area near Belt three days ago.

Since then, it's been almost like clockwork. A chopper—or as Rey calls them, a helo—will fly over as we're packing up, then another one or sometimes two when we stop for lunch, and then again before dark.

Nervous or not, this roadblock puts us even closer to our new home and makes me want to celebrate. We're just over forty miles from their ranch west of Great Falls, outside the tiny town of Simms on the Sun River. With Jennifer and me mostly recovered from our injuries, we've been averaging ten miles a day again. If we can keep it up, we'll reach the ranch in four days.

"Passing through, folks?" the uniformed guard asks.

"That's right." Rey gives a smile, his accent pleasingly Midwest.

"How far you going?"

"Our friends have a ranch just the other side of Great Falls."

"Still in Cascade County?"

"Barely. We're almost right on the county line with Lewis and Clark." Jennifer bobs her head. "Not far from Simms."

The Airman looks over our ragtag group. "Welcome home."

Tears fill my eyes as my hand goes to my mouth.

Jennifer steps forward. "Thank you, thank you so much. Do you know anything about Simms? Is it safe?"

"Sorry, ma'am. I don't have that information. There're several aid stations set up in the area that may be able to help. The nearest is only a mile or so ahead, at The King's Arena."

Jennifer crinkles her forehead. "The boarding stables?"

"Yes, ma'am, the former horse boarding stables. You can't miss it. I'll need all your names and hometowns. We're keeping track of county residents for our records. Identification if you have them, especially for the owner of the home you'll be staying at."

Jennifer hands over her driver's license and answers a series of questions, including if she has any proof of ownership. "At the house, yes."

"But not on you?"

She gives him an incredulous look. "Why would I?"

He tilts his head to the side. "There've been several situations where people have been using a version of salvage law."

Jennifer shakes her head. "I don't know what that means."

"Like for boats?" Rey asks.

I chew on my bottom lip, remembering the long nights I helped Jon with his law school studies. Salvage law is an old concept dating back to times when the sea was primarily used for commerce. When a ship was in distress, those who arrived and offered help were often only there to pillage the cargo, not to provide actual assistance. Salvage law was about rewarding people who were honest and risked their lives to help the vessel in trouble.

The reward was often substantial, sometimes even the vessel itself. Salvage law continues today with very strict rules on when the salvaged vessel can become the salvor's property. Quite a bit goes into determining the reward, and it's not always the boat. But I've never heard of it being applied to homes or land.

"How could a maritime law apply in Montana?" I ask. "Wouldn't squatter's rights be more appropriate?"

The Airman dips his head. "Right now, none of it's being done through the courts. Most likely, your neighbors will be happy to welcome you home."

"Humph," Atticus snorts.

After we register, the Airman says, "At the aid station, they'll help you map out a route to your place. Some areas are off limits."

"Like where?" Atticus asks.

"Downtown mostly. A few other places too."

"Downtown is off limits?"

"It's been claimed as sovereign property by a group."

"A gang?"

He lifts a shoulder. "They may be able to answer more questions at the aid station."

"Can we camp there?"

"No problem. Stay a couple of days if you need."

"Just the night," Atticus says. "We're ready to get home."

The converted stables still smell of horses. The former indoor arena, which Jennifer says used to be a spot for private horse shows, is the main hub. There're several outbuildings, loafing sheds, a barn with indoor stalls, and more—all converted and being used to help weary travelers.

The aid station is teeming with Airforce personnel, plus a variety of National Guard and Reserve, along with Civil Air Patrol and plenty of civilian volunteers. Not to mention it's full of travelers. After checking in at the main gate, being given an overview of the setup and where everything is, plus told the rules, we're each provided a pass for a meal and a shower.

"Shower?" Nicole squeals. "Like a real, hot shower?"

The check in lady smiles. "Close enough. It's outside and sun heated, but I promise you'll enjoy it." She then directs us to where we'll set up our camp in one of the former boarding runs.

As we reach the fenced-in area, we discover several tents already set up. The space is plenty large, and the covered loafing shed has even been converted to an outdoor kitchen complete with a campfire ring and tables.

"Howdy, folks," an older gentleman says as we reach the gate of the fenced-in run. "How long you staying?"

"Just overnight," Rey answers.

"Heading west?"

"That's right. You?"

"Yep, with my wife and young 'un." He motions to a woman holding a child around LJ's age. The wife is around the same age as Patti, maybe a couple years older. The man looks older than me by a decade. Of course, in today's world, looks can be deceiving. I know I look much older than I did a year ago. Maybe I also look like I'm in my sixties instead of fifties.

I self-consciously raise a hand to my scraggly hair. What used to be smooth and dyed a deep brown is now a brittle salt and pepper mess. At least the shower will get it clean.

I sneak a glance at Kimba. She, too, has noticeably aged since Nate's death. She's a natural beauty. Even on the road, she was stunning.

The beauty's still there, but she's more haggard looking. Her once shiny blond hair is now matte and straw-like. Her eyes sport dark circles and her lips are pale. Her body looks okay because of the intense workouts she subjected it to while we were camped after Nate's death. Not as sculpted as she was from the makeshift weightlifting, but still good.

Rey, an incredibly handsome man, has experienced physical changes. His blond hair has turned gray at the temples almost overnight. He has lines on his forehead and around his mouth I hadn't noticed before.

I'm so lost in my thoughts of how we all look, I barely pay attention to the conversation between the man and Rey, not until the man says, "We're staying here a few days, heard they're going to try and clean up the downtown area. Thought we'd wait before moving through."

"Oh?"

"That's the rumor going around."

"From whom?" I ask.

He shrugs. "Everyone. 'Course, that's all we hear—rumors. Rumors they're cleaning up the downtown. Rumors about World War III . . . rumors, rumors, rumors."

Rey gives a nod and says we've been hearing plenty of rumors too. Months ago, when we were in Billings, there was talk of skirmishes and fighting in other countries, even nuclear detonations.

Rey had said we shouldn't put much stock in those rumors. Maybe he's right. We haven't heard anything official. Not that it matters. Whatever's happening in other countries really has little to do with us reaching the Dosen ranch.

Once we get our tents set up, Atticus says he's going to the aid station to see about the best route to the ranch. We'd talked about this while traveling, not knowing what we'd find here. Atticus and Axel think we should take a main road until we hit the confluence of the Missouri River and Sun River, then walk along the riverbank to the ranch. Jennifer insists the river is too overgrown and travel will be difficult.

Rey, Axel, Brett, and Jameson all join Atticus to look at the map while Kimba and her daughters go in search of the showers. Jennifer and I, along with Patti and her children, stay at camp. I'm ready for a long rest before going in search of anything. Even the draw of the hot shower is secondary to reclining.

It's been eight weeks since I broke my arm, and I've only had it fully out of the splint once, when Daniela Reynolds undid it, put some medicine on it, and rewrapped it. She gave me solid instructions to leave it wrapped until early August.

Today, August 2, seems like a good day to remove it, especially with having a shower available. I can get this splint off and wash my stinking arm.

And stink it does!

I can smell it wafting off me. The sling, once a pretty pink color, is now a dingy faded gray. A few of the wood shims, which were supposed to help hold the bones in place as they knit back together, snapped during the last few weeks. Patti helped me remove them without disturbing the rest of the makeshift cast or the duct tape, which is holding the upper part of my arm to my body in an effort to further reduce my movement. The tape has also been replaced and added to.

"Patti?" I motion to my sling when she looks at me. "You think we can take this off before I shower?"

"The sling? Sure. I have a garbage bag we can put around your arm."

"The whole thing."

"You sure?" Jennifer asks.

"It's been long enough. Daniela Reynolds said I could undo it and then start with the salve, but to keep it in the sling so I don't use it much for a few more weeks."

"It's probably a good idea," Patti says. "I have a fabric bandage we can wrap it in if you think it's needed."

"We'll see. I'm going to give my arm a good cleaning first."

Patti smiles. "Good idea."

"Do you want to go to the showers?" Jennifer asks. "I can keep the children. I'll help you bathe them later if you'd like."

"I'll wait. You all go first. I have some time."

"Meaning?" I ask.

Patti tilts her head and gives a shrug. "We're here, in Great Falls."

Jennifer's eyes go to the children, happily playing with small wooden toys. "I guess we are."

I shake my head. "You're just going to stay here? At the aid station?"

Patti's voice is low. "Thought I'd check with the man who said they're heading west, see which route they're taking." She lifts her chin in the direction of the older man. He's playing with his son while the wife looks on, a small smile on her lips.

"How far is it to your friend's place? The ones you said you can spend the winter with?"

She lifts a shoulder. "Around a hundred miles, probably."

"You can't make it." Jennifer's aggressively shaking her head. "Not before winter. It'll start getting too cold at night."

"I'll get a ride. It'll be fine."

"No," Jennifer insists. "It's too cold for the babies. You should— " She takes a deep breath, then her words come out in a rush. "You should spend the winter with us and start again in the spring."

My head swivels to Jennifer.

She meets my eyes. "Is that . . . do you agree, Victoria?"

"Yes, of course. But it's not really up to me. You should ask Atticus and Axel."

"Oh, I have little doubt what Atticus thinks." She gives me a wink.

"Thank you," Patti says. "But we've been enough of a burden."

"Ha!" Jennifer retorts. "Hardly. Your preplanning kept us from starving and gave us additional firearms and ammunition we may need. And your nursing skills may have saved my life."

Patti's head dips slightly. "Perhaps. Let me think about it. Rey and Kimba still plan on leaving soon after you get to your ranch?"

I tighten my mouth. Jameson asked Rey a few days ago if, because it's getting so late, they'd stay the winter. Rey's no was abrupt, leaving zero room to question.

Kimba's sure, with just the four of them, they can make good time and travel the less than two hundred miles to Bozeman in under a month. None of us choose to remind them what can happen along the way to cause delay. They know what can go wrong as well as any of us do.

"Should we free your arm?" Patti asks. "If you're ready, I'll get my supplies."

Chapter 32

Aid Station
Two Miles East of Great Falls, Montana
Sunday, August 2, After Supper

Victoria

The lady was right about the shower being wonderful. My newly freed arm is shriveled and wrinkly, but it's clean.

And the meal they offered this evening was unbelievable. Grilled burgers! But no buns. Instead, we got a homemade tortilla and a large portion of fresh lettuce and spinach from the garden they tend. Other than the sprouts Patti makes and what we forage, we rarely eat anything green.

After dinner, Jennifer, Patti, LJ, and I are walking around, trying to digest our meal, when Patti stops and points. "I can't believe it." She rushes off to some bushes along a fence and spends a minute pawing through her messenger bag. Like all of us, she carries a smaller bag of essentials she doesn't want to be without. Pulling out her handwritten book of herbs, she flips through the pages.

Jennifer's and my eyes meet, and we both shake our heads. "What is it?" Jennifer asks.

LJ, holding tight to Jennifer's hand, asks to be let go so he can run to his mom.

"It's okay, let him come." Patti's smile is wide. "Do you know what this is?"

I step a few feet closer. "A salad weed?"

"Even better. Comfrey. It doesn't grow wild here. Someone must have planted it. I'm going to ask if we can cut some. We'll use it fresh and dry some by the fire. Maybe even get a root ball so you can grow it on your ranch."

"Comfrey . . . the stuff for my broken arm?"

"Exactly. See?" She shows me the water pencil sketch from the herb and wildcrafting book Daniela made her. "It's the same."

I take the book from her and adjust the distance with my arm. Once I find the sweet spot, my vision evens out. I nod my agreement; the drawing and physical description appear to be the same.

From my side, Jennifer says, "There aren't any flowers on the ones growing here. Are you sure it's comfrey?"

"They flower late spring or early summer. See?" She points a finger to a line of writing. "Daniela noted it here."

"The leaves do look the same," I agree. "Maybe we should ask. But we do have that salve."

"Not much salve. If they'll let us take cuttings, by next summer we could have our own comfrey garden."

"Daniela gave us a start of turmeric for the garden," Jennifer says. "I'm not sure how well it's holding up, though. We've been on the road a lot longer than expected."

A quick visit with one of the civilian volunteers led us to someone who used to work at the horse stables when it was still operating. She said the arena owners planted it several years ago to use as green manure for the gardens. It's taken over in several spots, and they're happy to share.

We not only harvest leaves from the comfrey but she also loans us a shovel so we can dig up a few plants by the roots. She even gives us a ratty pillowcase to carry them in, then a reminder to plant them where we won't mind if they make a nuisance of themselves as they grow and spread.

Once back at our camp, Patti uses instructions from her herb book to soak several of the comfrey leaves in hot water. Then she wraps them around my newly freed arm, covering them with a towel to keep in the heat. "It's a poultice," she says.

With my comfrey poultice doing its magic, she lays the rest of the leaves out by a small fire in hopes of drying them for travel.

Atticus spreads out our Montana map. "If we take Tenth Street to the confluence of the Missouri and Sun Rivers, we'll avoid the issues in the old part of the city."

"Are you sure they destroyed the Hotel Arvon?" Jennifer asks.

Her son lifts a shoulder. "That's what we heard. The area caught fire—or it was set purposely."

"I loved that old hotel."

Atticus puts a hand on his mom's arm. "I know it was your place, yours and Dad's."

Jennifer spends many minutes reminiscing on how she and her husband would get away for just one night each year for their anniversary. They'd stay at the Hotel Arvon, requesting a different room each time.

"Will the road take us all the way to the ranch?" Jameson asks, bringing the conversation back to the present.

"Only through the city," Atticus answers. "Then we follow the river."

"I still say the river will be too difficult," Jennifer says, shaking her head, "too tangled with brush."

"It should be okay, especially the parts near Interstate 15."

"And after that?" Jennifer raises her eyebrows at Atticus.

"We can get off if it gets bad, but I think we'll be fine to where Sun River meets up with Highway 200. Plus, along the river we'll have more food opportunities. Deer, fish, even wild stuff. It's pretty cool Patti found the comfrey." His eyes travel to the young woman. "You've decided to spend the winter with us?"

Patti dips her chin. "I asked around. You were right about not being able to catch a ride with the military. There's a civilian transport, taking trade for rides on I-15 to I-90."

"We're probably going to try and get on it," Rey says, meeting Kimba's gaze.

She gives a reluctant nod.

Rey gives his wife a vacant smile. "But it won't help Patti since she wants to go to Ovando, where her friends are."

"That's the best way for me to go without Ledger." Patti shrugs. "I have another cache between here and Orvando, and at their place. If you're sure, Jennifer, I'd like to accept the invitation to stay the winter. I'll work hard and earn our keep."

"I have no doubt." Jennifer clears her throat. "Here, in front of everyone, I want to apologize for the terrible way I was. I was . . . it was not the way I should've behaved. I'm ashamed of myself. Over the last several weeks, as you've selflessly helped me get well, I've come to realize . . . "

Jennifer purses her lips. "I've realized how un-Christlike I've been. How I've let my history, my *flesh*, determine how you've been treated."

Patti opens her mouth to respond, but Jennifer raises a hand. "I need to finish, to tell you—*all* of you—how sorry I am. I'm so grateful that, thanks to God and who He is, I can now look at you with love. He has taken this . . . this . . . "

"Racism?" Axel offers.

"Um, well, I guess." Jennifer's cheeks color. "I was going to say thorn. But yes, Axel's right. Please forgive me, Patti. Please know I love you and your children as Christ commanded. Even more than that." She smiles at LJ and Trish. "They're special to me. *You're* special."

"Thank you." Tears fill Patti's eyes as she reaches for Jennifer's hand.

Jennifer not only takes her hand but pulls her into a hug as she whispers more apologies. After several moments, they release. Wiping her eyes, Jennifer says, "So, I guess the river it is."

"The only problem . . . " Rey says. "Well, not really a problem but something to be aware of, there's a lot of bear activity."

"Nothing new. We have plenty of bears around Simms." Jennifer makes a circling motion with her arm. "Around this entire area even."

"That's what I told the lady." Atticus lifts his hands. "She said it's not just the black bears but the grizzlies, though we know black bears can be dangerous too."

There're several nods as we remember PJ Cameron being attacked by a black bear last winter while out hunting near the ski lodge. Rochelle Bennet, his hunting buddy and also one of our traveling companions, killed the bear and saved PJ's life.

Rey leans forward slightly. "Seems they've been making a nuisance of themselves, even breaking into homes—both occupied and unoccupied."

"The bears? How're they doing that?" I ask.

Rey lifts his shoulders. "Don't know. I guess with people hunting their food, they're resorting to other measures to feed themselves?"

"It doesn't even make sense. People may be hunting, but just like in Billings, Great Falls lost a considerable amount of their population over the last year. There should be enough wildlife to go around."

"Even a small change in things can affect bears." Atticus holds up his thumb and index finger, showing a little bit. "At least that's what I learned from my dad. Years ago, we only had black bears here. But now there've been more than just small changes, so who knows? Black bears mainly eat plants, but they'll also eat dead things they find. You know, deer, rodents, rabbits. We know about the issue with rabbits dying, thanks to hemorrhagic disease. I don't know if they'll eat the diseased ones. Grizzlies will take down a deer or elk."

"Or a human?" I ask.

"It's pretty rare," Jennifer says. "There's maybe a couple of fatal bear attacks a year."

"They gave us a can of bear spray," Axel says. "And we have our firearms."

"It's good we have those. But still, this is nothing new," Jennifer states. "They've been increasingly prevalent in recent years as they expand east from Glacier and other areas."

"Right." Atticus nods. "That's what I think too. We'll just need to be smart about it, especially if we bring down any game or catch fish. We've lived here all our lives. We know what to do."

Chapter 33

Fergus Peak Lodge
Monday, August 3, After Supper

Sadie

It's been just over a month since my mom was married and widowed in the same day. Daniela and Chuck managed to keep the infection away, and she's slowly healing. The burns on the palm of her hand were the worst, still needing to be bandaged. The smoke really did a number on her lungs. Even short, slow walks leave her out of breath.

Surprisingly, her spirits have been good. Well, not exactly good but not terrible. She's grieving. Definitely grieving. The sparkle she had while with Donnie is gone.

He brought out something special in her. Something I hadn't seen since my dad was alive. And even something more. The way he made her laugh but could also get her fired up and angry, it was true passion. True love.

I'll admit, I expected her to fall apart. Last year, after the terrible things we went through—being captured, Uncle Wes being killed, and then finding my grandma and grandpa dead—Mom was a wreck.

She became someone I didn't know. With the tragedy of losing her new husband, it would make sense for the hopelessness, the anger she had then, to return. Instead, she's leaning on God and her belief Donnie, who'd also accepted Jesus as his Lord and Savior, is now worshipping with the Father.

I know this brings her a lot of comfort. Whether it's true or not is something else. Yeah, I'll admit that when I was praying the night of the fire, I felt something. *Heard something.* The way the wind sounded through the trees truly resembled a voice. It must have been my overactive imagination. Nothing else makes sense.

But still . . . I can't stop thinking about it and wondering if God was speaking to me. Sebastian is convinced God speaks to him. Could He reach out to me also?

In the days after the fire, my brother rarely left our mom's side. He slept on the floor next to her bed and cuddled with her during the day, making sure he was there for anything she needed. He knows how close we came to losing her. He's also heartbroken over Donnie's death. The man became a father to him.

I'm sad too—surprisingly so. While I was mostly happy about the marriage for my mom, I realize how much I truly liked Donnie. He was gruff and rough around the edges, difficult at times, but I know he did things out of love and a sense of duty, a desire to protect.

Chuck Rice is here a lot to check on Mom and lead church service every Sunday. He visits Daniela, too, though both of them pretend that's not why he's here. He still makes fun of her herbs, and she makes a point of calling him *Mr. Rice* and acting like she doesn't like him.

Each week after church, we have a potluck. With the gardens doing well and food plentiful, we're taking advantage of it. We also do plenty of preserving so we'll have food over winter, but the preaching gives us a reason to get together. Soon, the weather will turn and we'll all be stuck at home, so it makes sense to take advantage of it while we can.

Getting everyone together lets us catch up on the news too. Sometimes, being back here away from everyone else feels like we're disconnected. The men—and some women, now that mom was a trailblazer—still go into town to trade.

There're more travelers in Lewistown and more news coming over the ham radios. We still don't know what's truth or rumor, but there's a lot of talk about the entire world being in peril. *World War III.* There are even rumors of foreign troops on both coasts. Considering we heard that many of the coastal towns were nuked, we don't know if that's true at all.

Someone said maybe the nukes are a rumor and there never were any ground detonations, just the EMP caused by the high-altitude nukes. But we know there was at least one since Ben Ferguson and his family saw the mushroom cloud when they were escaping Oregon.

The more rumors we hear, the more confusing it all is. I'm glad to be safe at the lodge with Aunt Karla, Mom, and Sebastian.

I'm starting to like Chuck Rice and his preaching. Like that first time he preached, the things Chuck says, and the way he says them, are easy to understand. More than any time growing up and attending weekly service, I want to listen. It's much like when we were traveling with our friends and they'd read from the Bible and then discuss it.

I didn't participate in the discussions, and often acted like I wasn't even paying attention, but sometimes I did. Often those verses felt like they were directed at me. I'd get swept up in it and make more out of it than I should.

It's the same now. When Chuck's preaching, which he says isn't preaching but reading from the Word, it *feels* personal.

I know I'm not the only one who thinks this. Afterward, people are always talking about how much his talk meant to them. I guess he has a knack for choosing things we can all relate to.

The origins of the fire are a mystery. It was several days after the fire when Mom scribbled in a notebook what she remembered from that night, left-handed since her right is bandaged.

She says they'd already extinguished all the candles and went to bed. She was asleep when something woke her. The smoke was everywhere; the snap and pop of the fire was probably the noise she heard. She started coughing immediately.

Waking Donnie was hard, he may have already been affected by the smoke. They were both confused and couldn't make good decisions. She doesn't even know how they managed to find the window, how she was able to get out. Or why Donnie didn't.

Something that's been nagging at me since that night is how quickly Jack showed up to help. He said he couldn't sleep and was out walking. I asked Aunt Karla about it, what she thought, and she said I was making a mountain out of a mole hill. Maybe. But it's still odd.

And making it even odder is Jack's absence at the Sunday services and potlucks. He hasn't attended any of them. He doesn't come around at all, not really. He was here the day after the fire, helping make sure it was out and checking on Mom a few times. Then he came back a few days later to help with cleanup and to see how she was doing.

Aunt Karla says it's a busy time right now with the cattle and harvesting crops. I'm sure it is, but for someone who begged my mom not to get married, I'd think he would want to make sure she's healing okay.

I take in a deep breath. The sweet aroma of the flowers growing around the patio is heavy in the warm air. It's a beautiful evening. Still hot from the heat of the day but with a gentle breeze.

I'm helping Brooke and Cassie with the saddle tack again, cleaning it and making sure it's all in good shape. Sebastian and I ride a few times a week; although, he doesn't ride Old Rosie any longer. Now he rides Gordie. Mom said Donnie would've wanted him to have his horse.

Mom's reclining on a lounge chair, under a patio umbrella to protect her damaged skin from the end of the day sun. Even in the heat of summer, she's wearing a long-sleeved shirt and pants. The long-sleeved shirt is not only to cover the burns on her arms, but to hide the pistol Kimba gave her. She'd left it in the drawer in Aunt Karla's room on her wedding day and didn't grab it after the ceremony, so it was spared from the fire.

Brooke and Cassie are talking and laughing. Sometimes, if I have something to add, I'll join in. But mostly I just listen to their banter.

My eyes catch movement coming up the road—Samantha's walking with a purposeful stride. I go back to my work, glancing up every now and then.

As Samantha nears us, it's obvious her usually pretty face is twisted with anger.

"Uh-oh," Brooke mutters. "Wonder what's wrong with her?"

A sly smile crosses Cassie's face. "Oh, I have a good idea."

"Whadda ya mean?" Brooke asks.

"I s'pose you'll find out in a minute or so."

It doesn't take long for Samantha to reach us. She's still fifty yards away when she yells. "You! How could you? You . . . you hussy!"

Cassie lets out a laugh. "Now c'mon, girl."

"Girl? Don't girl me. I'm not the one . . . the one who's a man stealer."

Standing near the table, Samantha's voice is still loud. Screeching.

I glance at Mom. Her eyes are open, but she looks unconcerned.

"Calm down. I'm sure he explained it to you and told you how it is."

"He expects me to share him. *Share him!*"

"You know we don't have enough men in our community." Cassie is calm. "It's only smart. We'll be able to— " She gives a quick glance toward my mom. "It's logical."

"It's gross! You can have him. I'm not interested in sharesies."
Cassie shakes her head. "You're being childish. It's logical."
"You already said that. But it's not. It's gross and . . . and immoral."
Samantha bursts into tears before running to the back stairs. None
of us say anything as we listen to her feet hitting the wooden steps and
then the decking. The door to her room slams.
"Are you . . . are you dating Randy?" Brooke asks.
"I've been wanting to talk with you about that." She smiles at her
fellow wrangler. "Let's go for a walk. Um, Sadie, why don't you come
too."
I look to my mom. She makes a slight movement with her
shoulders before giving a barely perceptible nod. Even though Mom's
doing okay after the fire, she doesn't talk much. Her throat is still raw,
her voice is hoarse, and her breathing's sometimes labored. She says
it's easier just to keep quiet.
She continues to sip all sorts of tea concoctions Daniela puts
together to help her heal. Carrying around a notebook also lets her
rest her voice, while still allowing her to converse.
"Uh, okay." I slide my chair back.
I meet Mom's eyes again. From her look, I know she's as curious
as I am about this. It's clear whatever Cassie has to say, she doesn't
want my mom to hear.
Cassie sets off toward the stables. We're barely out of Mom's
earshot when Brooke asks what's going on.
"Something wonderful." Cassie smiles. "I'm going to have a baby."
"A baby!" The look on Brooke's face registers surprise followed by
disgust. "With Randy?"
Cassie's head bobs. Her smile covers her entire face.
"Congratulations," I say, poking Brooke in the arm.
Brooke makes a snorting sound.
"Thank you," Cassie gushes. "At least someone has manners." She
shoots a dirty look at Brooke. "Isn't it wonderful. And I won't be the
only one. We're going to build a huge happy family. Randy and I
want you two to be part of it."
I crinkle my brow.
"Samantha too, of course. He really likes her, and since she's also
pregnant . . . " Cassie lifts a hand.
"Wait," I say. "Samantha's pregnant? With Randy's baby?"
"Mm-hmm. I told you it was wonderful. We'll be sister wives."

My blood runs cold. *Sister wives.* That's what crazy James who kidnapped Sebastian and me kept talking about. He wanted Becky, who thought Sebastian was her dead son, to be his wife. And he wanted other wives and lots of children. He kept talking about a television show depicting the life.

I narrow my eyes. And he mentioned a guy he met to the west doing the same thing.

"You don't happen to know a guy named James, do you?" I ask.

"James? James Stahl? Edna's husband?"

"Who?"

"The old couple who live closest to Jack Mosher," Brooke says. She turns back to Cassie. "What do you mean *be part of it?*"

I shake my head. "Not him. Some guy who may have lived here before."

The two women give me an odd look.

"Never mind," I mutter.

Brooke grabs Cassie's wrist. "You want Sadie and me to be a part of what? To share Randy?"

She shakes her arm free. "Jeez. Calm down."

Crossing her arms, Brooke taps the toe of her boot on the ground. "A part of what?"

"We want to build back society, create something wonderful out of all the terrible things that happened."

"You keep saying *wonderful.* This whole thing sounds wrong. Like Samantha said, gross."

Cassie lifts her chin. "It's not gross. It's . . . it's beautiful. We'll create a wonderful new family. Samantha and me, we'll have so much fun raising our babies together. You'll see. I want you with us."

She looks at me. "You too, Sadie. I know you're only sixteen, but that's not really too young in today's world. Randy and I've talked about it, about *who* we should have, and you two have the qualities we want."

"What qualities are those?" I ask, feeling sick to my stomach.

"You're both pretty and smart. We get along well."

"I'm not sharing a man with you." Brooke crosses her arms. "Especially not— " She looks toward the horses. "You might call it sister wives or whatever, but it's a harem!"

Cassie releases a laugh. "Oh, puh-leeze. Call it whatever you want, but there's nothing wrong with it. It's even in the Bible. Tell her, Sadie!"

My eyes go wide.

"I mean, you and your family, your Aunt Karla, everyone's so religious. Surely you know about the guy who killed the giant and then became a king. He had a harem, right?"

"King David?"

She nods knowingly. "Randy told me all about him. That was what they did to make sure their bloodline thrived. The women all lived together—*worked* together. King David would go and . . . " She raises her eyebrows.

"Visit?" I offer.

She winks at me. "Sure. That works."

Brooke turns to me. "Is that true? I mean, I've heard some of Chuck's preaching, but he doesn't talk about that stuff."

"I'm not— " I let out a breath. "I'm not an expert or anything, but I know the story of David and the things he did."

"He was after God's heart, right?" Cassie looks at me expectantly. "Because of the things he did?"

I shake my head. "I don't think it's quite like that. He did some bad things, and it caused a lot of heartache. He found his way out of it, repented, and then turned back to God."

As I say the words, a new understanding washes over me. It's the repentance and turning back to God that makes the difference, that made David a man after God's heart.

It's what I want too.

I want the same kind of love God gave David to be given to me. I swallow hard as tears sting my eyes. I want what David had, what my mom and brother have. I want God's love.

"I don't care if it's in the Bible." Brooke kicks the bottom rung of the corral. "I'm not interested. And you shouldn't do it either. What does Jack think about this? You know how he wants to— "

"Keep us for himself?"

Brooke's eyes go wide. "Jack? No. He treats us with respect. We're here, separated, so men like Randy won't ogle us."

Cassie sneers. "That's what he wants you to think. Jack's no angel. Is he, Sadie?"

"What?" I shake my head. "I'm sorry, I was thinking of something else."

"You know, after what Jack did to your mom?" she prods.

"My mom?"

"How he got her pregnant and then cheated on her?"

I blink my eyes several times, trying to sort out what Cassie's talking about.

"Oh . . . you don't know. She never told you?"

"My mom worked at a clinic. Well, not really a clinic. Is that— "

"Really?" Her hands go to her chest. "Oh, that's so sweet. She used her tragedy to help others. Of course, the woman's right to choose— "

"I don't know what you're talking about," I interrupt. "My mom's tragedy?"

I clamp my hands over my mouth. Suddenly, things make sense. The hints she's dropped, her passion for helping women who felt they had no choice, the few things she said about Jack and how they had history. I thought she meant he dumped her for someone else. But this . . .

"I need to go." I take a couple of quick steps before turning back. "Oh, and like Brooke and Samantha, I'm not interested in being part of your . . . whatever it is."

Cassie takes several long steps and grabs my arm. "You can't tell anyone. I've taken you into my confidence on this." She motions to Brooke. "You too. This is private."

I let out a snort. "This is nuts."

"She's right." Brooke nods. "You aren't going to find anyone interested in going along with this crazy idea."

Cassie gives a sly smile. "We'll see. But I'm serious. I expect both of you to keep quiet about our plans."

"About you and Samantha being pregnant?" I ask.

She lifts a shoulder. "For now. She'll calm down and see how this is for the best. Then we'll make a big announcement about it. I wasn't supposed to say anything to you two yet. Randy will be angry at me if he knows you know already. Just give it a few days."

Brooke shakes her head. "Nuts. That's what I'm saying. You're both nuts."

Cassie's still grasping my arm. I shake it loose and walk away. When I reach the patio, Mom's eyes are closed. I plop on the lounge chair near her knee. She calmly opens one eye and then the other.

"Drama?" she mouths.

"Did Jack Mosher cheat on you?"

She lifts a hand. "Yes," she croaks.

"He got you pregnant? And you . . . you had an abortion?"

Her face goes pale as she vigorously shakes her head. "No!"

Tears fill my eyes. "You lied? All this time, the work you did, it was all a lie?"

She continues to shake her head as she grabs her notebook and madly scribbles: *Miscarriage. I had a miscarriage.*

"Oh . . . I'm sorry, Mom. I didn't know."

She writes again: *Jack wanted me to have an abortion. I said no. He was mad. He went to a girl he knew from school and cheated on me. I was upset. I lost the baby a few days later.*

"What a jerk. How can you even be friends with him now?"

She tilts her head and then returns to her notepad. She holds it close to her so I can't see what she's writing and spends a good minute on it. Finally, she turns it to me:

I was so hurt, so devastated by his cheating. I thought maybe I should do what he wanted. I was actually thinking about it! Then, when I lost the baby, I thought it was my fault, that I'd caused it to happen by thinking the way I did. Afterward, I wanted to help other women. Help them with options, help care for them and their baby after he or she was born. It was my way to apologize to my own child.

I shake my head. "But you didn't do that, right? You had a miscarriage. It wasn't your fault."

She shakes her head, then whispers, "Felt like my fault. When I had the losses after you were born, I thought I was being punished."

I reach for her.

She opens her arms and pulls me close. After several minutes, Mom asks, "How?"

"How do I know? Cassie told me."

Mom pulls her head back to look at me—with fear in her eyes. She mouths, "Cassie? How?"

"She's dating Randy, you heard that?"

Mom nods.

"I think he told her. Maybe Jack told him?"

Mom scrunches her mouth. She turns her head and looks at the mountains in the distance. "Why?"

Chapter 34

Fergus Peak Lodge
Tuesday, August 4, at Breakfast

Sadie

So much for keeping things quiet. I had breakfast duty this morning, and Samantha and Cassie were the main topic of conversation. Now, as we finish setting up and people are drifting in, it's obvious the entire lodge knows. And not just about both women dating Randy, but also about the pregnancies.

I've just put out a second bowl of sautéed greens when Cassie walks in, her head held high and a smirk on her face. Brooke is behind her, staring at the ground. She lifts her eyes in time to meet mine. With a slight raise of her eyebrows, she shakes her head. I lift my chin in response.

It seems the stuff Brooke and I were told about the sister wives is still a secret. I didn't even tell my mom. I wanted to—and still want to—but the whole thing is so nuts it doesn't even really deserve a conversation. Like Brooke said, no one will go along with it.

And not to be mean, but Randy? Really? Part of me could understand if it was someone like Jack Mosher, good looking and kind. I make a face. Not kind. Not after what he did to my mom when they were young and the way he's been acting since Donnie died, not even coming around to make sure Mom's doing okay. No. He's definitely not kind.

I look to my mom. She and Sebastian are already at their table. She looks tired, worn out. She and I talked late into the night, discussing what I'd learned about her and Mosher.

She said they were so young and she thought—*believed*—they were in love, that they'd get married and be happy. She didn't expect him to freak out over the news of the baby. To cheat on her. She didn't want to tell anyone—not her aunt, who she was staying with and working for during the summer before her first year of college, and definitely not her mom. She knew how disappointed they'd be in her.

Then, when she lost the baby, she told Jack. He was relieved but also kind. He held her while she cried. But she couldn't look at him without thinking of the baby and what he'd done. So that was the end of it.

Like Cassie said, Mom's dedication to helping women grew out of her own experience. Even when she saw Jack again, a few weeks ago when we arrived here, all those memories came rushing back.

She said the first thing he did, after saying hello, was to apologize for his part in the whole thing. Like Mom, Jack is also a Christian now, and he feels guilty.

At the time, he thought there was no other option, so he told her she needed to get it *taken care of.* And when she refused, he was so mad at her, finding another woman was an easy out. She wouldn't want him any longer.

Now he knows it was the wrong choice. Aunt Karla knows about it too. Jack told her last year, after the EMP. She and Mom had talked about it several times since we arrived. Mom says she feels a weight lifted off her after keeping the secret for so long.

She'd had so much guilt over the years. When she married my dad, she told him, said she didn't want to start their marriage with a secret. Then she started doing volunteer work at the clinic and, after Dad died, became a full-time employee.

She did it all to try and make amends. It wasn't until we were kidnapped when she realized everything she'd done wasn't done in the right way. She needed to ask God's forgiveness.

When we talked last night, one of the things she wrote was:

I was embarrassed over what I'd done. So embarrassed, so sinful, I didn't think God could forgive me. I mean, really, why would He forgive me? After what I'd done? I truly believed I caused the death of my child. I tried to do good. I guess you know it didn't work out. I faked my Christianity for so many years and pretended to be all holy. I looked down on others. It wasn't until I begged God to help find you and Sebastian that I realized just how lost I was.

Mom says she now knows God has forgiven her, and she's working on forgiving herself. One day she'll be reunited with her babies, the one she lost with Jack and the three she and my dad lost between me and Sebastian. Part of me doesn't understand the guilt she felt—*still* feels. It wasn't her fault she miscarried.

Mom and I also talked about my epiphany at the corral, how I want to follow Christ—my *need* to follow Him. There was lots of hugging and tears. She said she's been praying for me. I'm happy but nervous, and I'm scared to even think about surrendering to Him. And as Donnie used to say, God has a heap of work to do on me.

Mom catches me staring at her and gives me a wave, motioning me to join them at the table.

"Hey, squirt," I say, plopping next to my brother.

"Hey yourself." He gives a big nod.

"Tired?"

"*Yeah*. You and Mom were making racket all night."

Mom breathes out a chuckle.

"Um, we weren't even in the apartment. We were sitting right at that table there." I point to a small table against the wall.

"Yeah, well, I heard you when you came back in. Then I couldn't get back to sleep."

I point to his plate. "Eat your greens."

After breakfast, Cassie says she feels sick and is going back to bed. Brooke asks if I can help at the stables.

Because it's getting so busy with harvesting the garden and crops, there's no school right now, so Sebastian also volunteers to help. When winter arrives and we can't do the outside work, the children will have school several hours each day to make up for the limited lessons during the rest of the year.

"Run ahead and pick out your pitchfork," Brooke tells Sebastian.

He gives me a questioning look, which I answer with a nod.

Once we're alone, Brooke whispers, "I can't believe everyone knows. Cassie blamed me, but I didn't say anything."

"Me neither. It sounds like Samantha was the one."

"Yeah, that's what I think. But she only talked about the pregnancies. Not the . . . " Brooke makes a face. "What does Karla think?"

"I didn't talk with her. I know she likes both Cassie and Samantha. Everyone here is family to her."

"Do you think we should tell her? Then maybe she can talk with Jack. They can do something about Randy's weird ideas."

"We promised we wouldn't."

"Don't you think . . . " She leans closer to me. "I've been listening to Chuck when he preaches. Cassie might think this plan of theirs is Biblical, but I don't agree."

"Maybe we should tell my aunt. I'll think about it while we're working."

"You and your brother are okay with the mucking? I need to work with one of the horses."

I lift a shoulder and make a face. "Sounds totally fun."

Mucking isn't terribly fun, but taking out the soiled bedding from the stables is part of the horses' needs.

"Hey!" Sebastian yells.

"What?" I lean against the pitchfork.

"You got that . . . that stuff on me."

I don't even try to hold back my chuckle. "Oops. It wasn't on purpose." I dip the pitchfork tines into the straw bedding and then flip it in his direction.

"Hey!" he yells again. "You did that on purpose."

"Yep!" I flip a little more at him. It's soon nuts, with straw and debris going everywhere. We laugh and carry on for many minutes before I raise my hand for a truce.

I'll admit, this feels good. We have so little laughter in our lives. The entire last year has been one tragedy after another. And just when I thought we'd seen the last of it, thought we'd finally found happiness, Donnie died and Mom got hurt.

"What do you think Jack's going to do?" Sebastian asks, digging his pitchfork into the mess we made.

"About what?"

He lifts a shoulder. "About Cassie being sick."

I furrow my brow. "Why would Jack do anything about it?"

"You know last night, after we finished our martial arts practice?"

"Yeah?"

"Some of the others were talking. They said Samantha and Cassie are having babies."

"You heard about it last night?"

He looks around, making sure we're alone, then steps closer to me. "It was Hayley—you know, the redheaded girl with a braid down her back?"

I lift a hand for him to continue.

"She said Randy told her. And he isn't happy just making Cassie and Samantha have babies. He wants to make lots of babies. I don't— " Sebastian shakes his head. "I don't think he knows he's supposed to marry the mom before they have a baby."

"How does Hayley know this?"

He glances around again. "He wants to give her a baby."

"What?" I jerk my head back. "She's . . . how old is she?"

He lifts a shoulder. "Don't know. As old as you, maybe?"

I shake my head. I don't think so. She may look my age because she's taller than me, but she doesn't act sixteen. She acts more like twelve. I'm suddenly sick to my stomach. Cassie and Samantha are adults. Brooke's an adult. I'm almost an adult, but Hayley is nowhere near legal age. Randy's plan has gone from gross to criminal. Predatory.

Sebastian leans on his pitchfork. "She said she's going to use our self-defense moves on him if he gets too close. She'll pop him in the nose with her elbow."

I give a slow nod. "We're not going to let that happen."

He gives me a serious look. "I know. You'll keep him from hurting anyone."

With a questioning look, I ask, "What do you mean?"

"Don't know. I just know God is going to use you to make sure nothing bad happens to anyone else. You believe in Him now, right?"

Looking at my pitchfork, I give a slight nod. "I guess I do. I mean, it wasn't so much I didn't believe before, it was . . . " I lift a hand while shrugging.

"And now?" A wide smile covers his face.

"Now I want what you and Mom have, the things Chuck talks about. I want to know more. I guess I want to be part of your Jesus club."

He wrinkles his brow. "Are you making fun?"

I let out a laugh and shake my head. "Not even. I fought it, but now . . . I'm one of you."

"All right!" He offers me a high five.

I smack his hand and then pull it away. "Ewww. Gross."

He shrieks out a laugh. "Oops. Sorry."

Without any more horseplay, but still talking about my newfound relationship with Jesus Christ, we finish the work. I know the right thing to do. Keeping Cassie's secret is wrong, maybe even sinful. I need to tell Aunt Karla and my mom. Then they can handle it from there. Hayley is too young to even be talking about stuff like that.

After washing my hands, I go to Aunt Karla's apartment. With Donnie's death and the cabin destroyed, we're still living with her.

A twin-size bed was found for Mom and put in Aunt Karla's bedroom. A second twin-size bed for me is in the corner of the living room with a shoji screen set up in front of it to give me a little privacy. Sebastian sleeps on the couch. At some point, we may move to our own place, but for now, this feels right.

Mom still has a lot of healing to do until she's completely well. We all know it's a miracle she's doing so good. I know it's frustrating to her, though, to not be able to do much but lie around. Daniela keeps telling her she'll soon be able to move more but now is a time of healing.

I'm surprised by how nice Daniela is compared to the first day we met her. Now she has a ready smile and is always wanting to teach us things. I enjoy working in the gardens with her and the nature walks we take to look for edibles and medicinals. Mom has said many times how she owes her life to Daniela and Chuck.

Aunt Karla is in the recliner doing some mending. Mom is stretched out on the couch.

I close the door quietly.

Mom's eyes pop open, and she gives me a smile. "Baby girl," she whispers.

"Hey." I chew the inside of my mouth. "Can I talk to you? To both of you?"

Mom motions to the side chair with her hand.

"Something wrong, dear?" Aunt Karla asks, setting her mending aside.

"Well, maybe. It might be nothing, but . . . " I lift my hands in the air as I plop into the chair.

Neither woman says anything. I wait several seconds before I blurt out everything, starting with Cassie talking to me and Brooke and finishing with what Sebastian just told me about Hayley.

Mom sits up and motions to the spot on the couch next to her. I move beside her, letting her wrap an arm around me.

Aunt Karla shakes her head. "I wish I could say I'm surprised. Cassie and Samantha, I warned both of them. But they're adults and can make their own decisions. Hayley, though, she's only fourteen. Just a child! I told Jack— " She gets a hard look on her face.

"And he's interested in you?" Even with being this close to my mom, I have to listen closely to make out her soft words. "Like Hayley, you're just a kid."

I want to argue and remind my mom sixteen is hardly a child, especially in today's world. But for this, she's right. "I don't know for certain about Hayley. Just what Sebastian said she told him."

"Where else would your brother come up with it?" Aunt Karla's mouth is a firm line. "We need Jack here. Take the horse and go after him."

My eyes go wide as I swallow the lump that instantly forms. "Me? Alone?"

Mom pats my shoulder. "Take Brooke if you need."

"No." Aunt Karla shakes her head. "This needs to be people we can trust."

"Brooke was grossed out by it too."

"I said no." Aunt Karla's voice is harsh. "She and Cassie are too close. You go. Bring Jack back. We'll discuss it with him before bringing anyone else in the loop." She gives me a slight smile. "You'll be fine, dear. I've seen you ride. You can do this on your own."

I dip my chin to my chest as I let out a shaky breath. "Can I have Brooke help me saddle Boot? He does that thing that makes it hard to tighten the saddle."

"I'll help you," Mom says.

"No, Leanne," Aunt Karla asserts. "It's too much. I'll go with Sadie and see her off. She'll be fine."

I change out of my dirty work clothes and into jeans and a long-sleeved shirt. We haven't found any boots in my size, so I wear my tennis shoes. When I step out from behind my privacy screen, I'm surprised to see Aunt Karla has changed. She's in jeans, a button-up shirt, and boots.

"I've decided to come with you. We'll ride over and talk with Jack. Less chance of . . . " She lifts a shoulder.

"Where's your bag?" I ask, looking for the large purse she always carries—the one Mom told me holds a handgun.

"I'm not bringing it." Aunt Karla puts a hand to the small of her back. "But don't you worry none. We'll be fine."

I tilt my head at her and then look at Mom, who gives me a slight nod before pulling me into a hug. "Don't worry. Your aunt knows how to handle this. I'm glad you came to us. See you soon."

We leave through the side doors, stepping onto Aunt Karla's private patio. Sebastian's done with his chores for the moment and is playing in the yard with some of the other kids.

Seeing us, he runs over. "Whatcha doing?"

"Running an errand," Aunt Karla answers, continuing her stride toward the stables. With her ankle injury now many weeks old, she doesn't even limp.

"For what?"

I make the quiet motion Rey and Kimba taught us.

His eyes go wide. "Is this about . . . " He tilts his head toward the lodge. "You know."

I do the quiet motion again, this time bugging my eyes toward him for effect.

He nods. "Can I come?"

I shake my head as Aunt Karla says, "Not this time. You go on into the apartment and keep your mom company."

His disappointment is clear on his face. "Okay. But are you sure you should walk that far? What about your ankle?"

"We're riding."

His eyes go wide. "Oh . . . okay. Want me to help you saddle?"

We finally convince Sebastian we're okay on our own and he should go stay with Mom. Aunt Karla puts me to work brushing Boot and a horse named Jasmine, Aunt Karla's favorite, while she gets the rest of the tack together. We're to the point of being ready to put the saddles on when Brooke shows up.

"Need a hand?" she asks.

"Thanks," my aunt says. "If you could put the saddle on Jasmine, I'll get her cinched. Then we'll do Boot."

"Going for a ride?"

"Yeah. Seems like a good day for it. First time I've been out since my fall."

We ride out at a leisurely pace, with Jasmine leading and Boot on her tail.

Once we turn the corner and are no longer in view of the stables and lodge, Aunt Karla twists in her saddle. "Can you trot?"

I give a shaky nod.
"All right then."

Chapter 35

Fergus Peak Lodge
Tuesday, August 4, Late Morning

Sadie

We slow the horses before reaching the checkpoint barricade, continuing with our ruse of being out for a ride. The men are surprised to see Aunt Karla and comment on how good it is that she's getting out again. She even tells them how she's feeling right at home in the saddle and is ready to add some speed.

With that, we again take off on a trot. I had no idea my aunt was so smooth.

When we reach the top of the long hill, Aunt Karla slows us to a walk. "Kick Boot to bring him alongside me. We'll go in casual."

The stubborn horse requires some serious coaxing to convince him to move from his usual trail spot.

"Good." Aunt Karla smiles. "You're really doing well with him. He can be stubborn. Here's the plan. We continue with our ruse of being out for a ride, but we stop to visit with Jack—something I used to do often before I fell and he started coming to me."

"Why?" I ask.

"Why'd I visit?" She lifts a shoulder as I answer with a nod. "Mostly so I could continue to be a nosy old broad." She snorts out a laugh. "I guess you know Jack's in charge of things, but . . . " She tilts her head.

"But he wants your opinion."

"We need a leader. Jack's the right person to do it—contrary to what Randy Loomer may think—but he looks to others for help. Me, Chuck, Daniela too. There're a few others."

"What's with those two?"

"Chuck and Daniela?"

"Yeah."

"They're something, aren't they? Acting like they can't stand each other but then getting all googly eyed. It's only a matter of time until they realize what the rest of us can already see."

We ride in silence a few moments before I ask the question I've been wondering. "How can you even stand him?"

She looks to me with a question covering her face. "Stand who?"

"Jack Mosher," I spit out his name.

She furrows her brow before her features smooth and she releases a slight *oh* sound. "Because of your mom? And their baby?"

"He cheated on her. He didn't want their baby. And now, with the way he is . . . we shouldn't trust him."

Her mouth becomes a straight line. "You know he came to me last summer, after his mom died, right?"

I lift a shoulder. "He told you about it, yes."

"He didn't just tell me, he . . . he cried. He was broken. He wasn't a Christian back when he was with your mom—she wasn't either, though I had no idea. Quite the actress she was."

I give my aunt a small smile. Mom fooled everyone. All my life I'd gone to church with her, prayed and read the Bible with her. I had no idea she was living a lie and had never truly followed Christ. She knew the words to say and the things to do, but deep down, she didn't believe.

Last year, when Uncle Wes was killed and we found Grandma and Grandpa murdered, Mom stopped pretending and lashed out at God. It wasn't until recently she had a true conversion.

"Anyway," Aunt Karla continues, "Jack was only home for the summer. He was in college at the University of Montana–Missoula. He met Ledger Hyde at college. Did you know that? They were on the rodeo team together. Ledger moved here because of their friendship."

I shake my head. "That whole thing, it doesn't make much sense."

"It makes a lot more sense to me now than it did before. You've filled in some missing pieces by sharing Randy's plans. I can see now how Randy set it all up, framed Ledger to get him out of the way. Randy always had a thing for Patti, Ledger's wife. She wouldn't give him the time of day. She was so head over heels for her husband. But Randy was always making a nuisance of himself. Makes sense he went after Samantha. She resembles Patti some. Jack . . . "

She shakes her head. "He's been under a lot of stress. He never should've believed Randy as far as Ledger was concerned."

"Why did he?"

Her pause is so long I think she didn't hear my question. Before I can ask again, she lets out a sigh. "I don't know. Not exactly. Ledger was mad about the gun rules. We didn't have the restrictions at first, that wasn't until after Daniela joined us. When Jack saw how distressed she'd get over the firearms, how she became so vocal about them, that's when he said only those trained and part of the protection squad could carry a gun in open sight."

"In open sight?"

She gives a knowing look. "Daniela and a few others, they get upset seeing the guns. It makes sense with what happened to them. Daniela was a complete basket case when Jack found her. She's told me she was comfortable with firearms before, even had a rifle and knew how to use it. I guess she has some kind of PTSD or something now. Jack tried to be understanding of her situation."

"I didn't know about all of that."

"But anyway, back to your original question about Jack. When he came to me last summer, he was broken. He'd accepted Christ a year or two after college, that was Ledger's doing. He found God and couldn't stop talking about Him. I think Jack went to church with him just to shut him up!" She cackles out a laugh.

"But it worked. Jack became a Christian, and soon his entire family followed suit. After Jack's mom died, I think he realized your mom could be dead and he never got a chance to make things right with her. So he came to me, hat in hand and tears staining his face. I can forgive him because he didn't know any better."

"Didn't know any better?" I scoff. "He knew—he had to know."

"Jack was of the world then. He followed the desires of his flesh and thought a baby would ruin his life."

"But— " I catch myself before I blurt out my next sentence.

"But what, dear? You think I should judge Jack on things he didn't know then? Things he didn't understand?"

"Lots of people aren't Christian but still know, still understand . . . " I lift a hand as I struggle for the words I want to use. Words that'll say what I'm thinking without telling Aunt Karla that even I, a brand-new Christian, understand what happened between my mom and Jack was wrong. How could he not?

"There he is." She lifts a rein in the direction of one of the pastures.

Jack and several other men are on horses, doing something with a herd of cattle.

"Let's head that way." When we reach the fence line, Aunt Karla calls out to him.

I swallow hard, still not wanting to see the man. Aunt Karla may say he's changed, but I don't believe it. Not with the way he was the day of Mom and Donnie's wedding, and not with how he's been since Donnie died—never coming around to make sure things are okay and not even joining the church services.

Jack gives a look of surprise followed by a smile. Then he turns to another man before trotting over to us.

"Hey, Karla. Glad to see you back in the saddle."

"It feels good. I almost waited too long, though. Walking may be difficult after this ride."

"Ain't that the way it goes?"

"I need to talk with you. Can you take a minute?"

He glances back to the men. "Yeah, they'll take care of things. You want to go to the house?"

"Let's ride."

He tips his hat back slightly and runs his hand across his sweaty forehead. "Meet me at the gate."

Once Jack is on the same side of the fence as us, we head overland, picking our way slowly across an unfenced area.

"What's going on?" Jack asks once we're well away from anyone else.

"Sadie? Tell Jack what you know."

I clear my throat before beginning my story. I give the facts, not embellishing with what I think about it all. And not once do I look directly at him. I keep tabs out of the corner of my eye, watching as his calm expression changes. He begins to work his jaw, clenching and unclenching. He's mostly quiet, only asking the occasional question for clarification or making noises to urge me on.

I finish with, "That's what I know."

"How sure are you of this?" Jack asks.

"I know what Cassie said. It was an invitation for Brooke and me. Have you heard about the babies? About Samantha being mad that Cassie is pregnant too?"

"Rumors travel fast around here," Jack says. "There was scuttlebutt about it last night. Randy came to me as soon as the gossip started. His story is different. He and Samantha were already over when he started dating Cassie. He broke up with her and she was basically stalking him. She showed up at his place one day, and they . . . " He tilts his head.

"Anyway, he says he feels terrible about it and will help Samantha with the baby, but he's going to marry Cassie. He wants to move to the lodge and follow the plan we had for Donnie there."

"No." Aunt Karla's voice is harsh. "That man is not living at my lodge. Cassie can move to his place, but . . . no. Just no. And for what it's worth, I'd believe Cassie over him any day. My guess is she jumped the gun on her invite for Brooke and Sadie. And poor Hayley . . . " She shakes her head.

"Let's head back to your place. I want to talk to Hayley and Samantha. Brooke too."

"How will you keep it quiet?" I ask. "If Cassie sees you there, talking to everyone, she'll tell Randy."

"Yup. I suppose that's true. Maybe we'll need to lock her in her room until I can sort this out."

My eyes dart to him, checking to see if he's kidding. From his determined look, he's not.

We talk little as we ride back to the lodge. Once there, Brooke, who was working in the gardens, comes over to help us unsaddle. "Hey, Jack. I didn't know they were meeting up with you to ride."

"Yup. When I saw Karla back on her horse, I couldn't resist."

"You staying awhile? Or do you want to leave Silver saddled?"

"Leave him saddled."

I start to unsaddle Boot as Jack helps Aunt Karla off her horse. Brooke wastes little time working on Aunt Karla's horse. As she works, Jack says, "I wanted to ask you something."

Brooke keeps at what she's doing, until Jacks says, "Brooke?"

"Oh, me? Sorry, I thought you were talking to Karla."

Jack relays his questions, pretty much repeating everything I told him and looking for confirmation. She keeps looking nervously toward the lodge and occasionally at me while he talks.

"Did Sadie tell you this?"

"She did. Is your recollection of the conversation similar?"

She kicks a clod of dirt . . . or something. "That's pretty much how it went. But Cassie, you know how she is, all dramatic about everything."

"So you think it was just her . . . what? Imagination?"

She lifts a shoulder. "Randy can't really think he could— " She makes a face. "I mean, he isn't a great catch or anything."

"Well, he must be somewhat. Both Cassie and Samantha were— " Jack clears his throat " —dating him."

She makes another face. "I don't understand it. You should ask Randy."

"I thought I'd see what you know, talk to Samantha and a few others, then go find him."

"Won't take much to find him. He's in Cassie's room right now."

Aunt Karla's face goes pale. "In her room? She knows the rules."

I start to ask what it matters now—Cassie's already pregnant— when Brooke says, "It sets a bad example for the younger girls. Hayley was asking me about him going in there."

"Where is Hayley?" Jack asks.

"Aren't you going to go talk to Randy now?" Aunt Karla crosses her arms.

"Let me talk with Hayley. We know where Randy is, so . . . " He lifts his hands, palms up.

"I'll take you to her," Brooke says.

Aunt Karla cocks her head at Brooke. "Please do, dear. I'm going to check on Leanne. Sadie, walk with me?"

I look to Jack, making sure he's finished with me.

He dips his chin slightly. "I'll be there shortly, Karla."

Aunt Karla's first few steps are cautious. "Ugh. I was right about hurting tomorrow. Let's plan on doing this regularly. You're a great riding partner."

I smile at her comment. "Maybe Mom can ride too? It wouldn't be too much exertion."

"We'll talk with Daniela and Chuck about it."

Mom's face is a question mark when we enter the apartment.

"Do you have any sixes," Sebastian asks. When she ignores his question, he persists, "Mom, I'm looking for sixes." He motions to the cards in her hand.

"Oh, sorry, go fish," she says. "Um, let's pause this game a minute so I can talk with your aunt and sister."

"'Kay." He puts his cards face down on the coffee table and leans back in his chair.

I give my brother a look. "You should go outside and play."
"Says who?" He crosses his arms over his chest. "What's going on? I couldn't go riding with you, and now—" His eyes go wide. "*Oh* . . . is this about Hayley?"

Chapter 36

Fergus Peak Lodge
Tuesday, August 4, Late Morning

Sadie

"I doubt it'll matter much if your brother stays," Aunt Karla says. "Like Jack said, the grapevine travels fast around here."

Sebastian gives me a cheeky look.

I point my finger at him and open my mouth when a yell comes from outside.

"What's that?" Sebastian's eyes go wide.

Aunt Karla steps to the still ajar patio door and shakes her head. "I'll take care of this."

"Stay inside." Mom orders as she rises from the couch. "Watch your brother."

I grab Mom's hand. "Are you sure you should go?"

She gives me a nod and darts out the door, moving quicker than she has since the fire.

As soon as the door closes, my eyes meet my brother's. Without speaking, we run to the front-facing window.

"Is it Jack?"

I nod as I watch what I can only describe as a wrestling match. Jack's on top, and then suddenly he isn't. "And Randy."

"Wow. Randy did a good move. You think they're fighting about— "

His words are interrupted when Cassie runs into view, yelling and screaming. She distracts Randy, allowing Jack to toss him off.

Jack scurries to his feet and hollers, "Stop!"

"Randy!" a female voice yells. "You're making things worse."

"Who was that?" Sebastian asks.

I scan the area, finally seeing Samantha along the edge.

"You shut up!" Cassie yells.

"Make me." Samantha flips a hand in the other woman's direction.

Letting out a growl, Cassie runs toward Samantha and hits her hard enough to send her flying.

With Jack's attention now diverted to the new conflict, Randy whips out his pistol and shoots. I let out a yelp as the impact of the bullet sends Jack spinning. He lands on his stomach.

Randy fires again, this time into the air. There're screams and complete chaos as those gathered around scurry away.

"Get down." I yank on my brother's arm as I hit the floor.

"Enough!" Randy yells. "I've had it with all of you. Cassie, get off Samantha. And you'd better hope you didn't harm her or our child. I've told you over and over, the two of you are a team. You've been chosen to be part of something special."

The screaming has stopped and is replaced with weeping.

I motion for Sebastian to stay put as I cautiously look out the window.

"Y–you shot Jack." Cassie points at the prone body on the ground.

"We talked about this and how it might be necessary." Randy points at her with the muzzle of the gun.

Cassie flinches before dropping her gaze. She gives a slight nod before muttering something I can't make out.

"Now then," Randy says. "Help Samantha up. You shouldn't be treating your sister like that."

Cassie reaches for Samantha, who yanks her arm away. "She's not my sister. This whole crazy thing—I'm not going to be a part of it."

My eyes dart back to Jack. How bad was he hit? There's no way to tell from here. I scour the area, looking for my mom and aunt.

"We need to help him," Sebastian says, now crouching at the side of the window.

"Not while Randy has a gun."

"He'll . . . he'll die."

"Randy Loomer!" a voice calls out. "You get on out of here."

I swivel my head, looking for the source.

Daniela Reynolds. She's leaning against the side of the house, partially concealed, a long gun in her hand.

"Well, well." Randy smirks. "If it isn't Miss High and Mighty. Thought you were anti-gun? Betcha don't even know how to use the thing."

"Try me."

"Aren't you something special? I've bested real men, so I don't find a busybody like you to be much of a threat. By the way, where's your handler? She hiding out in her apartment? Letting you be her bulldog?"

In a low voice, Sebastian says, "You should get Aunt Karla's gun."

I let out the breath I've been holding. "I don't know where she keeps any of them."

"Get the one out of her purse."

My eyes dart to him. "You know about that?"

"Go get it."

I search the yard again. *Where are they?* "We're too far away to use a handgun."

"Why are you doing this, Randy?" Daniela asks.

"We're starting a new world. Cassie, it's time for the next part of our plan."

"Are you . . . are you sure, Randy?" Cassie's voice is tight. "I think . . . this isn't what we talked about."

His head spins toward her. "This is *exactly* what we talked about. Eliminate any threats in our way. We took care of Hyde and Nelson. And now Mosher's there, bleeding all over the ground. Won't be long for him. Next we'll get rid of Miss High and Mighty."

Daniela makes an audible gasp.

I don't know if Randy hears Daniela, but his gaze drifts back to her. He smiles in a disgusting way before adding, "Then the old broad and a few others we don't need. Although, I might let the widow live. Thought the fire would take care of her along with that Donnie character."

My hand goes to my mouth.

"Is he talking about Mom?" Sebastian's voice is tight and squeaky.

I shake my head and put a finger to my lips. "Stay back so he doesn't see us."

"You!" Daniela shouts. "You started the fire? You could have . . . you could have killed us all!"

"Oh, calm down. Jeez. You're always so melodramatic about everything. What? Did you think it was an act of God? Or maybe you thought it was Jack? Yeah, I got a good laugh out of that. Cassie told me how the rumors were flying. Jack just happened to be out walking. There's plenty who thought he was the one responsible. Definitely worked in my favor. But nope. It wasn't your precious Jack."

Randy sticks out his chest. "It was me. Donnie was trouble. I knew from the first day I laid eyes on him that he'd mess up my plans. He had to die."

Cassie looks at Randy with adoration. "You did what you had to do, honey."

Samantha looks sick. "Wait—what? You killed people? And you started the fire?"

He scratches his chin with the hand holding the gun, causing it to bob around. "You really aren't very bright, are you?"

Samantha cowers at his words.

"You didn't catch on the day Mosher and I showed up here? The day you were my alibi for Gray Nelson's death?"

She shakes her head. "I never thought . . . I figured you were just . . . why, Randy? Why'd you kill them?"

Randy groans.

"Because it was the only way." Cassie's voice is light, almost cheerful. "He had to eliminate the competition. The rest are too weak willed to be a problem, to stand up to Randy and his brilliant plans. Most of them anyway." She shoots Loomer a smile. "There's a few others that'll— "

"Enough, honey. No need to spoil all the surprises."

"You two— " Samantha wildly shakes her head. "You're both nuts. I don't want any part of this."

"Me neither!" another girl—woman, really, since she's around the same age as Cassie and Samantha—yells out from where she's cowering on the far side of the lawn.

Several other voices, some I recognize and others I don't, yell out similar things, declaring they want no part of the sister wives plan. *So much for secrets.*

Aunt Karla and Jack were right about the rumor mill. Or . . . did Cassie go to others? Not just Brooke and me? Maybe she and Randy have been drumming up support, talking to women to convince them of their crazy idea.

And what about Hayley? The way Sebastian put it, Randy talked with her directly. Are others already pregnant? Not just Cassie and Samantha?

"Randy, whatever you were planning, it doesn't seem to have the support you thought." Aunt Karla's words carry across the yard.

He spins in the direction of her voice and wildly fires.

Sebastian lets out a yelp. "Did he hit her?"

I bite my lip while shaking my head.

"Sadie?"

"I don't see her. I don't know where she is. Or Mom."

In an instant, everything turns to chaos. Samantha launches herself at Randy. He yells and then shoots, which sets off a cascade of firing from several weapons along with more screaming.

How many guns are in this supposedly gun-free zone? I guess Aunt Karla was right about people keeping them out of sight.

"Down!" I grab Sebastian's arm. We put our hands over our heads. As quickly as it started, the shooting stops.

"Wh-what just happened?" Sebastian tremors next to me as someone outside cries out.

I shake my head. "Just wait. We need to wait."

It feels like forever before someone yells, "I need some help here!"

Sebastian looks at me with wide green eyes. "Was that Aunt Karla?"

"Stay here. I'm going to look."

He shakes his head and darts up. "Me too."

"Sebastian!" I hiss. "Stay out of the window."

"It's Aunt Karla," he says as I'm getting to my feet. "Mom too."

"They're okay." I blink rapidly to clear my vision.

Mom's kneeling by Jack while Aunt Karla is next to Cassie. Samantha is sitting nearby, cradling her arm, blood dripping from it.

"Stay here," I order my brother. "I'm going to help."

"Me too."

"No! Stay. Here. I'll call you if we need you."

He drops his shoulders and dips his head. "Fine."

I slide out the patio door, cautiously making my way to the edge of the building—the same location Daniela was at when she was using the lodge not only as cover but also as a gun rest. She's gone from the spot, but the rifle is laying on the ground. The odor of gunpowder wafts through the air.

I glance to the lawn. Daniela's by Samantha's side. Others from the lodge are coming out from hiding. Daniela yells for Brooke to go for Chuck and anyone else who can help with the injured. Someone hollers they've been hurt.

"Sadie!" Aunt Karla yells. "Grab the first aid kit in the dining hall."

I run to do her bidding and find several people crouched in the dining room. I'm bombarded with questions about what's happening and if it's over. I motion to the windows. "People are hurt!"

"Is he dead?" Hayley, the girl Sebastian said was approached by Loomer, asks.

"I don't know. I don't know anything. I need the first aid kit."

"I hope he is. He's . . . he wants bad things."

Our eyes meet. "Loomer?"

Her face crumbles. "I don't want to be a sister wife."

"He's already . . . ?" My stomach turns sour.

Hayley looks at her toes. "When you started teaching us how to fight back, I decided I was going to do it. I'd hit him and get away next time he . . . anyway, it's better if he can't hurt us."

"Here." One of the women thrusts a bag of first aid supplies at me. "I'll go with you. I can help."

When we reach the injured, it's clear to see Randy won't be bothering Hayley or anyone else. There's a puddle of blood surrounding him and a knife in his chest.

"Open the bag," Daniela demands, now by Cassie's side while Aunt Karla has moved to Samantha. She starts barking out orders of what she needs.

"Karla, how's Samantha?" she asks.

"Needs a better bandage."

"Go," Daniela orders me. "Then take the bag to your mom so I can tell her what to do for Jack."

"Is he— " I glance to my mom.

"He's alive," she mouths.

After getting Aunt Karla what she needs, I go to my mom's side. Daniela's instructions are little more than to stop the blood leaking from Jack's shoulder. "I'll get to him as soon as Cassie is stable," she says.

A few more people, all with minor injuries from falling when they tried to escape the carnage, are brought to what's now the treatment area. It's a crazy time that seems to drag on forever. Eventually, Chuck Rice and several others from the community show up.

When Chuck takes over for Mom, she motions for me to help her stand.

"Are you okay?" I ask once we're upright.

She shakes her head. "Trouble breathing. Help me to the room?"

I glance back at Randy's body. "What all happened here? There was so much shooting."

"What *did* happen here?" Chuck asks. "Brooke told me about Randy shooting Jack, but then she went into hiding. Heard the screaming and then some shooting, but only saw the aftereffects before going for help. Looks like quite the bloodbath."

"He wanted to make us all sister wives," Hayley says. "Well, most of us anyway. He said he was going to kill Karla, Daniela, and some others. But the rest of us . . . " Her entire body shudders. "Samantha attacked him. See her knife?"

"He fired his gun," Samantha says. "When I stuck him, he shot me, but then it . . . somehow the bullet also hit Cassie. She'll be okay, right?"

Daniela gives her a slight smile. "The bullet went through her side. I don't think it hit anything vital, but . . . Chuck will look at her when he can."

"Looks like the knife isn't Loomer's only problem." Chuck gestures his head toward the dead man.

"Karla shot him. And, uh, me too." Daniela's voice is quiet.

Chuck makes a chuffing sound. "That's my girl. I knew you had some serious fight in you."

She shoots him a dirty look. "I still hate those things. And I'm not a *girl*."

Chuck points to two of the men who arrived with him. "Go get the stretcher board. We're taking Jack inside. He's lost a lot of blood, but the wound looks clean. I think he just might make it." He turns back to Daniela and gives her a wink. "Notice you didn't say you weren't *my* girl."

Chapter 37

Along the Sun River
West of Great Falls, Montana
Wednesday, August 5, Evening

Victoria

On Monday morning, with the pillowcase of roots tied to Patti's backpack bouncing along with each step, we set off on the final leg of our journey. The first day we traveled only from the aid station at the stables to a beautiful, treed park with a view of the confluence of the Missouri River and Sun River.

Another aid station was set up for camping, but it wasn't nearly as elaborate. No food or other services, but we did learn things are still volatile in parts of town.

The next day, we made our way to the north side of the Sun River. Jennifer was right, traveling along the river is a challenge.

It's not flat enough to push the babies in the stroller, so they're in the fabric carriers. Trish is tied to the front of Patti—which makes it easy to nurse her while walking—with LJ sometimes walking, sometimes riding on someone's shoulders, and sometimes in a carrier strapped to someone's chest.

We still drag the stroller and wagon along to carry extra goods, but it's certainly awkward. What we didn't expect, though, was a path to be etched out because of so many people traveling along the river, making it somewhat free of heavy brush.

Last night, we found a field where several others were camping. We caught a few fish for dinner but haven't seen any large game to add to our stores. This close to the ranch, we're okay on food, so we aren't worrying much.

When we left the camping field this morning, another family of four hiked with us. They stopped a couple of miles back when their young children had enough for the day, while we continued on.

When we decide it's time to stop, we realize continuing wasn't terribly smart. Where the family stopped was a nice, open camping area. We're in thick brush. After using my axes and knives to clear it out a bit, we're still forced to space our tents out in little open spots instead of keeping them together as we prefer.

I'm wearing both axes again, one on each hip. Although everyone has cautioned me not to throw it because my arm is much too weak, it feels good to have it back in place. Before Nate's death, he was wearing this ax as we walked each day.

As I put it in place this morning, all those sad memories came rushing back. Sniffing away the tears, I realized I was also remembering some of the happy times with Nate. How he was so helpful to me after my arm was broken. His kind smiles. The way he'd poke fun at his sisters but was also fiercely protective of them.

Remembering Nate also reminded me of Asher. The Hoffmann and Dosen families have lost so much.

I also realized losing my husband of so many years wasn't nearly as traumatic and lingering as Asher's and Nate's deaths. Jon died, I was sad, but also . . . I squeeze my eyes tight and will the feelings away.

I don't even like to admit this to myself, but the truth is, I was relieved when he died. What a horrible person I am! To feel relief at the death of my husband, my children's father, what kind of woman does that make me?

"I hate this closed-in feeling and not being next to the others," Jennifer says as we finish setting up our tent. "We can't even see them!"

Since there are plenty of branches and limbs along the river, we're using my sons' broken tent. Good thing, since the bug population is terrible.

Patti's tent is in the largest clearing, about twenty feet from us, and the little tent the Hoffmann girls are using is a few feet beyond that. Rey and Kimba set up the smaller of the tarps too. The boys are setting up the large tarp near Patti's tent.

Because of the increased bear activity, we're using a separate clearing upriver for cooking and to store our bags and food. Even though I thought having a separate cooking and storage area seemed a little excessive, as we're cleaning up from supper, Jennifer says it's better to be safe than sorry.

"Especially since we're seeing bear signs," Atticus adds.

"Black bear, right?" Axel asks.

"Right. Still, it's smart."

A shudder runs through me as I look over my shoulder. The feeling of being watched is heavy in this wooded stretch along the river. More than once today, someone has commented on it.

At first, we assumed it's people on the other side of the river or staying out of sight in the trees. But with seeing the bear signs, it's possible bears are watching us without us seeing them. To avoid surprising a bear, we've been talking and not trying to walk quietly. Surprising a bear, especially a sow with cubs, whether black or grizzly, could be deadly.

Because of the creepy feelings, we're even having three guards on overnight watch. Jennifer and I are on the last shift—starting at four o'clock and going until six—along with Nicole. Atticus, Axel, and Rey are on first watch, with Kimba and my sons on the second.

"I thought I'd read from Ephesians 4 tonight." Atticus opens his Bible. He reads about maturing and growing in Christ when we speak the truth in love.

I bite my top lip. Some of what he reads seems directed at me, especially when he reads about being separated from the life of God because of the hardening of the heart.

Rey surprises me when he says, "You know Chaplain Rick from the ski lodge did a sermon on the difference between being nice and being good. He said many believe Christians are called to be nice."

He looks around at our gathered group. "I thought so too. If I wasn't nice to people, I wasn't a good Christian. But after talking with Chaplain Rick, asking questions on what he meant, I realized I'd been nice in ways that weren't okay."

"Meaning?" Jameson asks.

"Christ calls us to be good, not nice. He, as Atticus just read, wants us to speak the truth in love, not just go along. Nice people smile and go along, they don't confront evil. Biblically good people stand up in the face of evil. They call it out. Nice people are weak. Good people are strong."

"That's right." Atticus nods. "Jesus was kind. He was compassionate and caring. He was *good*. But He wasn't nice, not the way we think of nice today. Instead of simply pasting a smile on His face, He stood up for what was *right*. He was here to do the business of the Father, to stand for the truth. It cost him His life."

I feel my forehead wrinkle. Even though those verses are what Atticus was reading, it wasn't what stuck with me. What stuck with me was my heart, the hardening of it, will keep me from going to Heaven. And I realize that isn't what I want. How amazing that the same passage can speak to each of us differently.

Could there be something to this part, too, as far as I'm concerned? Does not deeply grieving the loss of Jon, who had done such evil things, make be terrible? Or is the fact I never stood up and spoke out against his evil the real problem?

Am I guilty of being nice? Of playing along while he schemed and plotted? And not just for the takeover of the ski lodge, even before. In the years leading up to the attacks on our country, he'd done some rotten things—things I knew I should speak out against.

Not just in the way he treated his sons and me, but in the conniving deals he put together, underhanded for sure and sometimes even illegal. He was a successful attorney, but some of his success, some of the deals he helped arrange, were built on lies.

I stood by him, even knowing what he was doing. I was the devoted wife. *Nice*. Always smiling, never arguing, never disagreeing. And not just because I was afraid of what might happen if I did, but because I liked the life we had. I liked the money, the comfort.

It was easy to look the other way to preserve our way of life.

After all, I reasoned, it was for the boys. To give them the best of everything. To make their life easy. They'd never know what it was like to be poor and go without.

And now here we are. Living out of our backpacks. Fishing, hunting, foraging, or scrounging for our next meal. Trading for things we need to survive. Stealing.

I never imagined we'd live in a world where money meant nothing. Even those who planned ahead and had gold or silver don't find it terribly useful. Sure, when we traded in Lewistown, one guy took the jewelry we found at houses along the way, but it was worth little, not even close to the value of ammunition or food.

Being nice isn't what Christ commands. Being good is. Standing up against evil. Against wrong. Learning to love like Christ, being kind and compassionate but also unflinching when standing for the truth.

That's the person I want to be. The only way to be that person is to completely accept God and His Son, Jesus Christ.

A sob escapes from Kimba. "I don't . . . I've been so angry, so mad at God for taking Nate from me. I feel so . . . lost."

Rey wraps an arm around his wife and pulls her close as their daughters scurry to their side. The four of them huddle together. Soon, through his tears, Rey calls out to God and asks—*begs*—for forgiveness, pleading with God to help them, to carry them through their grief.

With tears streaming, I feel my own need to call out to Christ. A need for Him to be in my life. To be Lord of my life. Even when attending church in the past, I'd never felt the urge before.

Seeing and experiencing Jesus as part of my life has changed things—watching as Jennifer dealt with Asher's death with such dignity because she knew it wasn't really the end, that she'll be with him and her husband again. When she was so awful to Patti, I wondered if it was all fake, if the things she said about treating others as she wished to be treated was a lie.

But as Jennifer went to God for help with her prejudice, and publicly asked for not only Patti's forgiveness but all of ours, I witnessed something amazing: a transformation that could only come from God and His love.

Kimba and Rey, as newer Christians, have had a more difficult time with losing Nate. While they tried to use the right words, saying how Nate was with Jesus, they pulled away from God.

I'm not even sure they realized they were doing it at the time, but Atticus did. And God used him, letting the young man step up to become a leader in our group, to bring the Hoffmann family back to Christ.

To bring me to Christ.

After the Hoffmanns release each other, Atticus asks Rey if he'll lead us in prayer.

I clear my throat. "Before that, I, uh . . . " I shake my head as my tears continue to roll. "Something's different for me." My hands go to my chest as I struggle to find words.

Jameson's damp eyes are wide. "Did you just ask Jesus into your heart? Because . . . because I want to. I'm just . . . what do I do?"

"I don't know," I say with a tear-filled laugh. "I didn't do anything special, but I think that's what I did or want to do." I turn to Jennifer, the one who's followed Christ the longest out of our group. "Is there something special we need to do?"

She reaches for my hand and then motions for Jameson to come to her also. After he kneels next to her, his hand in her other, she says, "There's no magical formula. The Bible says if we confess with our mouth and believe in our heart that God raised Jesus from the dead, we'll be saved."

"I believe." Jameson rapidly bobs his head. "I never really knew about that before. I mean, I did from Sunday School. But I never thought about how it applied to me. I thought it just sort of . . . happened. I knew Jesus was, uh, crucified. I thought it was just history, but now I think maybe it wasn't. I think He did it for me. He died so I can go to Heaven."

His watery eyes meet mine. I answer with a smile and a nod.

He smiles back before continuing with, "Asher tried to tell me about it, about how if I was the only person on earth, Jesus would still have gone to the cross just for me. Asher believed it. Nate too. Even though Nate was young, he loved Jesus. He didn't say much about it, but it was obvious. How he went out of his way to help all of us. The way he kept us fed and how he helped my mom when she was so hurt." He drops his head and whispers, "I was kind of mad at first."

I wrinkle my forehead. "Really? Why?"

"Because . . . because he was being a better son to you than I'd ever been. And he had his own mom. Why be so good, so helpful to you? I confronted him about it and told him to knock it off. He apologized for upsetting me but said he felt God was commanding him to help. By doing this, he wasn't trying to make less of my role as the son, but to be obedient and let Jesus shine through him. I thought it was a bunch of hooey."

He lifts his head to meet my gaze. "I thought he was just trying to look good, to make me look like less. But now I realize . . . "

Jameson's eyes travel to Kimba and Rey. "Nate was just good. He was exactly how Christ wanted. He wanted to show Jesus' love by helping my mom, by giving us food, by making himself useful. It may have been annoying to me." He lets out a small laugh. "It was annoying. But now I wish . . . I want to be more like Nate. I want what he had. I want to *be* like he was."

Kimba walks on her knees to embrace Jameson. I rest my hand on my son's back. When Kimba releases him, Rey and then Nicole take a turn.

Naomi gives him a wave and smile. "You're my brother now."

Confusion paints Jameson's face. "What's that?"

"Having Jesus in your heart makes you my brother, since He's in mine too. We're like one big family. Your mom too. She'll be my— " Naomi crinkles her nose. "My older sister?"

I let out a laugh. "Much older."

"So, is that it? Am I one of you?" Jameson asks. "Should I pray or something?"

"You can," Jennifer says. "Many people recite The Sinner's Prayer. But there aren't magic words in the prayer that give you salvation. Salvation comes through faith in Jesus alone."

"Is the prayer where I admit I'm a sinner?" Jameson asks, then mutters, "Because I am."

"We all are. It's because of this sin we need—*we want*—God's forgiveness. You already said you understand Jesus died for you so you can go to Heaven?"

Jameson gives a solemn dip of his chin. "Asher said Jesus' blood would cover me. When God looked at me, He'd only see the blood and not my sin. I didn't really understand it then, and maybe I don't completely now, but I want to be better, to *do* better. To be like Him, be more like Jesus."

"Welcome to God's family." Rey reaches for Jameson again before turning to me. "You too, Victoria."

After hugs all around, Jennifer says, "This is an answer to prayer. Atticus, can you read Psalm 51? I think it'd be wonderful to hear right now."

Atticus takes a minute to flip through his Bible before clearing his throat. His voice is low, deep. "Have mercy on me, O God, according to Your unfailing love; according to Your great compassion blot out my transgressions. Wash away all my iniquity and cleanse me from my sin. For I know my transgressions, and my sin is always before me."

I close my eyes as the words wash over me. *Have mercy on me, O God. I don't deserve it, but I want it. I need it.*

"Yes, Lord," Jennifer says quietly.

"Create in me a pure heart, O God, and renew a steadfast spirit within me," Atticus continues. "Do not cast me from Your presence or take Your Holy Spirit from me. Restore to me the joy of Your salvation and grant me a willing spirit, to sustain me."

Once the reading is finished, Patti quietly sings a perfect tune that reiterates parts of the verses Atticus read. As the others join in, I'm again floating on the words. When the song is over, there's more hugging and joyful tears.

Brett embraces me and then his younger brother. "It really is an answer to prayer. This is a new life for us, for *all* of us. And it can be our best life if we put God in the center of it."

Chapter 38

Along the Sun River
West of Great Falls, Montana
Wednesday, August 5, Night

Victoria

"Did you say something?" Jennifer pokes me in the arm.

"Huh?" I ask, rousing from my near sleep.

"I thought you said something."

"Oh, uh, sorry. I might have been talking in my sleep. With the nightmares . . ."

"Were you having a nightmare?"

I shake my head, then realize she can't see me in the dark. "I don't even know if I was asleep. I don't think so."

"Hmm. Maybe it was one of the guys on patrol."

"Mm-hmm. May have been." I turn over and reach my hand above my head, feeling for my ax. I usually leave them in my backpack at night, but since we stored the packs where we were cooking and away from our tents, I decided to bring the axes in with me.

The creepy feeling of being watched during the day left me on edge. Now they rest in their sheaths within reach. Jennifer's revolver, which is always kept with her, is in the same general area. My pinky brushes against the handgun's leather holster as I search for the second ax.

Closing my eyes, I let out a long breath. I can't help but smile as I think about what happened earlier—the revival we experienced, Jameson and me joining Brett in walking with Jesus.

Sleep begins to take me when a slight chuffing noise pops my eyes open. That didn't sound like someone on patrol. That sounded . . . beastly.

Sitting up, I grab my glasses out of the storage pocket. I lean forward to look out the mesh window. A loud ripping sound comes from Jennifer's side of the tent, unsheathing it in one smooth move as the nylon peels away.

"What?" Jennifer gasps.

The next thing I know, she's sliding away. Her high-pitched, frightened screams shatter the night as her arms flail.

I grab her with my free hand and catch her elbow. The other hand is grasping my ax and comes down smoothly and solidly, connecting with the animal holding her.

It shakes its head, yanking the ax from my hand and sending slobber in all directions as Jennifer screams again. The creature lets out a roar and gives a yank.

My grip on Jennifer is weak.

She shoots out of my grasp.

My hand lands on her revolver. I unholster it and scoot to the gaping hole in the tent, my eyes following Jennifer's screams. A giant bear has her head in its mouth. Her bloodcurdling scream seems to send the animal into a frenzy.

"Play dead," I yell.

The bear lifts its head, it's eyes boring into me. It lets out a grunt.

I lift the handgun and aim. I squeeze the trigger, jumping when it goes off. The bear drops its head.

"Shoot it again!" Jennifer cries.

A terrible crunch sounds. She screams.

I fire her gun again. Another shot—not taken by me—quickly follows, then another.

The bear gives a low growl and shakes its head. Jennifer screams. He still has ahold of her.

"Use the spray!" someone yells.

There's a hiss, and the odor of hot peppers fills the air. My eyes begin to water.

"Is it leaving?"

"It's going!"

Jennifer's soft cries are the only sounds for several beats.

I crawl the rest of the way out of the tent. "Keep watching for it," I whisper. "I'm going to help her."

"Axel, go to the other tents. Tell everyone to get in with Patti. Stay there," Rey commands. "Be ready in case he comes back and tries for someone else. Atticus, you're with me."

"Mom?" Axel asks hesitantly.

"We'll take care of her. Go. Protect the rest of our group."

Axel hesitates and takes a step toward his mom, then quickly rushes toward the other tents.

On my knees, I scoot next to Jennifer. In the light of the nearly full moon, my breath catches at what I see. Her face is a bloody mess. I swallow the lump in my throat. "Hey, we're going to take care of you. You'll be okay."

"Mmm," she mutters, then says something else too garbled for me to make out.

Rey is by my side. "We need to move her and get away from here."

"I don't . . . I don't think we should."

"No choice."

"Take my rifle." Atticus thrusts it toward me. "We'll carry her. You need to be on guard. Make sure he doesn't— " Atticus shakes his head.

I wipe at my watering eyes, stinging from the bear spray. "Your mom's gun, I left it in the tent."

"We'll come back for it."

As the men gently pick her up, Rey at Jennifer's head and Atticus at his mom's feet, I cradle the firearm, ready to defend us as needed.

We reach the clear space with Patti's tent. Axel, Kimba, Nicole, and both of my sons are outside, weapons at the ready.

"Should we take her inside?" Kimba asks.

"Build a fire. A big one," Rey says as he and Atticus gently put Jennifer on the ground.

"What . . . why'd this happen?" Axel asks, going to his mother.

"Patti, we need you." Rey's voice is low.

"I'll go in with the children," Nicole says.

Within seconds, Kimba's lighting the fire as Patti evaluates Jennifer. Axel and Atticus are both by their mom's side. I hand the rifle back to Atticus. He gives me a nod.

Patti barks out orders, telling us what to do to stop the bleeding. There's so much blood, I don't even know how Patti can determine where it's all coming from. Jennifer's completely silent, her breath barely moving her chest.

"Did she pass out?" I ask as I put pressure on Jennifer's arm, my eyes still blurry from the spray. I blink a few times to try and clear them. Atticus is working at his mom's leg while Axel is by Patti's side.

Patti answers with a nod. "Probably best." She bows her head. "Father God, lay Your hand on our dear friend. Help her through this. Help us know what to do to treat her. We pray this in Your Son's Holy Name."

"Amen," Jennifer's boys' say in unison.

I mutter my amen while lifting a shoulder to my face to wipe away the tears. The light from the now roaring fire illuminates Patti as she works.

Several hours later, with a band of light on the horizon, Patti leans back. She lets out a sigh. "I don't know what else we can do."

The arm I was holding has been bandaged. The bone above the elbow was crushed in the bear's powerful jaws, same with her ankle. Patti put together a mixture of the dried comfrey combined with fresh yarrow she picked yesterday, making it into a paste and putting over Jennifer's wounds.

"Maybe now, with the bleeding stopped, you should stitch her up?" Axel asks.

"I don't know. I think we need to leave them to drain . . . maybe. This is beyond anything I know."

I look at Jennifer's face. Her jaw's hanging loose, broken by the grizzly bear. She has bite marks across her forehead. The amount of damage done in the short time he had her is unbelievable. Him attacking at all is hard to understand.

As soon as it's full light, Rey, Atticus, and Brett plan to look for blood to see if they can track him. I think it's best just to let him go, but Rey says we're in danger unless we know he's no longer a threat.

"We need to get going," Patti says. "Get her some help."

"We're not far from Vaughn," Atticus says.

"How far?"

"Once we get off the river, we can hit the highway. It's a couple miles to the east."

"And your home is to the west?"

"Yeah."

"I think someone should run ahead and find out if we can get help. I don't want to take Jennifer any farther than we need."

"How will we carry her?" I ask.

"We'll make a stretcher. Use a couple of branches, blankets."

"A travois?" Kimba suggests. "Maybe the tent?"

"He tore it up," I say. "I'm not sure how stable it'll be."

Rey crosses his arms. "See what you can work out while we check for the bear. Atticus, Brett, Axel, you're with me. Kimba, Nicole, Jameson, you'll stand guard here. Give us an hour, then we'll be back and ready to leave."

"There isn't enough light yet," Kimba says.

"It's close. We'll start with the flashlight."

Her mouth is a tight line as she reaches for her husband. "Be careful."

Atticus and Axel kneel by their mom, talking softly to her and telling her to rest so she can heal.

I turn to Brett.

Before I say anything, he nods. "We'll be careful." Then he wraps me in a hug.

While Nicole and Kimba start breaking down the camp, Naomi plays with Patti's young children, Jameson stands watch, and I help Patti figure out some sort of stretcher.

Jennifer is impossibly pale. The amount of blood she lost and the shock her body has been subjected to . . . she needs care beyond what we can give. I swipe at my eyes. They finally stopped stinging from the bear spray, but now they sting from the tears that keep reappearing.

What can we do to help my friend? How can she survive this?

We use two long, straight branches for the sides of the stretcher and shorter ones for the body. Everything is lashed together with twine, rope, and even duct tape.

"Should we add the tent?" I ask. "Stretch the fabric across to give more support?"

"Wouldn't hurt," Patti agrees.

Jameson and I go back to my tent. The scene in the daylight causes my stomach to churn. I squeeze my eyes tight as the memory of Jennifer's terrified screams replay in my head.

He lifts the tattered fabric of the tent. "Here's her gun. I can't believe you shot at the bear."

I lift a shoulder. "I got him with my ax, but it didn't stop him. I . . . he took it with him, I guess." I glance around, looking for my missing ax.

"You should carry it."

"Carry Jennifer's gun?" I shake my head. "I'll stick with the ax. The second one should still be in the tent." I bend over and rifle through the tent for it.

"Um, I think we should probably hurry." I glance at Jameson as he points to the ground. "The blood . . . "

My stomach churns at the large patch of brown on the ground. "We should've brought Nicole or Kimba. Two to carry the tent and bedding, one to be on watch."

He tilts his head. Not bothering to empty the tent of the bedding, Jameson begins to drag it. "Here." He extends the rifle stock toward me. "You be our guard."

My heart pounds in my ears as we move through the brush. Jameson struggles with the tent, catching and ripping it. There might not be anything left to use on the stretcher by the time we make it back.

Kimba meets us at the clearing. "You made good time. As soon as you left, I realized— "

"That we should've taken someone to watch our backs?"

The corners of her mouth drop. "Sorry. I'm not . . . it seems I don't quite think straight these days."

"I need to get dressed." I look around the space. "Did you grab our packs from the other clearing?"

"They're here." Kimba lifts her chin to a pile of supplies. "Move over near the brush. I'll stand guard while you change out of your night clothes."

Patti gives me a nod. "Good idea. I'll do the same once you're finished. Then we'll figure out how to make the best use of the tent."

I rummage through my pack, getting out my clothes for the day. Once I have them and step into the brush, I fumble with buttons and zippers. My nervous fingers aren't operating as they should. Even though I know Kimba's on the other side of the foliage, I feel exposed. Vulnerable.

When I'm finally put together, I return to watching Jennifer while Patti gets ready. The rest of our group had already changed from their nightwear to day clothes at some time since the bear attack.

Or, as in the case of my son, they slept in day clothes. I've told him many times he should change, but more often than not he'll pop up in the morning wearing everything but his belt, socks, and shoes. He was the same before our world changed, often falling into bed fully dressed. *Teenagers.*

Patti and I add the torn-up tent to the top of the stretcher. When it's done, she stands back and cocks her head. "Not the work my ancestors would've done, but I think it'll hold."

"Did we even need to add the tent?"

"Probably not, but it's on there now. Let's add her mattress pad to make it more comfortable for her."

"Use mine too. Double it up."

"All right." She nods.

With the stretcher built, we get Jennifer ready to travel. Patti dribbles water in Jennifer's mouth to keep her hydrated.

Kimba sets her husband's fully loaded backpack on the ground. "They should've been back by now."

I look to the east, trying to judge how long they've been gone by the change in the light. It's still early, maybe only an hour after sunrise. "I'm sure they'll be here any minute, just as soon as they can ensure it's safe to travel."

Kimba kneels next to Jennifer. "Any change?"

"No," Patti says. "She seems to be holding her own . . . if she can just keep at it until we can find someone who has the knowledge and medicines she needs."

"Do you think the Air Force brought things to these small towns?" I ask.

"Maybe?" Kimba shrugs. "From what we heard at the aid stations and walking through Great Falls, they've been doing a great job of caring for the area."

"I still think we need to send scouts ahead and see if they have medical personnel," Patti says. "We'll be slower pulling the travois anyway."

"I'll do it," Jameson says. "I'll go with Axel or Atticus since they know where the town is. We can jog ahead."

I quickly shake my head. As I open my mouth to voice my opposition, I suddenly stop. The year before everything fell apart, he ran cross-country and did track in school. He could do it. "Let's see what Rey thinks."

A rustle in the brush brings us all on high alert.

Chapter 39

Along the Sun River
West of Great Falls, Montana
Thursday, August 6, Early Morning

Victoria

"We didn't find him," Rey says as he steps out from the thicket. "We followed the blood trail until it crossed the river."

"He was hit?" I ask.

Atticus gives a nod. "He was bleeding pretty good. Thought he might have gone into the water and died, but we didn't see his carcass. We did find this."

He hands me my ax. It's been washed, but there's still blood where the head meets the handle. The head is also looser than it should be.

"An injured, angry bear is out there?" Kimba asks.

Rey presses his lips together. "We should assume so. Are we ready to go?"

"I want to run ahead," Jameson says in a rush. "Like Patti said, to find help for Jennifer."

"Me too," Axel says.

"Safer with three." Atticus shakes his head. "I need to help carry Mom. Brett?"

"I'll go," Nicole says. Kimba begins to protest, but Nicole shakes her head. "I'm the logical choice."

Rey lets out a sigh. "Let's figure this out. One person to pull the travois. We'll need to swap off every so often."

"Someone to manage the stroller," I say. "And another pulling the wagon. Plus, we have the babies. And we need to watch for the— "

"Yeah, definitely need to watch for the bear."

"I don't like it," Kimba says. "We should stay together and get out of this brush. Then we can wait while Axel and Jameson run ahead."

"I'm just as capable as they are." Nicole crosses her arms. "Just because I'm a girl— "

Kimba scoffs. "This has nothing to do with you being a girl. This is about all of us being safe. Staying *together*, with a savage bear on the loose, is smart. Separating isn't."

"She's right." Atticus nods. "Make lots of noise while we move, he and any other wildlife should keep their distance."

"But my mom— " Axel points to Jennifer " —she needs help now."

Rey rests a hand on Axel's shoulder. "We'll get her help. Let's get moving. Get out of the thicket and then you can run."

"But first," Kimba says, reaching for her husband's hand, "we need to pray."

After a quick prayer, we're moving through the brush, dragging a severely injured Jennifer and watching for a crazed grizzly bear.

Even with stopping several times to give Jennifer water and rotate who's pulling the travois, we make good time.

"There's the road." Atticus points ahead.

"Let's get to the clearing." Rey motions to a swampy looking spot ahead. "Then we'll stop."

A few minutes later, in a wide-open, wet area that soaks my shoes, we move to the edge of the marsh where it's dry.

I help Patti check Jennifer and give her water while Rey lays out the plan. "I'll go with Axel and Jameson."

Kimba's breath catches. "That's probably safest."

Rey turns to Atticus. "How far you think it is to the town?"

"Not far. Three or four miles."

Rey scratches his whiskered chin. "We should be back within two hours. If we're not back in three, start heading west, toward Simms."

"There's no doctor." Atticus shakes his head. "Probably not in Vaughn either, but definitely not in Simms."

"Do you know a nurse? A veterinarian? Anyone?" I ask.

"The school nurse," Axel says. "She lives somewhere around the school. And Mr. Jenkins—he's part of the volunteer fire department, an EMT. Most of the fire department has EMT training. Remember the lady in Belfry who helped Donnie when he was shot? She was an EMT. And look at Patti." He nods in her direction. "She's not even as trained as that lady was and she's doing great and is keeping my mom alive."

Patti gives him a small smile.

"Good thinking," Rey says. "Hopefully, we'll find help in Vaughn and be back in the allotted time. Let's get ready to roll. Survival items only in your packs."

As the three of them empty out their backpacks to lighten them for the speedy trip, I lean close to Patti. "What do you think?"

"She's doing much better than I'd have thought. The bleeding is under control. There isn't even much showing on the bandages. She's still out but doesn't seem to be in distress. Her jaw . . . I have no idea how to fix a broken jaw."

"Don't they wire it shut or something?"

"Yeah, but how? That's beyond emergency training."

"You ready?" Rey asks Jameson and Axel.

I make my way to my feet and shuffle over to my young son. "Be careful." I open my arms to embrace him.

"Be back soon."

Rey hugs his wife and daughters.

Axel and Atticus clap each other on the shoulders before they both kneel by Jennifer. "I'll be right back, Mom, with help for you. You'll be okay."

After they leave, Nicole asks, "Should we set up the tent?"

"The small one," Kimba answers. "The babies and Naomi can rest."

"I'm not tired," Naomi responds around a yawn.

"Oh, I know you aren't. But I'll need you to watch LJ and Trish while the rest of us stand guard and help Jennifer. It's a big job, and the tent will make it easier."

Naomi gets a very serious look. "I'll be the babysitter."

The tent is barely up when Atticus says, "They're back."

My head darts toward the road. Sure enough, Jameson and the others are coming into view.

Kimba and Atticus run to meet them. There's little discussion before they all quickly make their way to us.

"Town's gone," Atticus says, his voice hoarse with emotion. "There was a fire. Everyone moved out."

"How do you know?" I ask.

"Found some people camped up the road," Rey says. "They told us."

"And you believe them?"

"We used the binoculars too. Even with the distance, we could see charred remains."

Atticus shakes his head. "We'll do what Axel said and find the firefighters and school nurse to help."

"Let's do it." Rey motions. "Start Jennifer moving. Axel, Jameson, and I need to repack."

"I'm ready to go," I say.

"Me too," Kimba and Nicole reply in unison.

"Go." Rey motions. "We'll get the tent down and the babies moving. Patti, can you go with Jennifer? I'll take care of your children. We'll catch up."

My heart is pounding in my ears as we climb the embankment, carefully moving Jennifer a foot or two at a time. The loose ground reminds me of the hill I slid down when I broke my arm. If we drop Jennifer, all the work we did to get the bleeding stopped . . . I force the thoughts from my mind.

We're doing this. She's going to be okay. We'll get her to the top of this hill. We'll be fine. Then we'll start moving along the highway, faster than we've ever gone. We'll make good time. We'll find help for Jennifer.

As we reach the two-lane highway at the top of the hill, I let out a loud breath of relief. I glance back; the rest of our group has the tent down and is beginning their walk.

"I'm going to stay here," Kimba says. "I'll help Rey get everyone up this hill. It's a doozy."

"Want me to stay too?" I ask.

She touches my arm. "Keep going. We won't be far behind."

We make quick time, moving faster than we have at any time on this journey. As fast as we're going, Kimba, Rey, and the rest must have been sprinting because they catch us in no time.

We all know today won't be our normal *ten miles at a leisurely pace.* Today, we'll keep going until we get Jennifer the help she needs.

A quick stop for Patti to evaluate her and rehydrate Jennifer, along with everyone else, and we're off again.

The stroller holds not only LJ but extra gear. The wagon, rickety from going cross-country, has Naomi and more gear. She's too big for it, and we all know the wagon isn't designed to hold so much weight, but her being able to ride allows us to keep up this crazy pace. Little

Trish is strapped to Rey's chest so Patti is unencumbered in case Jennifer goes into distress.

"Let me check the lashings and make sure the travois is holding up as it should," Patti says. "Then we can move again."

A quick check and an adjustment or two, then we're off. The process repeats. As our shoes pound the pavement, echoing across the land, we talk little. Even the children are nearly silent.

Sometime later, Axel says, "We're almost to Fort Shaw. They might have help."

"Slow down," Rey orders. "We're approaching a town?" He drops his voice and mutters, "I should've checked the map."

Atticus shakes his head. "It's not much of a town. But yeah, something."

"Everyone on alert! Atticus, you have the lead. Standard procedure for approaching a roadblock."

Although we slow and spread out—our usual method for populated areas—there's no need. No barricade, no one checking. We don't even see any people.

Nicole, who's pushing the stroller, lets out an exaggerated sigh. "That got my heart pumping, more than it already was. Any more towns between here and Simms?"

The Dosen brothers look at each other. Atticus shakes his head. "Simms is next. Sorry. I wasn't . . . I wasn't thinking."

"Worry will do that," Rey says. "Combine that with the sadness and fear you're experiencing, it's hard to think straight. And we're all guilty of it. I should've asked before we left. I'm not— " He shakes his head. "Since Nate died, my brain has been muddled."

Kimba reaches for her husband's hand. "Let's have a quick break and then finish this up. How much farther?"

"Not far," Axel answers. His cheeks are ruddy from the exertion . . . or maybe from realizing what a dangerous situation we could've walked into.

Just over an hour later, we slow our pace as the brothers declare Simms is less than a mile ahead. Unlike Fort Shaw, we can already see activity in the distance. An outline of their barricade is evident.

"Atticus, you and Axel know these people. You have the lead," Rey declares.

We approach the barricade without drama. Atticus knows one of the women, and we're soon in and sent to the school, where a medical clinic and emergency shelter have been set up. He also tells them about the bear.

One of the barricade men rushes off, saying he'll let someone in charge know.

"Let me check on her," Patti says as soon as we clear the barricade.

"We're almost there," Axel argues as he continues to pull Jennifer.

"She doesn't . . . let me look."

Axel lets out a huff before gently resting the travois handles on the ground.

As Patti goes to Jennifer's side, someone from the barricade asks if everything is okay. With her mouth in a tight line, Patti meets Atticus's eyes first.

"I'm sorry." Patti shakes her head.

A whimper escapes Axel as he drops to his knees by his mom. Atticus drops his chin and momentarily closes his eyes before he joins his brother. Both young men seem transported to mere boys next to their mom's lifeless form.

It must have just happened. I was right behind her as we approached the roadblock. She was breathing, I'm sure of it. I thought I even saw her move.

"Sorry, Mom," Axel says. "We tried to get you here so you could get more help. I'm sorry we let you down."

"We didn't let her down," Atticus says in a quiet voice. "We did everything we could to get her help. Let's take her home. We'll— " His voice catches. "We'll bury her at the ranch."

Axel's agreement is barely audible. In a stronger voice, he says, "Then I'm going back and finding the grizzly. I'm going to kill it."

Rey drops a hand on the grieving boy's shoulder. "It sounds like the town may be putting together a hunting party. The bear is dangerous, and they know it."

"I'm going to be a part of it."

"How far is it to the ranch?" Kimba asks.

"Just over five miles," Atticus answers. "Do you think . . . can we keep this pace and get her home before dark?"

I look toward the western sky. Sunset is an hour away, maybe an hour and a half. Can we make it?

The woman Atticus knows from the barricade is next to us and offers her condolences. "She was such a kind, wonderful woman."

I wipe my eyes. When Patti was working on her in the middle of the night, I thought we'd lose her then. When we didn't, I had hope we'd be able to find help, someone who knew enough to repair the damage the bear did.

"We're taking her home," Axel says with a squeak in his voice.

"I understand," the woman says. "Um, you left Scott to care for things, right?"

Atticus looks at the woman. "Have you seen him?"

"A few weeks ago. He came in, did some trading."

"Everything was okay?"

She lifts a shoulder. "He had the Brower girl with him."

"Our neighbor?" Atticus spits out the words. "Why?"

"They're a couple."

"No way." Axel shakes his head. "She's nuts. Most of that family— "

Atticus lifts a hand to silence his brother.

"It might be good," the woman says. "There's been issues with Lance Brower and his older son." She scrunches her face. "What do they call him?"

"Mouth," Atticus and Axel respond in unison.

"Yeah. They've been enacting squatter's rights, saying if people left their ranch or farm, then it's fair game."

"That's not how squatter's rights work," I say, recalling what we'd heard before.

"Tell Lance." She scoffs. "It's probably good Scott's there and is friendly with the girl. Do you need anything before you go? We have care packages set up for people. I can get you a couple."

Atticus shakes his head, but Kimba says, "Please. We'd appreciate it."

With two small bags added to our supplies, we set off at our brisk pace. Our goal is to get Jennifer home before dark so she can be buried on her land.

Chapter 40

Along the Sun River
West of Simms, Montana
Thursday, August 6, Near Sunset

Victoria

The sun is hanging low when Axel motions with his arm. "As soon as we reach the top of this hill, we'll see it."

I'm breathing hard as we climb. There's a collective sigh of relief when the sprawling ranch house and multiple outbuildings come into view.

"You have cattle." Naomi's voice is full of wonder as she points from her spot in the wagon.

"Looks like we do." Atticus nods, a slight smile moving across his grief-stricken face. "Looks like we do. The horses are still there too."

"There's a glow coming from a window," Rey says.

"Scott?" Axel asks. "Maybe he's doing something in our place."

"Where does he live?" I ask.

"One of the cabins. You can't see it from here. The smaller house is where my aunt Nina lived." He points at a place with a similar design to the main house.

"Let's get off this skyline and make our plan," Rey orders. After we've all taken several steps back, he lays out the plan. "Approach like it's a roadblock. Atticus, we'll take point. Call out to him, see if he answers."

"Me too?" Axel asks.

"You'll stay back with Kimba. It didn't look like there was a lot of cover."

"We can use the entrance timbers," Atticus says. "There's four good-sized logs attached together on each side of the driveway."

"Good plan," Rey agrees. "You and me, daypacks only. Kimba, you'll cover us from the entrance. Hand your tactical rifle off to Axel, and you use the hunting rifle."

"Are you sure announcing ourselves is smart?" she asks as she takes the long-range rifle from Axel.

"I'm not sure anything is smart," Rey answers. "But from what we learned in town, he's been taking care of things here."

"And the cattle." Atticus smiles. "They're still here."

Kimba dips her head before turning to me. "Can you handle the .22?" She motions to the rifle Nate used to carry.

I answer with a hesitant yes. I clear my throat and, in a stronger voice, tell her I can.

She removes the rifle from the sling on her backpack and thrusts it toward me, then hands Patti the walkie-talkie. "Keep Naomi with your children. Get in the ditch. Rey has the other walkie. He'll call you with the all-clear. If things go bad, follow the ditch back down the hill until you can find a place to hide out overnight. As soon as you have enough light to see, go back to Simms. Jameson, Nicole, you guys are with Patti."

My son gives a solemn nod. "Things won't go bad, right?"

"Always good to be cautious," Rey answers as he hoists the smaller pack onto his back.

"What about my mom?" Axel asks, motioning to the travois his brother was pulling.

"We'll keep her with us," Jameson says.

Axel purses his lips. "I suppose."

"Let's pray," Rey says, reaching a hand toward his wife.

As we circle up on the side of the road, Rey's voice goes soft. "Atticus?"

His mouth is a tight line as he lowers his chin to his chest. "Heavenly Father, we come to You with broken hearts. My mom— " He takes in a breath. "We're so close to home. We ask You to put a cover of protection over us. Let Scott be here, ready to greet us with open arms. We can't— " His voice cracks.

"Thank you, Lord, for Your love and guidance. Thank you as You are with us as we grieve our losses. Thank you for getting us this far, now if You could just help us the rest of the way. We pray these things in the name of Your Son, Jesus. Amen."

After joining in the chorus of amens, I pull Jameson into a hug. "I'm sure we'll be fine."

He nods. "I'll help Patti. I know I haven't always been helpful, but now . . . " He lifts a shoulder. "It's important. And you won't need to worry about me, just do what you need to keep everyone else safe. I'm glad you're taking the rifle."

I let out a quiet breath through my nose. "After shooting the bear, I realized they don't bother me the way they used to. I can handle it. Especially considering my ax didn't even stop him. Of course, the handgun didn't either."

Brett pulls his brother into a manly hug and says, "We'll see you soon."

"Ready to roll?" Rey asks.

Though he and Atticus switched to their daypacks, leaving the heavier bags with Patti and Jameson, the rest of us carry our full gear as we go back up the hill. I give a quick glance to my son. His determined look fills me with confidence. He's matured so much over the past few months, growing into an amazing young man—a man who now has a heart for God.

"You okay, Mom?" Brett whispers.

"I think we'll be okay."

"Me too, but it's good to be cautious."

We move toward the ranch. "Hey." Axel points to the crossbar log that frames the entrance of their gravel driveway. "Our sign's gone. The eye bolts are still in place, but the metal sign with our brand isn't there."

With a shake of his head, Atticus says, "Wind, maybe?"

We set up behind the logs as the two men head toward the house. Atticus is in the lead with Rey a dozen steps behind.

The distance from the entrance to the house is about the length of two football fields. When they've reached the halfway point, Atticus calls out, "Scott? It's Atticus Dosen. Scott Pierce? You there?"

Atticus calls out again before a faint voice responds. "Atticus? Wow! I can't believe you're here."

Axel lets out a quiet whoop and steps out from behind the log barrier.

"Wait," Kimba orders. "Wait until Rey gives the all-clear sign."

Stepping back behind cover, he mutters, "Sorry. I wasn't thinking."

Atticus and Rey continue forward, meeting a large man and small woman partway. Rey motions for us to join them.

"Should I get the others?" I ask.

"I'll go," Brett quickly offers.

"They're coming now." Kimba gestures to the hilltop. "Rey must have called them on the radio."

We wait the few minutes it takes for everyone to join us, then go as one to Atticus and Rey.

When we reach our friends, Atticus's jaw is set, his voice tight. "What do you mean, he might need some extra hands?"

An attractive raven-haired woman around Atticus's age puts a hand on her hip. "Just what I said."

"This is our land, has been for over seventy-five years."

"What's happening?" Jameson whispers.

I shake my head.

The young woman smirks. "Your folks owned the land, not you. And you just told us your mama died on the way here." She looks over Atticus's shoulder, her green eyes peering at our group. "Don't see your daddy. He dead too?"

"What's she saying, Atticus?" Axel moves next to his brother, his fists clinched tight.

"She thinks her dad owns our land. Squatter's rights."

I shake my head. "That's not how squatter's rights work."

The girl darts her eyes in my direction. "Oh yeah? Says who?"

"The law."

She lets out a coarse laugh. "There is no law."

"Let's just . . . " Scott puts a hand on the woman's shoulder. She shrugs it off. "Let's figure this out tomorrow. We'll talk to Lance." He turns to Atticus. "You all can stay in Miss Nina's house tonight." He looks at our group. "She isn't with you either?"

"We'll stay in our home." Axel steps forward.

"It's not your home!" the woman shouts. "You abandoned it. Can't you get that through your thick skulls?"

"C'mon, Tara." Scott's voice is low, pleading. "We'll sort it out tomorrow. After we bury Mrs. Dosen. She deserves a proper burial."

"Humph," the woman scoffs. "She should've been a proper neighbor, then maybe things would be different. Do what you want, Scott. I'm going to bed." She spins on her heel and stomps away.

Scott waits until the front door slams before turning back to Atticus. "I'll help you with your mom. We'll sort it out. Lance, he'll probably be reasonable."

"This is our land." Atticus steps into Scott's space. "*You* know that."

The big man nods. "Things are just . . . different now."

"You're with Tara?" Axel makes a face. "She isn't nice. Lance and Mouth—they're not either."

"Tara's younger brother Connor's still here." Scott bobs his head several times. "He'll be happy to see you."

Axel's face softens. "We'll have to tell him about Asher."

Scott drops his head. "Atticus told me. I'm sorry. Your brother was a good guy, and a good friend to Connor." He lifts his gaze. "Tara's okay once you get to know her. We're, um, we're getting married."

Atticus opens his mouth to say something, then seems to think better of it. With a shake of his head, he turns to Rey. "I'll show you to my aunt Nina's place. I'm going to put my mom in the root cellar— " His head spins back to Scott. "If that's all right with you?"

The man lifts his hands. "Yes, yes, of course."

Atticus narrows his eyes and then turns back to Rey. "I'm staying with my mom until we bury her. Axel?"

"Me too, I'll stay with her too."

"We'll figure this out tomorrow," Scott says again. "Lance will be reasonable. I'm sure we can work it out."

Atticus turns back to Scott. "Lance will be leaving us alone. And you'll need to decide where your loyalty lies. The Double D belongs to us. To my brother and me."

Chapter 41

Fergus Peak Lodge
Thursday, August 6, Late Evening

Sadie

Jack and Cassie are awake and talking. Or, in Cassie's case, crying. Early this morning, she miscarried.

Samantha's bullet wound was just a graze. When Randy shot her, it caught her bicep and just left a scratch, then slammed into Cassie's side. The other injuries from the stampede to get to safety are all relatively minor—a broken ankle and many bruises.

Several other women have come forward, saying they, too, were seeing Randy. At least one of them is pregnant.

Another says she may be. After talking more with Hayley and some of the other young girls, it doesn't seem he did anything too disgusting. Hayley says he grabbed her and tried to kiss her once, but she turned her head and it landed on her ear. Thankfully, that's the worst of it for the children.

Even though Chuck and Daniela refer to Jack and Cassie as critically injured, because of the blood loss and the potential for infection, everyone's hopeful they'll make a full recovery.

Sebastian says he's sure they'll be fine and we won't have any more deaths from the trouble Randy caused. My brother and his *feelings* are often correct. I have no reason not to believe him this time.

While working together over the past day and a half, it's plain to see Daniela and Chuck have resolved whatever issues they previously had. As I sit with Mom, who's sitting by Jack while the two of them quietly visit, Daniela and Chuck are on the other side of the room. She laughs at something Chuck says.

"Won't be long now," Jack says.

"Until what?" I ask.

"Another wedding."

The light smile Mom had falters.

Jack closes his eyes. "Sorry, Leanne. I wasn't thinking."

"It's good to see happiness. Daniela and Chuck—they deserve it."

"So do you," Jack says.

I turn to Jack. "You didn't think that before."

A flash of pain crosses his face.

"Sadie," Mom whispers.

"It's true, though. You were happy with Donnie. You were in love. And he— " I motion toward Jack. "He tried to ruin it, tried to steal you from him."

"That's true." Jack's voice is low. "I realized the mistake I'd made all those years ago."

"Well, your timing stinks." I drop my chin and let out a breath. "Until . . . I thought . . . " I clear my throat as I try to get my words organized. "Until Randy said he set the fire to the cabin, I thought it was you."

His eyes go wide, and he shakes his head. "No. Never."

I lift my shoulder. "Why were you there so quickly? You said you were out for a walk? In the middle of the night?"

"Sadie," Mom says in her husky whisper. "This isn't the time for an interrogation."

"It's a fair question. I couldn't sleep. I knew what I'd done." Jack glances from me to my mom. "Going to you like that was wrong. Disgustingly wrong. I wanted you to be happy. I truly did. I just thought maybe . . . maybe you'd realize I was the one for you. I knew as soon as I asked you to leave Donnie for me, it was a mistake. I hope you can forgive me."

Mom bobs her head one time. "Of course. I already have."

"Why'd you stop coming around?" I ask. "After Donnie died and Mom was hurt, we didn't see you. It was . . . suspicious."

His mouth goes in a tight line. "Yeah, I heard the rumors."

"I never believed them," Mom says. "I didn't know how the fire started, not until Randy made his proud confession, but I knew it wasn't you."

"No. Never. I'd never hurt you—not like that. I just want you to be happy."

"I am happy. My children are safe. I love . . . I *still* love Donnie and wish he was with me. But knowing he's gone to Heaven, and that Sadie will too— " With her good hand, she reaches for mine.

"We don't know what the future holds. We never did. Since the attacks, we've lost many people we love. Donnie. Asher. My brother Wes. My parents. But even before that, before things became so awful, people died. My first husband was taken from me by cancer."

She gives my hand a squeeze. "The Bible tells us death is temporary. These troubles on earth are temporary. Glory is eternal. I've been praying for the safety of our friends who were traveling with us, that they'll be sheltered at the Dosen ranch, and for the people we left behind in Bakerville—Ben and his family, plus the others we met in our short time there."

Jack clears his throat. "You know Chuck's put a prayer chain in place? If the rumors are true that World War III has started, then not only the country but people across the globe need our prayers. He's started with the infirm—the ones who can't do the physical work—making them prayer warriors."

My mom smiles. "I'm one of the infirm. He came to me last week."

"Oh, of course. I should have— "

Mom waves Jack off. "I'll admit, I wasn't sure I wanted to be a part of it. I've been . . . with Donnie dying . . . ." She shakes her head. "I didn't know if I had it in me to pray for others. And it seems like such a little thing, like it can't possibly make a difference. The Bible says to pray for each other, that the prayers of the righteous are powerful and effective. I don't claim to be righteous." She lets out a tinkle of laughter.

"But it's helped me more than I can say," Mom continues. "It's giving me a purpose. And if we really are at war, if this chaos and mayhem is worldwide, then we need all the prayers we can get."

I look at my hand, still nestled in my mom's. "We're safe now. But others may not be. Our friends may not be."

"We are safe," Mom says, her voice stronger than it's been since the fire. "We're building a new life a life that guarantees plenty of hard work. It won't be easy."

My heart fills as I squeeze my mom's hand. "But with each other, and God beside us, we'll get through it."

"Amen, Sadie. Amen."

Also by Millie Copper

Montana Mayhem Series

Unending Havoc: Montana Mayhem Book 1

Ruthless Havoc: Montana Mayhem Book 2

Merciless Havoc: Montana Mayhem Book 3

Havoc in Wyoming Series

Wyoming Refuge: A Havoc in Wyoming Prequel

Havoc in Wyoming: Part 1, Caldwell's Homestead

Havoc in Wyoming: Part 2, Katie's Journey

Havoc in Wyoming: Part 3, Mollie's Quest

Havoc Begins: A Havoc in Wyoming Story (Part 3.5)

Havoc in Wyoming: Part 4, Shields and Ramparts

Havoc in Wyoming: Part 5, Fowler's Snare

Havoc Rises: A Havoc in Wyoming Story (Part 5.5)

Havoc in Wyoming: Part 6, Pestilence in the Darkness

Christmas on the Mountain: A Havoc in Wyoming Novella

Havoc Peaks: A Havoc in Wyoming Story (Part 6.5)

Havoc in Wyoming: Part 7, My Refuge and Fortress

Nonfiction Books

Stock the Real Food Pantry: A Handbook for Making the Most of Your Pantry

Design a Dish: Save Your Food Dollars

Real Food Hits the Road: Budget Friendly Tips, Ideas, and Recipes for Enjoying Real Food Away from Home

Stretchy Beans: Nutritious, Economical Meals the Easy Way

Find these titles on Amazon:
www.amazon.com/author/milliecopper

Acknowledgments

Thanks to:

Ameryn Tucker, my editor, beta reader, and daughter wrapped in one. I had a story I wanted to tell, and Ameryn encouraged me and helped me bring it to life.

Dee from Dauntless Cover Design.

My husband, who gave me the time and space I needed to complete this dream and was very patient as I'd tell him the same plot ideas over and over and over.

Three more daughters and a young son, who willingly listen to me drone on and on about story lines and ideas while encouraging me to "keep going."

My amazing Beta Readers! Thanks to Barbara, Becky, Ilona, Judy, Katrina, Linda, Marquita, Tammy, Tonya, and Tracy for your help in creating the final story. Your insights and abilities to see the things I miss are very much appreciated! And a special thank you to Tim, specialist in all things that go boom, for always answering my questions and pointing out things I wouldn't even think about.

And to you, my readers, for spending your time with our band of weary travelers. If you have five minutes, you'd make this writer very happy if you could leave a review. I appreciate you!

About the Author

Millie Copper, writer of Cozy Apocalyptic Fiction, was born in Nebraska but never lived there. Her parents fully embraced wanderlust and moved regularly, giving her an advantage of being from nowhere and everywhere.

As an adult, Millie is fully rooted in a solar-powered home in the wilds of Wyoming with her husband and young son, milking ornery goats and tending chickens on their small homestead. In their free time, they escape to the mountains for a hike or laze along the bank of the river to catch their dinner. Four adult daughters, three sons-in-law, and three grandchildren round out the family.

Since 2009, Millie has authored articles on traditional foods, alternative health, homesteading, and preparedness-many times all within the same piece. Millie has penned five nonfiction, traditional food focused books, sharing how, with a little creativity, anyone can transition to a real foods diet without overwhelming their food budget.

The twelve-installment *Havoc in Wyoming* Christian Post-Apocalyptic fiction series uses her homesteading, off-the-grid, and preparedness lifestyle as a guide. The adventure continues with the *Montana Mayhem* series, scheduled for release in the summer of 2021.

Find Millie at www.MillieCopper.com
Facebook: www.facebook.com/MillieCopperAuthor/
Amazon: www.amazon.com/author/milliecopper
BookBub: https://www.bookbub.com/authors/millie-copper

www.ingramcontent.com/pod-product-compliance
Lightning Source LLC
Chambersburg PA
CBHW050838190726
48286CB00007B/2136